The Manifest

J. Anthony Torino

Published by J. Anthony Torino

Cover Illustration by J. Kent Holloway

Library of Congress Control Number: 2017908524

ISBN 978-0-692-89709-6 (Paperback); 978-0-692-90165-6 (EBK)

Dedication

To my wife,

who inspires me every day

to be true to myself.

To my family,

for the unwavering,

unconditional love.

And, to my mom,

who once told me,

"Dare to be different".

Table of Contents

Preface

Let me be perfectly clear. I believe the Earth will be hit by the comet 73p Schwassmann-Wachmann (SW3) in May and June of 2022. I came to this conclusion by decoding some of the writings of the controversial seer, Nostradamus while validating my assumptions with scientific facts. Yes, I know this is a bold claim as others have suggested that they too have deciphered his cryptic writings before, only to be debunked. And yes, his quatrains are written in such a way that interpretations can vary widely. In fact, I've read books that have been written solely to discredit the man. So, I get it. Why should my prediction carry any more weight than the next guy's? Yet, I know what I know. Using science, historical references, language lexicons, software, and common sense; combined with what I describe as divine inspiration, I believe I've stumbled onto something. I've decoded some of Nostradamus' quatrains that reveal the time and place where a known comet will strike the Earth. Truth be known, I'm hoping my prediction will also be debunked. Because if what I believe comes to pass, in 2022 our planet and civilization may be in for a rough time.

In 2007, I treated myself to an awesome 42nd birthday present; a 6-foot-tall, 12-inch reflector telescope that was delivered to my home in a huge box. Eagerly, I put it together and when fully assembled was ready to use what resembled a big cannon. I purchased several different lenses to ensure I could see all that captivated me both near and far. It's surprising what the moon actually looks like! For as long as I can remember, I've been fascinated with the heavens above. I can't tell you why. Perhaps it's the explorer in me. Or maybe the scientist. Really, I think it's the philosopher. Thinking back, I can see how, as a young boy, I was influenced by a documentary in which Carl Sagan explained the Drake Equation. Based on Drake's 1961 formula and hypothesis, I was convinced that there were, no that there *are*, other beings up among the stars. I love to think about that. Whatever the reason, I can remember lying on the roof of my parent's garage during the warm summer evenings, quietly gazing at the worlds above. That passion continues today. At times, I wish I had gone into the field of Astronomy.

The year I bought this behemoth telescope, planetary tracking software was just coming of age. There were no planetary "apps" at that time, only software that could be loaded onto my laptop. As such, I was determined to use whatever other technology was available to me to get closer to answering my lifelong nagging question...is there life out there? Enter the computer program, *Starry Night.* When I first purchased the program, I was immediately consumed by it. It had all the capabilities I desired including an on-screen look at real-time placement of stars, planets, comets, asteroids, and other out-of-this-world celestial bodies. It allowed me to change the view to different Earthly vantage points (just in case I was wondering what the night sky looked like while standing in Paris) as well as the ability to vault forward and backward in time using its built-in ephemeris generator. In other words, one could track the movement of these bodies into the future or review past movements, much like that of today's weather apps that have the ability to view past or future radar. Although I knew these up-close pictures were artist renditions, I still looked with wonderment. As one educated in the world of IT, what I appreciated most was the effort that went into designing the code that created these representations. The program creators decided to use actual data gleaned from database sources like the Jet Propulsion Laboratory where celestial data was streamed live into the program. Another great feature was the ability to click on a body in the sky whereby a short description would appear. The program allowed me to zoom into the body and even place my virtual self upon it to see the rest of the sky from that vantage point. And, the different views it allowed were nothing short of electrifying. I could even view these heavenly bodies while displaying the zodiac and constellations drawn into the night's sky. I was set. I could find a target, point my telescope and peer into the heavens.

I've always felt plugged into the universe in an unexplainable way. I would describe it as a heightened sense of consciousness or knowing and it's what ultimately led me to my conclusions. I believe it's at least conceivable that some of us may be plugged into feeling or foreseeing the future. Some would call it a sixth sense while others might describe this as inspiration. Nostradamus himself attributed his ability to see the future to God-breathed inspiration. Now, just to be clear, I'm not suggesting that I can foretell the future. I just have a feeling about it. Most of the time these feelings get validated, while other times, not so much. This connection I feel with the universe is a real thing though. This may sound like the stuff Sci-Fi movies are made of but consider this; isn't cause and effect a future-telling exercise? The older I get, I become more aware of the fact that there may not be such a thing as coincidence.

Then there's good ole Nostradamus. I was influenced early in life by a documentary on his works. What I found fascinating was the "possibility" of him knowing or somehow seeing the future. I've read many books about the man, and not just those about his prophecies. As I mentioned earlier, I've also read the books that attempt to debunk his prophecies and paint him as nothing more than a man who found a way to make money writing horoscopes for royalty. At one point, I was almost convinced that he might be a fraud. I suspect this is a natural side-effect that comes from being a critical thinker.

However, in mid-2007 I experienced something that I have trouble explaining. While watching another Nostradamus documentary I had a moment of exceedingly strong inspiration. Knowing that his quatrains were written in a cryptic fashion, I began to look for a pattern and found something fascinating. In his quatrains, he describes the placement of the planets, the moon, and the comet in relation to the zodiac and other celestial bodies. He used astronomy and astrology references to indicate where and when this comet could be found in the sky! As I panned his works, what I found was akin to striking gold. I found two huge nuggets that led me to the rest of the find.

Between 1555 and 1558, he released *Les Propheties* which includes many of the famous quatrains we know today.

In quatrain 2-15 he writes:

> *"Shortly before the monarch is assassinated,*
>
> *Castor and Pollux in the ship, bearded star:*
>
> *The public treasure emptied by land and sea,*
>
> *Pisa, Asti, Ferrara, Turin land under interdict."*[1]

Jumping to line two, I believe Nostradamus is referencing Castor and Pollux, two stars that help make up the constellation Gemini. The "ship" is the constellation Argo Navis (the ship named after Jason and the Argonauts). This constellation was broken into 4 different constellations by Nicolas Louis de Lacaille[2] in 1752 and now includes Carina (the keel of the ship), Puppis (the poop), Vela (the sails) and, Pyxis the compass. The bearded star is certainly a reference to a comet.

Here were two stars that gave me a starting point. I opened my Starry Night program, centered on these two stars, and scanned back

---

1 Nostradamus, M., & Garencières, T. (2001). *Nostradamus: his works and prophecies*. Urbana, IL: Standard Publications.

2 de Lacaille, N. L., (1763). *Coelum australe stelliferum,* H L Guerin & L F Delatour.

and forth in time until…WOW! There it was! SW3 was staring me in the face. On January 12, 2021, SW3 passes over Castor and then over Pollux on June 11, 2021. From there it heads directly to the "ship" Argo Navis (and also for a really close pass with Earth), for arrival in July of 2022. Because SW3 is broken into many fragments, I believe some will impact the Earth in May and June of 2022 while other pieces will travel on.

In the first line, Nostradamus foretells of the assassination of a monarch. But which monarch? If my assumption regarding the January 2021 date holds true, it will be sometime shortly before this and only time will tell.

In the last two lines, I believe he's referencing the evacuation of Rome where one would currently find the "public treasure" of Christianity. He references this again in other quatrains. As for Pisa, Asti, Ferrara and Turin, these Italian cities may be in the path of destruction.

In quatrain 10-50 he writes:

> *"The Meuse by day in the land of Luxembourg,*
>
> *It will find Saturn and three in the urn:*
>
> *Mountain and plain, town, city and borough,*
>
> *Flood in Lorraine, betrayed by the great urn."*[3]

---

[3] Nostradamus, M., & Garencières, T. (2001). *Nostradamus: his works and prophecies*. Urbana, IL: Standard Publications.

In the first line, I believe "The Meuse" Nostradamus is referring to is an observatory. My research led me to find the Observatoire des Cote de Meuse, an observatory located in Verdun. The central European maps of 1477 and 1547 show the observatory would still be in Luxembourg had the national boundaries not changed. For me, this confirmed that Nostradamus is giving us a clue that an observatory would find or "observe" Saturn and SW3 "in the urn". But, which observatory? And when?

Then, I find another nugget! In January of 1996, "*Hermann Boehnhardt (Universitaets-Sternwarte Muenchen - USM, Germany), and Hans Ulrich Kaeufl (ESO-Garching), using the ESO 3.5-metre New Technology Telescope at the La Silla Observatory (Chile) in remote observing mode from the ESO Headquarters in Garching (Germany)"*[4] observe Schwassmann-Wachmann 3. Where? In the Urn of the Aquarius constellation (the only Urn in the sky) along with Saturn! Coincidentally, the Universitaets-Sternwarte Muenchen (USM) a Germany observatory is located in Munich adjacent to a river that connects to the Meuse River.

It was from this point that I began to put more pieces together which has ultimately led me to believe that in May and June of 2022, 73P/Schwassmann-Wachmann 3 will strike the planet.

So now my dilemma. What if I've really uncovered (even if by

---

[4] ESO.org., Split Comet Schwassmann-Wachmann 3, http://www.eso.org/public/images/eso9608a/

pure coincidence) that SW3 is going to strike Earth in 2022. Who do I tell? And who's going to believe it anyway if my prediction is based on the works of Nostradamus? After all, there are many who have claimed to decipher his quatrains without offering proof. Then again, using his quatrains to find time and place, I was able to use other scientific facts to fill in the rest. BUT, what if I'm completely wrong and become responsible for inducing a panic of global proportions? I certainly don't want that.

In 2007, I wrote to Dr. Claudia Alexander of the Jet Propulsion Laboratory seeking her advice. I had seen her interviewed during a documentary about comets and asteroids as she was the foremost expert in the evolution and interior physics of comets and at that time, project manager for NASA's Galileo mission. Because she knew a great deal about the interior composition of comets and SW3 had continued to break apart, I thought she could perhaps offer some help. Despite her credentials and unique knowledge, the truth is that I reached out to her because she seemed approachable. I simply wanted to call her attention to my concern about SW3 and was hoping she would either scientifically validate my findings or debunk it. So, after exchanging a few emails, we spoke on the phone. I dreaded the conversation somewhat, as she had pressed me in previous emails to explain where my concern stemmed from. Until the call, I had put her off in hopes of convincing her to at least look into it. I won't soon forget the call. When I finally disclosed my research connection to Nostradamus' works she graciously offered me some advice. "Why don't you publish this on a few Nostradamus online message boards to see if you get any traction?" she asked. The thought had crossed my mind. However, what I really needed was someone in the scientific community to consider whether a real-life comet would potentially impact the planet. "Of course, you know I cannot bring Nostradamus back to my scientific community." she continued. Yes, I knew even before our phone call that this would never happen. We never spoke again. In 2015, I was saddened to hear of her death as she had succumbed to cancer.

After my call with Dr. Alexander, I did nothing. Although I thought about it constantly, I didn't talk about it or write about it...I told no one.

In 2013, completely unexpected, the topic came up in conversation with my wife over dinner. We hadn't spoken about it in a very long time and I mentioned that it had continued to be at the forefront of my mind. She suggested perhaps positioning it in the context of a fictional story. "Let the world decide for itself." she offered.

And so, after many years and several edits, I present you with "The Manifest". Let the world decide for itself.

Quatrain Century I - 69

The great mountain, seven stadia round,

after peace, war, famine, flooding.

It will spread far, drowning great countries,

even antiquities and their mighty foundations.

- Michel Nostradamus[5]

---

[5] Nostradamus, M., & Garencières, T. (2001). *Nostradamus: his works and prophecies.* Urbana, IL: Standard Publications.

Prologue

She woke to the sound of a dog barking. For a while, she lay in bed, listening to the animal, hoping it would stop, but it didn't. With a groan, she pulled the blanket from her face. It was dark. Not even a hint of sun came through the window.

"Michel?" she said.

There was no answer and, as she moved her hand to where her husband should have been, she found she was alone. She sat up and glanced around the room but Michel was not there.

She rose and, working her way carefully across the darkened floor, reached the door of the bedroom and opened it. The great room was quiet. The remnants of the cook fire beckoned with a warm, red glow from across the room. She crossed to the fire and used a taper to light a candle. When the wick caught, she lifted the candle and made her way to the stairs. Outside, the dog continued its insistent barking.

She started up the stairs, the old wood creaking beneath her feet, her way lit by the soft light of the candle. When she neared the top, she noticed that it was brighter. But the light was strange, blue. Puzzled, she continued on. As she reached the top she heard voices.

Her husband's room—the room where he did his work—was at

the end of the hall. She could see it was the origin of the strange light. It spilled from under the door, bright and blue, casting strange shadows on the walls. Almost as strange was that she heard two voices, yet she'd heard no one come in.

She crossed to the door and listened. She recognized her husband's voice; the other she did not know. They were talking too quietly for her to pick up any of the words. Around the doorframe seeped the light. It touched her hand where it rested on the door handle and she flinched. She noticed, then, that the dog had gone silent.

She turned the door handle and pushed open the door a crack. For a moment—a single, brief instant—the blue light filled the hall, blinding her. Then it was gone. She shivered, suddenly cold. Bravely, though, she pushed open the door.

Michel was at his desk. From her place in the doorway, she saw his shoulders move. She realized he was crying.

"Michel?" she said, stepping into the room. When her husband didn't respond, she crossed to him. On his desk, a candle was lit, casting meager light over her husband's work. She placed a hand on his shoulder and, slowly, he looked up. As she watched, it seemed as if he was returning from some place—a place far away. Despite herself, she shivered again. "Michel, who were you speaking with?"

The question seemed to puzzle him. His face was a question.

"No one," he said, as if words were new. "I was speaking with no one."

She looked past him, to the paper on the desk, the ink fresh.

"What did you see?" she asked gently.

His brow furrowed, as if he could not understand the question. Then his eyes turned to the paper on which he'd been writing. They went to the quill that he seemed surprised to see in his hand. When he turned to look at her again, fresh tears spilled from Michel de Nostredame's eyes.

"Death," he said. "I saw death.

Chapter One

Elena took the last few steps down to the platform, her heels sounding on the cement. A heavy bag slung over her shoulder. A heel threatened to catch on the last step and her fingers brushed the rail, quick enough that she hardly felt the cold of the metal. Then she was at the bottom, where she stopped.

It was nearly 11:00 PM. Only a handful of people milled about the platform. Those who had come with the train were gone, some of them passing Elena on the steps. To her left an old woman in a faded blue dress stood looking at a train schedule. Beyond her, a young couple leaning close, their conversation their own. No one else.

Her eyes went to the train windows. She saw few people beyond them, last stragglers along a waning line. She pulled out her phone, looked at the time. From Valle Aurelia she could just make it to Tuscolana before the system shut down for the night.

She heard the final boarding bell and slipped her phone away. She started for the train. Before she stepped onto it she turned her head to look down the line of cars, her eyes moving beyond them. Past the train there existed nothing but what seemed an unending line of tracks that looked to sink into the darkness that was the whole of the world beyond the meager reach of the platform lights. The knowledge of it stayed with her as she stepped onto the train and she shuddered despite the warmth of the car.

She put a hand on the rail and looked down the car. There were more people than she'd seen from outside but not many. Her eyes moved from one to the next, dismissing each in turn. Lingering on the young men a dozen seats away and moving on when none of them looked in her direction.

She could feel her heart beating along a vein in her neck. Her hand shook as she released the rail and started up the car. Away from the young men in the back. She picked a seat well away from anyone else and moved the bag to her lap.

Through the window, she could see the woman in the blue dress, her eyes moving from the schedule to the train and back. Confusion on her face. Elena watched the vignette play out through the frame of the window, and when the doors hissed shut and the train started down the track, the woman slid off the scene. For a time afterward Elena's eyes stayed on the glass, even as the tunnel wall rose up beyond it.

She only came to realize she was gripping the bag too tightly when her fingers began to hurt. The pain pulled her back to the train car and, after loosening her hold on the bag, she looked around the train again. Everyone in the same spots; no one looking. Yet she still felt her heart's too-fast beat. She wrapped her hands around the bag again and sat that way as the train made its way toward Tuscolana, as it rose from the tunnel and into the open air of Rome at night. She found herself staring at the bag, at the zippered top of it. Imaging through it to what was inside. Wondering if she should just get off the train at the next stop, find the first trash can and upend the bag into it. It would make things a lot simpler.

She released a sigh and retrieved her phone. She looked at the face of it, calculating the time in the States. After four rings, it went to voicemail.

"It's Elena. Call me when you can. I have something I need to bounce off of you."

She slid the phone back into her coat and sat thinking about things. Laughter pulled her eyes to the right, toward the spot where the young men sat. One held a phone for the others to see; lascivious smiles all. She almost smiled too, joining from afar their private joke, until something she hadn't expected caused her to tense. There was someone else sitting there—a man in dark pants and collared, striped shirt a few seats beyond the trio with the phone. Someone where, only moments ago, there had been no one.

She sat there looking at him, as if he were some puzzle to figure out. She didn't think she'd looked away for very long—certainly not long enough for the man to have walked from farther back in the train to claim a seat nearer the front. Except she could find no other explanation for his appearance. He wasn't looking at her; he held a tablet on his lap, his hand moving over the display. Yet, the very fact of him unnerved her. She watched him for a long while, barely disguising the act of surveillance, but he never once looked up.

When, less than a minute later, the train started to slow, she'd finally looked away, although she could still see him along the edge of her vision. She watched him that way for a while longer, until it pained her eyes to do it. When that happened, she blinked the strain out of her eyes and then gave a small headshake.

"Seeing shadows in every corner," she told herself.

The train stopped and she stood and moved to the door, bag in hand. She watched as others did the same, noticing that the man who'd unnerved her seemed content to travel the last leg down the line. Moments later she was off the train and heading for the passenger building.

The ring of multi-level buildings surrounding the space carved out by track, walkway, and terminal provided a curtain between Elena and the wide expanse of the city beyond. Little moved within the circle but beyond she could hear the sounds of heavy traffic that seldom eased in Rome. The air, cool for December, was good after the stale air of the train. As she neared the passenger building she glanced over her shoulder. The trio of young men from the car, having exited with her, were aimed toward the near empty parking lot to the right of the terminal. That left her taking the few steps up to the passenger building alone and, despite the fact that she'd watched her traveling companions with suspicion during transit, the loss of them now left her feeling more nervous than she'd been.

Once inside, she headed for the bathroom. It was small but bright and clean. She closed the door and locked it behind her. Turning away from the door she saw herself in the mirror hanging above the small sink. Her eyes were tired, her hair more tousled than she liked, but she was almost surprised to see that the woman looking back at her didn't seem as scared as she felt.

"Because there's nothing to be afraid of," she informed her reflection. She set her bag on the sink and ran a hand through her hair. She turned on the tap and wet her hands with cold water, then ran her hands over her face, massaging fingers into the corners of her eyes.

She dried her hands and pulled the phone from her pocket. Then she hesitated, her thumb over the display, considering what number to call. When she decided, the call again rang through to voice mail. She tucked the phone between cheek and shoulder, unzipped the bag, and pulled out a manila folder.

"I'm sending you a few files," she said. She opened the folder, withdrew the papers and set the folder to the side. "Can you take a look and help me figure out what it is I'm looking at? As soon as you can?"

After ending the call, she studied the papers she'd pulled from the folder—papers she hadn't had time to review properly before leaving her father's office. Her hand shook as she glanced over the text of the front page. It had her father's familiar signature at the bottom. An indictment of sorts. A finger pointing at her treachery.

"You didn't leave me much choice."

She set the papers on the sink and took a picture of the top page. Then, after moving that page to the back of the pile, she repeated the process. She took seventeen pictures. When she finished, she flipped through them to make sure the recipient would be able to read them. Satisfied, she keyed the phone number and sent the images off. When she'd finished, she toggled to her sent message box and deleted the evidence.

After slipping the phone back into her pocket, she took another long look at her reflection, wondering that the act of betraying the man who had raised her seemed to have left no indelible mark. What she did notice was that her hands had stopped shaking, as if her body knew that pushing the button that sent the pictures beyond her purview had robbed it of the need for hyper-vigilance.

She returned the papers to the folder and slid it back into the bag. She zipped it shut and slung it over her shoulder. She unlocked the door and pulled it open as her other hand reached for the light switch.

A short hint of motion before pain robbed her of sight. Then there were hands on her shoulders, pushing her back. By the time she thought to yell, the hands had turned her around and one was over her mouth. He was wearing a glove, the fabric of it pressing her lip hard against her teeth. She tried to bite him but when her mouth opened the hand pressed in further, robbing her of leverage.

When her vision cleared, she noted that the light was still off. She saw only shadows. Then the other hand closed around her throat. She froze for just a moment, until the reality of it came in a rush. Then she was motion, her body struggling against the arms, against the finality of what was happening. She twisted and pushed, rocking forward then back. From somewhere inside came sounds that sounded like growls through the filter of the hand pressed between her teeth. She felt strong fingers contract around her throat, could feel a fire kindling in her lungs. Tears came, fast and hot down her cheeks.

Her foot came up, then down on his instep. A slight loosening of his grip. She pushed herself backward, driving him into the door, and all of a sudden, the room was filled with light. She blinked against it as she drew a quick breath but the hand closed tight again before she'd had her fill. He held her tightly, pressed against him, his back to the door. She could no longer move, his grip seeming to tighten with each beat of her heart. The fire in her lungs was a searing flame now but she could feel it starting to gutter out, its fuel near spent.

Out of the corner of her eye she could just see the bathroom mirror, could see herself. She looked so still, quiet. She saw his arms, the striped shirt. A shadow of dark pants. Then her entire world was shadow. Then nothing.

Chapter Two

When his eyes opened, the light that made its way past the drawn curtain seemed to pass through a second curtain before it reached him—one that rendered the room in indistinct lines that moved in time to the pounding pain in his temple. He groaned and shut his eyes again as the phone continued to ring, not moving until it had gone silent, and then not for several minutes after that. But when the wakeup call came a second time he half-opened his eyes and allowed the room to resolve into some kind of clarity.

Blindly, he reached for the bedside table, where he felt around for his own phone. Once he had it he pulled it close and blinked until he could see the time. He returned the phone to the table just as the hotel phone stopped ringing.

He closed his eyes again and stayed where he was for another few minutes. Finally, though, he worked his way upright and slid his feet to the floor. He stood and made his way to the bathroom. When he finished, he moved to the sink and worked the grit from his eyes with cold water. Now that he was up he found the headache receding, which suggested it was only the last bourbon that had done him in.

He yawned at his reflection in the mirror, then showered and shaved. Less than ten minutes later he was dressed and stepping into the hall. At the elevator, he retrieved his phone from his coat pocket and thumbed through the calls he'd missed. There were three—and two from the same number.

He looked at the time of the first call, trying to calculate what time it would have been for her in Rome. If she was in Rome. For all he knew, she could have been calling to let him know she'd just landed in Washington. The thought made him smile but before his thumb could open the attachment—the one that looked to have come after her second call—the phone rang.

"Where are you?" the voice on the other end asked.

"Standing in a hallway, waiting for the world's slowest elevator."

The elevator door chose that moment to finally creak open and he stepped in and, switching the phone to his other hand, pressed the button that would take him to the lobby.

"You were supposed to be down here fifteen minutes ago."

"Fifteen minutes ago, I was in my underwear. And I'm pretty sure the hotel management—not to mention any guests who might be in the lobby—will be grateful that I took the extra time to put on pants."

"We're going to be late, Sully. The most important part of an event like this is the hobnobbing beforehand."

Before he could respond the elevator bumped to a halt and the doors opened. As they parted he saw a short, dark haired man standing just a few steps away, phone to his ear and eyes on him.

"I don't hobnob, Jason" Sully said, still speaking into the phone.

The other man gave him a pointed up and down look as the subject of the perusal lowered the phone and slipped it into a pocket.

"From the looks of things, you hobnobbed enough for the both of us last night," Jason said as he, too, lowered his phone.

Sully stepped out of the elevator. He looked up, squinting at the brightness of the lobby lights. The dull pain in his head threatened to become something greater and he quickly lowered his eyes. He looked at Jason.

"I'll occasionally bend the rule when there's good bourbon involved."

Jason's lip curled and he gave Sully a knowing look.

"Or a lovely astrophysicist?"

Sully started across the lobby, aiming for the bank of doors leading to the street.

"A close second to the bourbon," he called over his shoulder. Then, after a pause, "A very close second."

Outside, Sully found a line of cabs waiting and he and Jason slipped into the nearest. As the car pulled away from The Liaison and out onto New Jersey Avenue, Sully stifled a sigh and absently watched the passing buildings behind the elms that lined the street.

"From what I hear, Leggett's already submitted his proposal to the OST," Jason said. He paused until Sully turned away from the window. "So, unless you're ready to do the same—and I mean before this ride is over—our only card is face time with General Randall before he hits the buffet."

Sully answered with a half-smile.

"Leggett won't get the grant," he said.

"And what makes you so sure? Remember, he's got Senator Harper in his back pocket."

Sully was shaking his head before his friend finished.

"He won't get the grant because his proposal lacks the one thing sure to interest General Randall."

Jason raised an eyebrow.

"Nothing explodes," Sully said. He paused a few seconds, then added, "And I'm only half-kidding. If you look at the last seven projects our friend the general has funded, each one has had at least the potential of blowing up."

While the appraisal pulled a slight chuckle from Jason, he still looked unconvinced. As Sully watched, the other man's hand went to his breast pocket and then, after a moment, fell away. Sully wasn't convinced Jason knew he'd even made the gesture.

"How long's it been now since you quit? A week?"

“Something like that. And, just so you know, it only bothers me when someone reminds me.”

“So no cigars after dinner?”

Jason’s eyebrows rose in mock surprise.

“Cigars are a different matter entirely. I may have quit smoking but I’m not an ascetic.”

Sully smiled again and returned his attention to the sights of New York Avenue passing beyond the window.

“What it comes down to,” he said, “is that while Leggett might be able to convince a Senator or two that his research has national security applications, you can’t escape the fact that solar radiometry is boring.”

“So, we’re hanging our hat on the belief that the general will go for our proposal because it’s shinier?”

“Essentially.”

Jason seemed to weigh that before answering.

“I don’t think I’m as happy about that as I should be,” he said.

“We didn’t create the system; we just stand to benefit from it.”

Less than a minute later the cab rolled to a stop behind a line of like vehicles and the two men exited. Sully paid and then followed Jason toward the entrance of the building in which they’d spent a good portion of the last two days.

The Walter E. Washington Convention Center was an elegant

behemoth of stone and glass. Sully thought it something of an architectural spectacle—a glittering façade gilding an interior both utilitarian and ornate. If he'd had his way he would have spent his time exploring the whole of it rather than sitting through lectures that most of his undergraduate students could have delivered more adeptly, or swilling champagne with the thousand others who had shown up for the same kind of face time Jason seemed to think was so necessary.

"Conventions would be fun if you could have them without the people," he said.

"What?" Jason called over his shoulder.

"Nothing," Sully said. Then they were inside.

*****

Sully held back as most of the nearly four hundred people who'd crammed into the room to hear the morning's lecture rose and began to file toward the doors. Of those who remained, some were heading for the stage, toward the two men—one older but fit looking man in a dark suit, the other with three clearly visible stars on his uniform—who stood in easy conversation. Sully decided not to even glance in Jason's direction but the lack of acknowledgment didn't slow the other man.

"Would you like to tell me again how Leggett's not getting the grant?"

Sully, standing in the aisle ten rows from the stage on which the men talked, made a point of hardly glancing at Leggett and the General.

"I wouldn't worry," he said. "I was watching Randall during the lecture. He could hardly keep his eyes open."

"Maybe he had one too many bourbons with the lovely Dr. Hannah too," Jason needled.

Sully ignored the baiting. Instead, he held up the program. "And who can blame him. *Radiometric Attunement, Authentication, and Adjustment of Multispectral Photogrammetric Imagery*," he read. "My god, just reading that aloud makes *me* want to jump off a building and *I* know what all the words mean."

"So, I'm to assume then that our friend the General isn't discussing the finer points of what amounted to a two-hour long discussion of lens gels and frequency adjustments? That he's chosen this moment, on a stage in front of a number of the man's colleagues, to tell the good doctor that he's not getting the grant?"

Sully turned his back to the stage and started for the exit and, after a last glance at their competition, Jason followed.

"My guess is that Randall is playing nice because of Leggett's relationship with Harper," Sully said. "Remember, the Senator sits on at least half a dozen appropriations committees."

"Not to mention that their granddaughters play on the same softball team," came a voice from over Sully's right shoulder. A woman's voice; a hint of amusement in it.

Sully spared himself only a second to wonder how she could have appeared behind them from the midst of a nearly empty room before he turned to respond to the woman responsible for the last bourbon—or two—from the evening before.

"Good morning, Emily," he said to a flame haired woman who looked to have survived the previous night with a good deal more grace than he. In fact, but for a change from ball gown to a skirt that just began to hint at too short, and a taming of the red locks that had, last night, fallen where they would, Emily Hannah looked as if she could take a fresh glass of champagne from a passing waiter and pick up where they'd left off.

"It *was* before that bore of a lecture," she said, with just enough of a smirk to make Sully wonder if the critique was heartfelt or merely a conversational buy-in. Knowing her academic and professional backgrounds, he suspected the former. She turned her attention to Jason, adopting a more mischievous smile. "But I'm sure another bourbon will set things right again."

A hint of color touched Jason's ears but Sully knew his friend well enough to realize that he was seldom more than momentarily chagrined—a suspicion confirmed when the man assumed an impish look of his own.

"If I thought buying you a drink—or three—would improve my chances, I'd already have my wallet open."

Emily laughed and, stepping between them, hooked an arm through one each of theirs and started up the aisle.

"There's not enough bourbon in the world, Dr. Humphrey."

"Ouch," Jason said.

"So, no word about your grant proposal?" Emily asked, giving Sully's arm a squeeze.

"It's hard to get word about something we haven't submitted yet," Jason answered, his rueful smile only half theater.

Emily seemed genuinely surprised.

"You're kidding," she said, looking at Sully, who only shrugged. "Why would you come to this thing if you're not going to beg for money?"

"I don't know," Sully said. "The science?"

Emily gave up and addressed her next question to Jason. "What's the hold up? You've got at least a dozen marks from the Pentagon here and all of them have taxpayer money burning holes in their pockets." As she spoke, she began scratching at her forearm. Sully noticed a raw spot he hadn't seen the night before.

"Which is what I've been trying to tell him," Jason said. "Believe me, if I knew the password to his tablet I'd have submitted the damn thing myself."

Sully had kept quiet through the exchange but when the others went silent, and Emily raised an eyebrow in his direction, he decided to redirect.

"What's wrong with your arm?" he asked Emily.

She looked down at the hand that was once again scratching her forearm and she pulled it away.

"I'm doing some consulting for the Pentagon and they're testing microchips for building access so I volunteered." She raised her arm to show them the inflamed incision site. "It's supposed to get me in and out of the building faster but it itches like hell."

"So, they can track you wherever you go?" Jason asked. He shook his head. "Not in a million years."

Emily smirked. "Since the odds of you being asked to consult for the Pentagon are somewhere between slim and none, I don't think you have to worry about it."

"Ouch again," Jason said.

Emily turned to Sully. "Now, back to why you haven't submitted your proposal yet…" She raised a questioning eyebrow.

"Alright, you win," Sully said. "I'll submit before the next lecture. Even if I don't think we've established enough support for the causal relationship. And I think we're still shaky on factoring in the Lorentz Invariance."

It was Jason's turn to laugh. He made a sound that Sully could only describe as derisive.

"He thinks anyone actually reads past the first paragraph,"

Jason said to Emily. "After that they're just skimming for the word *weaponization.* And there's an added bonus if they spot the word *laser.*"

"It's like a Where's Waldo of military buzz words," Sully grumbled as the trio emerged into the lobby.

"Speaking of which," Jason said, "I'm not sure how he got out here ahead of us but I see a certain General heading for the canapés. So, I'm going to latch myself to his elbow and try to convince him that Leggett's a twit."

He hurried off and Sully watched him until the other man reached the general, with Sully having no doubt that his friend possessed the brazenness and determination to get the man to agree to a proposal he had not yet seen.

"Tell me, again, why you keep him around," Emily said, her own eyes following Jason's pursuit of largesse.

"Because he's not afraid to interrupt a hungry general." He paused, then added, "And because he's got enough dirt on me from our graduate days to keep me in thrall for the rest of my life."

"Is that a fact?" Emily asked. "If that's true then maybe I'll have to have that drink with him after all—just to loosen his tongue up a bit."

When Sully looked at her he couldn't interpret the meaning behind her smile, save that it had some correlation with the sly look in her eyes. Consequently, he chose to ignore it.

"And what about you?" he asked. "I'm betting you have a handful of suitors with deep pockets all lined up?"

"The usual suspects," she said with a shrug. "The typical interest from the DOD; a research partnership invite from MIT; and a project lead offer from NASA."

"And I'm guessing the DOD is at the top of that list."

"They can pay more," Emily said and Sully knew she was only half-kidding.

"Project lead at NASA could be hard to pass up."

Emily was shaking her head before he'd finished.

"They just went through another round of cuts. With the way things are shaking out there I'd be lucky if I had time to assemble a crew before they withdrew funding."

Sully proffered a sympathetic smile absent even a hint of sincerity.

"I'm sure you'll land on your feet," he said. "High energy density plasmas is a sexy field. MIT probably made the offer on the name alone."

Emily smirked.

"My project drills down to magnetic field topologies," she said. "Which doesn't look quite as sexy on the subject line. While yours falls under the experimental gravitational physics umbrella—which just rolls off the tongue."

Out of the corner of his eye Sully saw that Jason was still firmly attached to the general. He endured a moment of guilt that he'd held off on sending the proposal along but the feeling dissipated quickly; he knew how much Jason enjoyed the chase, despite the man's protestations. He turned his attention back to Emily.

"As long as you deliver it with a smile and a track record like yours you could probably leave off the title completely and still have people falling all over themselves for a piece of it," he said.

"I could say the same about you," Emily answered and Sully was observant enough to catch the precise moment when she wished she could pull the words back. He found himself amused at her discomfiture; and the cause of it was far enough in the rearview for him to be comfortable making her squirm a bit.

"Yeah, I'm sure no one here is at all concerned about seeing twenty billion flushed down the toilet because of a math error," he said, adopting a sly smile.

To her credit, Emily didn't take the bait. Instead, she gave him a knowing smirk.

"Which is the real reason you haven't submitted your proposal yet," she said. "Untenable causal relationship notwithstanding."

Despite knowing he'd played for the comment, hearing the truth of it put so succinctly gave Sully pause. He didn't say anything right away and when, after a time, he did, mischief had morphed into mild chagrin.

"Fortunately, the math is strictly theoretical this time," he said. "If I get something wrong, we don't lose a solar probe."

Emily's lip curled and she shook her head.

"Insecurity disguising itself as false modesty is unbecoming, Dr. Knight." Sully saw a flash of irritation in her green eyes but her expression softened almost immediately. "Our friend the general probably pissed away twenty billion before breakfast. Most likely on something with a few kilotons explosive yield."

The comment brought a smile to Sully's face and, apparently seeing her work done, Emily leaned close and brushed his cheek with her lips.

"I'm going to leave so you have time to press enter before the next lecture starts." She gave his arm a squeeze. Then she was gone.

He watched her walk away, his eyes following her as if she drew them along with some gossamer string. When she disappeared behind a group of men huddled in conference—her passing causing a lull in their own conversation—he aimed a derisive chuckle at himself and turned toward the buffet. Jason, plate in hand and absent a general, was one of a trio talking near the bar—the other women whose faces Sully found vaguely familiar, but not enough so to affix names to them. Sully caught Jason's eye and tried to wave him over but Sully begged off with a wink and turned the other way.

Outside, the air seemed cooler than it had been that morning and he took a few deep breaths, allowing it to clear his head. The exit he'd chosen came equipped with a low stone wall running the length of a landscape island and Sully settled onto it. For a while he just sat there, thinking and doing nothing, despite his promise to perform the last act that would transfer his and Jason's proposal from his tablet to the general's inbox. After a while, though, his mind began to wander and he was astute enough to recognize that he was avoiding clicking send—that, perhaps, Emily's analysis of the situation was more spot on than he wanted to admit.

Rather than give that thought any further consideration, though, he pulled his phone from his pocket. He'd missed two calls during the lecture—neither of which required an immediate response. But as he thumbed down, he saw the two missed calls from Elena—the ones he'd forgotten about as he'd left the hotel.

He listened to both: the shorter one with substantial background noise and the more intriguing one that promised attachments for his perusal. He smiled as he pulled the phone from his ear. While it had been a while since he'd heard from her, it was just like Elena to have sent him something to review without even a hint of an explanation.

Sully opened the file and then had to pull the phone close to even get an idea as to what it was he was looking at. It looked like a series of note pages—photos taken with a bright flash. He squinted and saw that the few pages he could see were in Italian and while he could speak the language passably, deciphering it from the screen of his phone was a different matter entirely.

He thumbed through the first few pages, all on what looked like the same letterhead. A shipping manifest perhaps? He could pick out a word or two from each page but not enough to get a feel for what he was looking at it. The next few pages, though, were only slightly more promising and that was solely because, on the same paper that made up the probable shipping manifest, Sully could see a series of numbers. His trained eye could pick out the math—a series of what looked like parabolic partial differential equations.

He frowned and paused over one of them, his thumb hanging over the advance button. It was a simple equation but, without a frame of reference, he had no idea what he was looking at. After several moments, he shrugged and brought his thumb down. The next several pages were more of the shipping documents—itemized lists with weights and international postal codes. Halfway through these Sully remembered that Elena's father owned a shipping company.

The more pages he went through, the more confused he became. Why would Elena have sent him pages of shipping documents that he could only assume belonged to her father?

As soon as that thought passed, it prompted another. Why would Elena have sent him the file and then not called him to follow up? Now that he reflected on it, there had been something in her voice during the second call. Agitation, perhaps?

By the time he reached the last image she'd sent him, he was well and truly puzzled. And the final page did little to mitigate that feeling. Unlike the others, the page was absent the letterhead prevalent on the others. Indeed, it was absent all but four lines of text, rendered in a neat and careful hand. Again, his suspect Italian kept him from translating the text with the confidence he would have liked but after he'd puzzled over it for a while he thought he'd adequately fleshed it out.

"Sudden joy to sudden sadness,
It will occur at Rome for the graces embraced:
Grief, cries, tears, weeping, blood, excellent mirth,
Contrary bands surprised and trussed up"[6]

He stared at the verse for several moments and realized that, if he wanted to make sense of any of this, he'd have to call the woman who'd sent him the file. He looked at the time and noted that the next lecture had already started—and that he had, as yet, not sent the proposal on—but the intrigue of a puzzle now held sway.

The call rang through to her voice mail and he ended the call without leaving a message. He sat on the landscape wall with the phone in his hand, frowning at nothing, parsing all of it in his mind. He called her again.

The phone was on the fourth ring before it was picked up.

---

[6] Nostradamus, M., & Garencières, T. (2001). *Nostradamus: his works and prophecies.* Urbana, IL: Standard Publications.

"Pronto?"

It was a man's voice and Sully, for a few long moments, found his own greeting latent on his tongue.

"Hello," he finally managed in his suspect Italian. "I'm looking for Elena Rossi."

The question was met with silence—one that lingered long enough for Sully to begin to suspect he'd lost the connection. But before he could try out the theory with another inquiry, the voice on the other end returned.

"This is Niccolo Rossi. Elena's father. Who is this?"

During his time in Rome Sully had only had occasion to meet the elder Rossi a handful of times. Elena had spoken little of him. The fact that the man had answered Elena's phone ignited an ember of unease in Sully.

"Mr. Rossi, my name is Solomon Knight. I was a colleague of your daughter at Sapienza."

There was another pause—one that only fanned the flame of Sully's unease.

"I remember you, Dr. Knight," Rossi said. The man sounded tired. "Elena spoke of you often."

Something about that set off an alarm bell in Sully's brain and it took a few long seconds for him to realize it was Rossi's use of the past tense.

"Sir?" he managed.

Another of the long silences ensued but, this time, Sully found himself hoping it wouldn't end—fearful of what waited on the other side of it.

"I'm sorry to have to tell you this, Dr. Knight," Rossi said, his voice heavy. "But my daughter is dead."

Chapter Three

The place smelled of antiseptic. Which Sully found strange because the building was, like many structures in this part of the city, old—the sort of age that hoarded memory and history and dust. The kind that manifested itself in worn wood and hairline cracks in the masonry.

But in this place, the wear, the cracks, the markers of countless thousands of visitors over the centuries, were glossed with polish and scent—pine for the wood, lavender in the viewing room. An old thing made more beautiful by age, yet sanitized for modern sensibilities.

Sully stopped just inside the door of the viewing room, taking the lay of it. There were fewer people than he'd expected considering the political and business connections of Elena's father. Then he reminded himself that he was late, that the visitation was into its third hour and many would have come and gone before his plane touched down at Fiumicino. He'd landed late, the plane delayed an hour in Washington, then parked into a queue over the airport. By the time he found himself exiting into Terminal Three he'd had doubts he'd be able to make the viewing at all.

But now he was here. He could see the coffin against the far wall. It was open but he couldn't see Elena from his vantage point. He didn't let his eyes linger long. Instead he sent them around the room. He spotted Elena's father near a pair of floral sofas against the wall to his right. Niccolo Rossi was talking with two other men. Even from across the room Sully could see the red rimming the man's eyes. Sully had met Rossi a handful of times when he worked in Rome and had always been impressed by the way he carried himself. He had the confidence of a captain of industry; the carriage of a lord; the keen eye and sharp instincts of a man for whom making money is a genetic trait. Now he just looked broken and bent.

Sully started toward Rossi and made it half way before Elena's father looked away from his companions and met Sully's eyes. The first second of that contact evinced a range of emotions that Sully couldn't hope to catalog, except to note that it included sadness, confusion, and supreme weariness. When Sully reached the trio, he held back a few feet, reluctant to intrude on a private conversation, if such could be told by body language. But Rossi immediately shifted his attention to Sully, extending a hand to bring him into the circle.

"I'm grateful you came, Dr. Knight," Rossi said. "I know Elena would have wanted you here."

"Mr. Rossi, I can't begin to tell you how sorry I am," Sully said. "Your daughter meant a great deal to me."

It was only half a stretch. At one time—when Sully had worked in this city—Elena *had* meant a great deal to him. But that was a long time ago and distance, other relationships, and the responsibilities of their respective careers had turned their time together into little more than warm memories. And the occasional reconnect when one or the other's business took them within proximity of the other.

"She spoke fondly of you, Solomon," Rossi said with a sad smile. "At one time, I'd even thought you'd end up in the family."

Sully chuckled. "And then your daughter came to her senses."

That pulled another small smile from the grieving father but it was also the kind of statement that lacked an obvious follow-up, considering the circumstances. Circumstances that Sully still hadn't quite figured out. The first time he spoke with Rossi, all the man could say was that Elena had been murdered. He didn't offer specifics and Sully, in shock at the news, hadn't pressed. On the flight over, he'd looked for what news he could find but there was little beyond the standard Italian news outlets: AKI, ANSA, La Repubblica. And these carried only the basics: the daughter of a prominent Rome businessman apparently strangled in a metro station.

"Mr. Rossi, I've been in transit most of the last twenty-four hours so I'm not up to speed. Can you tell me what happened? If they found whoever did this?"

As the questions left his lips, he wondered if the timing was appropriate? If, perhaps, jet lag and weariness had thinned the filters that would have kept the inquiries unasked. That thought was reinforced when Rossi did not immediately answer. Sully saw the other man's lips press together, saw the wince that flashed through his eyes. And something else. For the briefest of moments Rossi's eyes flicked to the other men in the group—the two he'd been talking with when Sully arrived, the two who had, to this point, remained silent.

For the first time, Sully turned his attention to these men. When he'd entered the room, he'd assumed the men were close friends or family. They'd stood near each other, leaning toward one another—hallmarks of an exchange of something more than pleasantries. But as Sully looked at them now, he wondered about that initial impression.

For one thing, there didn't seem to be a familial relationship. One of the men was fairer skinned, Nordic looking. The other was darker; perhaps Spanish. Both were impeccably dressed in dark, exquisitely cut suits. And both of them were watching Sully without even a hint of a smile. He glanced back at Niccolo Rossi, to find the man looking at him with something in his expression that Sully couldn't qualify. He only knew that it had something to do with the two strangers.

Sully turned back to them and forced a smile. One of the men proffered something similar in return but the other's face did not move, except to regard Sully as if he was a small fish on display in an equally small bowl. The look held coldness—calculation. It almost pulled a frown from Sully but he fought the impulse.

"I'm Solomon Knight," Sully said. "Elena and I used to work together at La Sapienza."

He offered a hand to the nearest man who, after a moment, took it.

"Mats Koning. A business associate of Mr. Rossi's."

Sully shook Koning's hand firmly and waited a few seconds before responding.

"I'm sure he appreciates you coming," Sully finally said. "At times like these we find that there are things more important than business."

He wasn't sure why he said it, why he was trying to goad the man, except that there was something about him—about both of them—that had raised his hackles. He couldn't put a finger on it; all he knew was that there was something going on here that wasn't quite right. Something he'd walked in on. Something he probably wouldn't have given a thought to were it not for the thing that had occurred to him during the flight from Washington.

What had struck him was that, if the timing of the news reports he'd seen were at all accurate, Elena was killed only minutes after leaving her last message on his voicemail. Sully couldn't help but feel guilty about that; if he hadn't missed her call, would she still be alive? Had he answered, would it have changed her path, her timing? Would she have, perhaps, lingered in one place long enough to miss the fate that became hers? He knew those were silly thoughts, that a person's life was comprised of a thousand different decisions and an untold number of external forces. There was no way to know if the choice between stopping for coffee or continuing on to the office would have some unforeseen effect. No way of knowing if letting a friend's call go to voice mail would end with that friend dying in a metro bathroom. He wouldn't excoriate himself, even as he mourned her loss. But he couldn't just overlook the coincidence of it. She'd left him two messages and sent him several pictures; then she was dead. What made things even more delicate was that several of the files she'd sent were photos of items on Niccolo Rossi's letterhead. He hadn't spared much time studying the pictures in detail. Most of his time in the air had been spent coordinating things with Jason—making sure that the proposal he'd promised to submit in-flight had, indeed, been submitted. Still, all of it made him uneasy. And the two icicles standing in front of him didn't help matters.

One of those icicles—Mats Koning—seemed not to realize he was being baited.

"You taught at the university, then?" he asked.

"Just for two years," Sully said. "I left for a position at MIT."

"Do you mind me asking what you teach?"

"Astrophysics," Sully said. "But I'm not teaching anymore. I'm privately financed."

Koning raised any eyebrow.

"Astrophysics," the man said. "Impressive."

"Not overly," Sully said. "It just means that most of my gray matter is wired for a single area, which generally indicates a person is woefully deficient in just about everything else. Elena was the brilliant one. Multi-discipline PhDs; five peer-reviewed books; and invites to teach just about anywhere in the world."

Sully kept his eyes on Koning but he could see Rossi and the other man in his periphery. The latter's expression hadn't changed but Rossi looked troubled.

"A great loss, indeed," Koning said and, from his tone, Sully doubted the man cared.

"If you gentlemen would excuse us, I'd like to have a minute alone with Mr. Rossi," Sully said.

He knew he was being presumptuous. It had been years since he'd seen Elena's father and, for all he knew, these men were close confidants, with more claim on the man than Sully had. Still, whatever undercurrent was making him uneasy also made him bolder than he might have been.

There was a moment's hesitation all around before, with a nod, Mats Koning moved off, his silent companion following. When they were gone, Sully turned to Niccolo Rossi.

"My apologies, Mr. Rossi. I was hoping we could have a private word."

"No apology necessary, Dr. Knight," Rossi said. "Those two had my ear long enough." There was a measure of levity in the statement but Sully thought it forced.

"Mr. Rossi, I just wanted to say again how sorry I am for your loss. I'm still having a hard time processing it."

"We all are," Elena's father answered.

Silence fell over the pair for several seconds. Sully wasn't at his best in situations like this; he doubted many were.

"Mr. Rossi," he began, "I may have been the last person your daughter called before she was killed."

Rossi's eyebrows went up in surprise.

"I was at a reception in Washington and my phone went to voicemail. She left me a message right before…" Sully trailed off.

Rossi was silent for a time, digesting this news. When he did speak, his voice was quiet.

"What did she say?" was all he asked. Sully thought he understood. Whatever message Elena left might well have been her last words.

"Not much, I'm afraid. She said she needed to talk to me—that she had something she wanted me to take a look at. I never got a chance to call her back."

Rossi seemed to absorb this. The normally confident, patrician eyes searched Sully's own.

"Nothing else?" the man asked.

Sully was slow in responding. It occurred to him that the photos Elena had sent him—at least the ones showing the Rossi letterhead—might have come to him without the approval of her father. He wondered if revealing them would mean a breaking of a confidence. The more he thought about it, though, the more he came to believe that Elena's death had freed him from the constraints of secrecy.

"She sent a number of pictures, Mr. Rossi. She wanted me to look at them and get back to her. I have a feeling she wasn't quite sure what she was looking at."

Sully didn't know what reaction he expected from Rossi but it wasn't the one he received. He saw Rossi's eyes widen, his mouth open almost imperceptibly. The first word that came to Sully's mind was *worry*.

"Mr. Rossi?"

The man composed himself quickly.

"You say she sent you pictures?"

"A series of photos. Most of pages on your company letterhead." He paused, trying to see if this pronouncement had any effect on Rossi. If it did, it was confined to a slight tightening of his eyes. "Do you have any idea why she would have sent those to me?"

Rossi's headshake came a shade too slow.

"I'm afraid I don't," Rossi said. "Elena had a good deal of control over our North American operations. There wasn't much she was required to run by me."

Sully remembered Niccolo Rossi's constant nudging of his

daughter toward the family business—something she'd resisted for a long while. Rossi was without sons; Elena his only heir.

"Can you tell me what was on the papers?" Rossi asked.

"I haven't had much time to review them," Sully said. "But they appear to be mostly shipping manifests. Which, I suppose, isn't that surprising for a shipping company."

Rossi chuckled at that. But the mirth was gone too quickly, leaving the two men in silence.

"And that was all?" Rossi finally asked.

Something about the way he asked the question, coupled with the strange vibe Sully had already picked up on, caused Sully to pause before answering. And to answer with less than honesty.

"That was it," he said, finding himself unwilling to reveal the existence of the equations that had accompanied the manifests. Or the partial Nostradamus quatrain she'd supplied, almost as an afterthought. A quick web search had revealed to him the source of the verse, as well as the ones before and after. However, rather than providing any kind of clarity, the inclusion of a five-hundred-year-old text with shipping logs and advanced math equations made Sully's head hurt.

He wanted answers and part of the reason he'd come here was to seek those answers. Yet, now that he was here, he found himself unwilling to show his hand. Something about this place—these people—had raised his defenses. He didn't know why but it was enough that he could feel it. All of a sudden, he wanted nothing more than to pay his respects to Elena and leave.

"If you'll excuse me, sir, I'd like to go pay my respects to your daughter." He knew it was an abrupt conversational exit but, right then, he didn't care.

He left Rossi and his secrets and made his way to the coffin, the one he hadn't settled his eyes on since the moment he walked in the room.

She looked like she was sleeping. There wasn't a mark on her—nothing to indicate that she'd suffered a brutal death less than forty-eight hours earlier. It had been more than a year since he'd seen her last but she looked just the same. Like she could simply sit up and flash him that full, warm smile he remembered—the one that would tell him this had all been a joke, a jest at his expense.

He placed his hands on the wood and looked at Elena, letting himself remember what she'd once meant to him. He wasn't a religious man. He'd never had much use for it. He wouldn't pray for her soul, or even for some phantom peace for her family, for himself. All he could do was to remember. He hoped that would be enough.

He stayed there for several minutes and, when he finally left, he did so without a word to anyone.

Chapter Four

As he stepped outside, he had to squint against the morning brightness that somehow made its way past the five-story buildings that lined the narrow street. Just beyond the doorway, he stopped to get his bearings. Despite the circumstances that had brought him back, he loved Rome and, although he had a flight that would take him back Stateside this afternoon, he wanted to absorb as much of it as he could.

He'd stayed at The Duke twice before and, if he remembered correctly, a handful of coffee shops and quaint breakfast places dotted the route from Via Archimede to Via di San Valentino. He could have eaten at the hotel restaurant—all five-star fare—but there was something about eating out among the locals, sampling the real food of a place.

He started off, following the sidewalk past the queue of parked mopeds and small cars that lined the street. Across the road, a two-tiered garden high-lighted with red blooms made concentric semi-circles along the outer wall of a curved apartment building. The air held a perfect crispness and carried with it the smells of a place both foreign and familiar. It was almost enough to let him shake off the pall of the last few days. Almost.

His dreams had been troubled by images of Elena. He'd slept

fitfully into the early morning hours until, finally succumbing to exhaustion and jet lag, he'd sunk into a deeper sleep that hung heavy on him after the wakeup call came. What had happened at the wake the day before also weighed on him. As he'd left the funeral home, and once the edge to his mood had softened, he was forced to review his short, strange conversation with Rossi. The whole of it, viewed from the inside, had been almost surreal and now, separated from it by several hours, it seemed no less so.

He wasn't certain what he'd been expecting. The requisite paternal grief, of course. Fatigue, confusion, a grasping for answers. All of those would have been appropriate and all were, indeed, present. It was the other, though, that unsettled him—the strange looks given to certain questions, the slow answers to others, the men who had seemed reluctant to let him speak with Rossi alone.

In truth, he wasn't certain why he was letting any of it bother him. Elena was dead and he was no longer beholden to whatever consult she'd wanted of him. Yet he knew himself well enough to understand that it would keep eating at him. It would stay with him after he returned Stateside. And while he and Jason worked at fleshing out their proposal. Maybe even well into the work. There was no way to tell how long it would stay with him. For that reason alone, he knew he had to do some digging—even just enough to sift the dirt a bit.

Ultimately it came back to the files Elena had sent him. He'd reviewed them again that morning on his laptop, where he'd sent them to enlarge the images. On the bigger screen, he could pull more detail from the shipping manifests but that hadn't been as helpful as he'd hoped. There were three distinct manifests marked by lot numbers and shipping dates. The listed items were marked numerically and Sully could only assume there existed a file somewhere that matched those numbers to the real items they represented.

In fact, Sully was only able to glean two things from the manifests. The first was that all three had their cargo going to the same place: Lisbon. The second—and the most intriguing—was that each of the manifests was signed by Nicolo Rossi, himself. Which meant that whatever cargo the numbers denoted was worth the notice of a man whose company routinely managed the transport of some of the world's most valuable items.

By the time he reached Via di San Valentino all he'd accomplished was to determine that he wouldn't get anywhere without breakfast. And coffee. And as if in answer to that need the first thing he saw when he rounded the corner was a small café, nearly hidden by its blending with the buildings on either side. In fact, the only reason Sully saw it was because of the signboard on the sidewalk. He crossed the street and entered, the smell of fresh cornettos hitting him the moment he passed the threshold. He stopped just inside the door for a moment, taking the lay of the place. There were a half-dozen people seated at small, white tables—most with cappuccinos and the customary cornetto in front of them. Sully took a table along the wall to his right, one that afforded him a view of the sidewalk running in front of the café but that also kept a table between him and the nearest patrons. The place was quiet and brightly lit and, working in tandem with the walk, served to improve his mood. It wasn't long before someone appeared at his table and, using the situational Italian that had served him well years ago, he ordered.

As he sat waiting for her to return, he let the dichotomous familiarity and strangeness of the place lead him. And before long it led him back to the puzzle of Elena and Nicolo Rossi. He pulled his phone out and opened the files. Smaller, nearly illegible on the screen. But he didn't need to read the manifests, or the strange Nostradamus quatrain. Instead, he was drawn to the math problem—the equation he had, as yet, had little time to ponder.

He brought the phone close and studied it, looking for whatever it was that had caught Elena's attention—and that had made her think it was something he'd want to see. It didn't take him long before he had the first bit; he had the astronomical units parsed out before the server set the cappuccino in front of him. That was the obvious part, the portion that his field made understanding second nature. It was the rest, though, that caused him to raise an eyebrow and keep it there. The astronomical units—positioning an object somewhere out there—were just part of some more complex problem. One that used Diophantine equations and Algebraic topology. He readily admitted the math was outside of his area. He suspected he could figure it out if he applied himself but the differences between the physics in which he worked and the math on the screen in front of him required a substantial learning curve. It would have certainly been beyond Elena who, while brilliant, had no education or experience with this field. In fact, there was only one person—maybe two—he suspected could understand what he was looking at with only a minimum of strain. He closed the file and called Jason.

The phone was ringing before it hit him that it was 2:00 AM in New York. With a perverse sense of pleasure, he let it keep ringing.

"You have to be kidding," came Jason's voice after the fourth ring.

"Morning, sunshine," Sully said.

He heard Jason shifting in the hotel bed, a few grumbled curses mixed in.

"The only thing that's keeping me from making a solemn vow to kill you when you get back is because I'm assuming you're calling for something really important. And I mean important like someone's died…" Jason's voice trailed off as his brain caught up with the flow of words, as he remembered why Sully was in Rome.

"Sorry," he managed.

"I'm the one who woke you up in the middle of the night," Sully said. "You don't have anything to apologize for."

After a pause he added, "And to make you feel better I knew perfectly well what time it was when I called and, no, what I need isn't that important. Which just made it fun to call."

That elicited more grumbling and Sully took it with a smile. While he waited, the server arrived with the cornetto, the chocolate showing through a hole in the side of the pastry. He nodded his thanks.

"So, what do you need?" Jason finally asked.

"I need your help with a math problem."

There was a pause on the other end of the call and Sully knew that his friend's love of a good math problem was warring with his righteous indignation.

"What kind of problem?" Jason asked.

"I have no idea," Sully said. "Except that it has something to do with astronomical point plotting."

Jason went silent again but only for a few seconds. "Does this have anything to do with those files Elena sent you?"

"It does."

Jason grunted. Sully heard more shifting noises through the connection.

"Can I assume there's something going on that makes this more than an old girlfriend asking for a professional consult?" Jason asked.

Sully didn't answer right away. He picked up the fork and poked at the cornetto. While he studied the pastry, the café door opened and a man entered. The newcomer stopped just inside the door. Sully looked up, took in the dark suit. A narrow face with an aquiline nose pinched by thin-frame glasses. The man scanned the room, much as Sully had before him. He took a table on the other side of the café.

"I'm not sure," Sully said. "Right now, I just want to understand what this stuff is. Elena seemed to think it was important."

He didn't go farther because, in truth, he didn't know if his own thoughts on the matter were organized enough to be coherent to anyone else. All he had were impressions—hints there was something just beneath the surface. It was just an itch; and he had to scratch it.

"Okay," Jason said. "Send it along and I'll see what I can do."

"Thanks," Sully said. "And get some sleep. Don't you know what time it is in New York?"

He hung up mid-curse and, with a smile, sent the file on to Jason. That done, he set to the serious business of breakfast. The cappuccino was still hot and he sipped at it. Then he dove into the cornetto, which was just as good as he remembered.

As he ate, he looked around the room, as if it, alone, stood in for the whole of Rome, which he would be leaving soon. He raised another forkful of pastry to his mouth as his eyes fell on the man in the dark suit, the one sitting with an untouched coffee. When his eyes lit on the man, Sully found himself frowning but he couldn't tell himself why. Almost as if he'd picked up on something on a subconscious level. Whatever it was, though, remained elusive. In fact, even as Sully watched, the man rose, pulled a few euros from his wallet, set them on the table, and left, the full cup of coffee sloshing as he brushed the table with his leg. Sully watched as he exited, then as he passed in front of the window. Sully frowned but before he could ponder it further, his phone rang.

"I'm going to have to pull Emily into this," Jason said. "That is, if you're okay with that."

There was a quality to the man's voice that Sully thought he recognized. On one hand, it was the intrigue of a puzzle. Coupled with that, though, was the knowledge that what he was looking at eluded him, too.

"If you think we need her, sure," Sully said.

"I think her experience with parabolic research will be helpful," Jason said. "Because I'm going to be honest with you, Sully. I only understand half of what I'm looking at."

Sully stifled a chuckle, understanding how that admission must vex his friend.

"Bring her in, then," he said. "And, Jason? I appreciate you taking a look."

"I'm not just doing it for you," Jason said. "I'm doing it for Dr. Hannah. This will give her another opportunity to see what she's missing."

"Always the altruist," Sully said. When he ended the call, he found that he felt better than he had since boarding the flight to Rome.

After slipping the phone in his pocket he downed the rest of the cappuccino, paid the bill and stepped out into the street. The mosaic light of early morning had given way to a sharper brightness, one that rendered the street in finer lines and contrasts. He stood for a few moments on the sidewalk. He still had a few hours before he had to be at the airport and there were undoubtedly places within walking distance that he could explore—bookstores, museums, historical spots. Even as he considered it, though, he knew it would just be killing time. He wouldn't enjoy any of it as much as he should. As it had with Jason, the lure of a puzzle now held sway.

With that in mind, he stepped off the curb, aiming toward the hotel. Even though most of an hour had passed there were still few pedestrians, and even fewer cars, in view, the section of the street he was on secluding the area from a good portion of the city traffic. As he walked, he considered all of the things on his plate once he landed in New York. Aside from the investigation into Elena's files he and Jason now had to put flesh to the proposal they'd submitted. Despite the reservations he'd voiced to both Jason and Emily, Sully didn't harbor any serious doubts that their proposal would be accepted. Jason was right; it had all the right buzzwords.

He saw it first as little more than a blur—some nagging thing at the edge of his vision. Something easily ignored by a man deep in thought. But on a nearly deserted street, any movement at all was worthy of notice. He was halfway across Via di San Valentino before he turned to look, before he registered the dark sedan coming toward him much too fast, before he glimpsed a man in a dark suit.

For just a moment Sully stood frozen, as the car made its approach, as time seemed to compress, bringing the car to a crawl that, try as he might, he would never be able to outrun. Then, as with the breaking of some spell, Sully moved. The car was only feet away when he threw himself forward. The fender caught him just above the knees, tossing him into the air, the thing happening too quickly for him to register pain. Then he met the windshield, the impact stealing his breath. Then the car was gone and the ground was coming up to meet him. Then all was darkness.

Chapter Five

Long before he was aware enough to put words to it, he knew that he was surrounded by pain. It was like coming out of a pea-soup fog, or rising from the black water of the deep ocean, floating upward toward the farthest reaches of light from the surface. Then, as the pain became something more solid, more recognizable, his upward swim stalled and the deep threatened to pull him back. He hung in that middle state for what might have been a long while, or could have been just a moment, but the urge to swim toward that light at the surface was too strong.

When he opened his eyes everything he saw was comprised of blinding white. He closed them again and, after a time, tried again, opening them a sliver. Working against the pain, which was localizing for him at various areas around his body—most noticeably the back of his head—he blinked through the brightness until shapes began to resolve themselves.

It took several more blinks before things lost their fuzzy edges enough for him to put words to them. Chair; television; heart monitor; IV line; nurse. In a flash, it came back to him—breakfast; the conversation with Jason; the car…

The recall did much to chase off any lingering cobwebs. It also made him want to sit up. But when he tried, two things stopped him. The first was a new, sharp pain that seemed to travel the entire surface area of his skull. The second was the nurse, a petite young woman with incongruously strong hands, which she placed on his shoulders and used to force him back down.

"Non ti muovere!" she said, frowning down at him. She kept her hands in place just long enough to ensure he wouldn't try to get up again and then she stepped back. "Mi metterò il medico."

Sully's Italian wasn't great under optimum conditions and his condition at the moment was certainly not optimum. So he simply offered a smile meek enough to convince her it was safe to leave. She returned less than a minute later, a doctor in tow. A young man; Sully wondered how many weeks separated him from the end of med school.

"Welcome back," the doctor said, his English almost without accent.

"Have I been somewhere?" Sully asked.

"Somewhere quite far off, yes."

He came to the bedside and leaned in, peering into Sully's eyes. After a few moments, he pulled a pen light from his shirt pocket and repeated his study.

"How's the headache?" he asked as he moved the light around.

"Manageable."

The doctor smirked. He straightened and returned the light to his pocket.

"It will become less manageable over the next few hours." At Sully's questioning look he added, "A blow to the head like the one you've taken can produce dizziness, nausea, and a good deal of pain. At least it will once the Dilaudid wears off."

Sully, who could hardly fathom moving his head more than a few inches above the pillow even with the aid of the intravenous medication, frowned.

"Did they catch the guy?" he asked.

The doctor's eyebrows knit. Then he looked again at Sully's chart.

"You were the victim of a hit and run," he said.

"Not news to me."

The doctor looked up. "There's a notation on your chart that the Polizia are to be called when you awaken. I imagine they'll want to see if you can provide a description of the vehicle."

Eyes still closed, Sully merely nodded. He had a response on his lips but before he could speak it he found himself sinking. Then the hospital room was gone.

Sometime later, through the fog, Sully became aware of an insistent chime—a familiar noise that titillated the edges of his consciousness for a time before receding into the auditory shadows. He couldn't quantify how long this coming and going of the noise occurred; only that it happened for an eternity before any part of his conscious mind could single it out from the rest of the cacophony.

His eyes fluttered open. He was in the same hospital room,

surrounded by the same machinery. The only difference was that the light coming through the window was different—the day faded. He lay there for a while, feeling the pain in his head, an ache in his back that he couldn't remember from the last time he'd been awake.

Whatever it was that had brought him back to consciousness had gone, leaving him alone in a quiet hospital room. He used the time to collect his thoughts. It was a difficult task, with so many variables jockeying for his attention. But before long he was able to settle on the thing that had consigned him to a hospital bed. The accident came to him like movie stills, detailed and vibrant. He could replay the entire scene in his mind up to the moment of impact after which, mercifully, the film came off the reel. He could see the car perfectly—a new sedan, a Peugeot he was almost certain. It had been traveling fast—much too fast for the narrow avenue. But the sun's glare kept him from seeing through the windshield, from seeing the person behind the wheel with any clarity. The only thing he knew for certain was that whoever had been driving wore a dark suit.

His body released an involuntary shudder. Fighting against the pain in his skull, he propped himself up enough to reach the pitcher of water on the bedside table. He took several greedy sips, only realizing how thirsty he was after he started to drink. When he was finished, he settled back into the pillow.

He had no idea what time it was but he knew he'd missed his flight. Worse, he didn't know how long they planned to keep him here, which meant Jason would have to handle the meeting with the

University of Chicago's Astronomy and Astrophysics Department himself. Sully sighed, pondering how a single step off a curb could throw everything into chaos.

Even as he thought it, though, he found that the observation didn't sit well. On one hand, the thing seemed like a simple accident. A step into the street in front of a speeding car. But try as he might to make that the official version of events, he couldn't shake the dark thoughts milling about in the background. The events surrounding Elena's death had already had him on edge, as had the strange conversation with Mr. Rossi at Elena's wake. He also remembered the man in the café, the uneasy feeling Sully had of being watched. How the man had risen and left the café without touching his coffee.

The more he thought about it, the more the accident served to put flesh to those dark shadows. When he'd come to Rome it had been solely to pay respects to Elena. The business with the files that she'd sent him had been ancillary. Now, though, he couldn't help but think that there was something bigger swimming just out of sight, the tip of a large fin just beginning to break the surface.

Sully had never put much stock in coincidence. He'd found that most things that caused him to raise an eyebrow ended up following a pattern, or having a design. As yet, he didn't know what the design was for this business but he was beginning to suspect that it was something intricate enough for his gentle probing to have engendered a disproportionate response. And to have cost a woman her life…

This progression of thought sobered him. It also unnerved him as he realized how vulnerable he was in a hospital bed in a foreign country. Even so, he couldn't bring himself to fully buy in to the burgeoning conspiracy theory. Coincidence was, after all, a very real thing.

When he heard the ringing of his phone coming from his pants, which were folded over a chair in the corner, he struggled to swing his legs over the side of the bed before the first chirp had faded. As he righted himself, the pain in his skull increased exponentially. For a moment, he thought he might pass out, collapsing to the floor next to the bed. But the room steadied enough for him to stand, bracing himself on the bedrail. It was his first opportunity to take stock of himself. He was naked, save for his underwear and an untied hospital gown. His clothes were all on the chair. He reached for the clip on his finger that fed his vitals to the heart monitor but then he stopped. The second the monitor stopped transmitting, someone would be in his room. He didn't know why that thought unnerved him as much as it did. He only knew that it was a feeling borne in his gut and he had no intention of ignoring it.

He pulled both the heart monitor and the IV pole with him as he moved to the chair, careful not to pull the power cord from the former. By the time he reached his clothes the phone had stopped. He pulled it from the pocket and looked at the last few calls. They were all from Jason. He considered calling Jason back but, instead, he slipped the phone back into the pocket, pulled the chair close enough so that he could sit in it and still remain connected to the monitor, then began the laborious task of putting his pants on. He was weak and his head was pounding and he was conscious of the way the heart monitor noted his increased adrenaline. He took a deep breath to slow things down a bit then moved on to socks and shoes. When that was done, he stood and fastened the belt.

He looked at the last two items remaining: a button-down shirt and undershirt. He dismissed the latter and reached for the button-down. Draping it over his forearm, he removed the tape holding the IV in place then slipped out the catheter, the hole welling with blood as the plastic slipped free. He grabbed for the undershirt and pressed down on the spot until the blood slowed. There was a table to his right, upon which were a variety of triage paraphernalia. Freed from the IV pole, he walked the heart monitor over to the table and applied a bandage to the catheter wound.

He dropped the bloody undershirt and slipped his arm into one of the shirt sleeves. He paused, taking stock of himself. His phone was in one pocket and he reached back and verified that his wallet and passport were in another. Then, with nothing left to do, he disconnected the clamp from his finger, slipped his arm through the other sleeve and was heading toward the door while buttoning. He didn't break stride as he stepped into the hallway and a quick glance around told him he'd been lucky—that his room was not within the sight line of the nurses' station.

He'd almost reached the elevator, moving more slowly than

he would have liked, before he sensed movement behind him but he didn't turn to look. Likely it was a single nurse coming to see if the clip had slipped from his finger. Luckily the elevator door opened only seconds after he reached it, bringing with it a woman in a wheelchair, pushed by an orderly. Neither so much as glanced at Sully as he stepped past them, still buttoning his shirt, and he pressed the button for the first floor. Only when the doors slipped closed did he feel a measure of relief. And even then, he couldn't really decide if what he'd done was necessary—if he wasn't creating a boogeyman where none existed.

When the doors opened on the first floor, he stepped into the lobby and took a moment to spot the exit. He threaded his way through guests, patients, and personnel until he put a hand on the door, gave it a push and was standing in the open air.

The change in temperature sent pins and needles arching over his skull and he had to resist the urge to run a hand along his head. It occurred to him that he hadn't taken a moment to look at himself in a mirror; he had no idea what kind of image he presented. It also occurred to him that the IV bag he'd left behind had been pumping Dilaudid into his system and that it wouldn't be too long before whatever pain the drug had been mitigating returned full-force.

As he'd navigated the corridors he caught the name of the hospital: Ospedale Sandro Pertini. He'd never heard of it; neither did he know the name of the street at which the exit deposited him: Via Del Tufo. But there were three taxis waiting and he got in the first one.

"The Duke Hotel."

The driver nodded and pulled away from the curb.

Sully relaxed into the seat, allowing the cab driver to shoulder the burden of his safety for the time being. But then the right front tire of the car dipped into a pothole and Sully nearly cursed at the sharp pain that rocketed through his head. He pulled out his phone and, as much as he was able in the cramped confines of the car, held it up and behind him and snapped a picture of his head. He caught the driver's eyes in the rearview but ignored them.

The image didn't show anything as ghastly as he'd imagined—nothing that seemed to account for how much pain he was in. But he supposed a skull fracture would not necessarily manifest itself visibly. What he did see was a dark discoloration just beneath the crown of his head. There were also a series of scratches, likely from contact with the pavement. He was pleased, though, to see that they hadn't shaved his head. Whatever tests they'd done to him while he was out must have revealed that the damage was almost all of the internal variety.

That thought sobered him. Despite his belief that getting out of the hospital had been a necessary thing, he had a serious head injury. He knew he'd need to get checked out sooner or later. He tabled that need for the time being, though, and dialed Jason's number. His friend picked up on the first ring.

"I've been trying to reach you all day," Jason said. Sully could hear exasperation in his voice.

"Yeah, sorry about that. I've been indisposed for the last few hours."

There was a pause; then Jason said, "A stewardess, right?"

"Not even close."

"Which probably means it's the kind of story you'll need to tell me over a bottle of bourbon."

Sully found himself pitched forward as the driver mashed the brake, then blared the horn at the car that had cut them off. For just a moment Sully felt like he was back in New York.

"Do I hear traffic?" Jason asked. "Are you back in DC already?"

"I'm still in Rome," Sully said.

The silence that pronouncement produced was of a different kind. Sully could see Jason doing the math in his head.

"Wasn't your flight supposed to leave six hours ago?"

"It's a long story, Jason. And I promise I'll share it with you over that bottle. Right now I'm heading back to my hotel to check out and then I'll catch the first flight back I can find."

That seemed to satisfy Jason, who let the matter drop.

"The reason I've been calling is because the lovely Dr. Hannah and I were able to figure out some of what you sent us."

"You and Dr. Hannah?"

"Okay, mostly her," Jason said grudgingly. "But in all fairness, gravity is really more her area than mine."

"Gravity?"

"Gravitational degradation, actually," Jason said. "In simplest terms, it's a probability scale. You start with an object with a known trajectory—one so straight you could predict it thousands of years into the future—then you toss a series of variables at it to see how they affect the course."

"Then the Diophantine equations?"

"Are processing object X's reaction to the variables." Jason paused and when he spoke again, Sully could hear genuine appreciation in his voice. "It's a pretty nifty bit of math. I'd like to meet the person who came up with it."

"You mean you wish you'd come up with it."

"Naturally," Jason said.

Sully took a few moments to ponder what Jason had told him.

"So, we have celestial coordinates and some high-level math that's supposed to account for the gravitational shift of an object," Sully said.

"Right. Except we only have partial coordinates. What you sent me is using a heliocentric elliptical model and we've got right ascension, declination, and hour. What we're missing is distance."

Sully knew that; he'd picked up on the missing variable before he'd sent the pages on to his friend. Not that it mattered. None of what he was uncovering made any sense. What would have been Elena's interest in celestial coordinates? And how would those have anything to do with her father's shipping manifests? Unless...

"What if there's no distance measure because the person who

wrote it is assuming a low earth orbit?" Sully asked.

"You mean a satellite," Jason supplied.

Sully shook his head even as Jason said it. "I really have no idea," he said. "I'm just reaching at the moment."

He didn't tell his friend that the growing insistent pounding in his head was making it difficult to give serious thought to much of anything.

"Anyway, thanks," he said. "That's a lot more than I had this morning."

"Save your thanks," Jason said. "You can thank me later with a nice Italian bottle of something or other."

"Done."

After he ended the call he leaned forward.

"You wouldn't happen to have any aspirin, would you?"

He saw the cab driver's eyes again in the rearview. A few seconds later the man proffered a bottle to Sully. He took it, dumped four Ibuprofen tablets in his palm, and then handed the bottle back. He swallowed the pills dry, willing them to do their work quickly.

When they arrived, Sully made a slow and less than graceful exit from the car, paid and generously tipped the driver, and entered a hotel he should have checked out of hours ago. He took the elevator to the third floor and was relieved when his key card opened the door. It meant they hadn't kicked him out and stuffed his luggage in some maintenance closet.

The door opened to darkness and he took a step in and flipped the switch just inside the door. Then he froze, his hand still on the switch.

The room had been tossed. The mattress was half-off the bed; the dresser drawers had been pulled and their contents dumped onto the carpet. Even the trash can had been overturned, the contents ostensibly sifted through.

For a time, Sully stood rooted to his particular piece of carpet near the door. He had a fleeting thought that whoever had done the deed might still be here. But he shook that off, suspecting that whoever had paid him the visit had done so hours ago. He advanced into the room, leaving the door open behind him.

He stopped near the bed and surveyed the room, hands on hips. There were a great many things clamoring for his attention—a jumble of thoughts all jostling for preeminence—but the one he latched onto right away was that what he was witnessing validated his decision to flee the hospital. It wasn't an affirmation that pleased him but it was all he had at the moment. It kept him from considering how serious this was—how the violation of his hotel room signified something even more dangerous than he'd considered.

With a sigh, he lowered himself to the bed, finding a perch on the askew mattress. His eyes moved over the room, taking it all in. They passed over the dresser, the desk, the open bathroom door. Then they moved back to the desk and, for what seemed a long while, he wasn't sure why.

When it hit him, he shot to his feet and he hardly noticed the stab of pain in his head. The desk was bare. His laptop was gone.

Chapter Six

The chair creaked with every shift of Sully's weight but he barely noticed. Neither did he give more than scant attention to the odors of old coffee and sweat that permeated the small room. His eyes were on the monitor as the man next to him ran the footage at four times the normal speed. The camera from which the footage was taken was positioned above and to the left of the elevator on Sully's floor and provided a full, if slightly askew view of the entire hall.

The man operating the controls said little and Sully did nothing to make him more amiable. It had taken a good deal of persuasion—and a few hundred euros—to convince the security guard to let him see the footage and Sully didn't want to do anything that might break their tenuous détente.

An hour earlier, as he'd taken in the violation of his hotel room, he'd considered calling the police. He had, in fact, had the phone in his hand to do so. But something had stayed him. Even now, sitting in one of the Duke's security rooms, he couldn't say for sure what. All he knew was that something was screaming *caution* into his ear. A part of him knew the reason for that insistent voice; it was the constant reorganization of the disparate pieces of a growing puzzle, finding the edges that met, the way the pieces seemed to hint at something much larger. It was the process of taking Elena's files, her death, Sully's unnerving conversation with her father, the fact that he'd been followed, hit, and left for dead, his hotel room tossed. Viewed together, it resembled something with enough tendrils to make Sully wary about trusting anyone—even the police.

On the monitor, people made their artificially accelerated ways up and down the hall, entering and exiting rooms, lingering by and spilling out of the elevator. A mixture of guests and hotel staff, pushing or carrying luggage or carts. Sully kept his eyes fixed on his own door but, while a number of people walked by it, no one's hand touched the doorknob.

The footage rolled for several minutes. By Sully's reckoning there was a six-hour block during which someone could have entered the room and even at four times the speed that left a good hour and a half of viewing. He hoped his few hundred euros would buy him that much forbearance. They were twenty minutes in and the security guy still hadn't spoken but Sully picked up on the more frequent shifts in position, the signs of boredom. He thought about the money still in his wallet, wondering if he'd have to dip into it again. Then something on the monitor pulled his attention away from anything else.

The elevator had opened, depositing two men in the hallway. Both wore dark suits and, despite the standard hallway lighting, sunglasses. The speed with which they moved was evident even through the speed of the video playback. Sully watched as they moved down the hallway, past a hotel employee pushing a janitorial cart. One glanced back once they'd past the cart, then he and his compatriot proceeded past Sully's door. Once they were out of the frame Sully, who had found himself leaning closer to the monitor, felt a wave of disappointment pass through him. The hotel employee paused at the elevator, then disappeared as the doors opened. Sully leaned back and sighed but the exhalation stopped as the dark suited men once again appeared in the monitor.

"Slow it down," Sully said, the first words he'd spoken in a half-hour.

Seconds later the playback slowed to real time and Sully watched as one of the men moved to Sully's door. The other turned to watch down the hallway in the direction of the elevator.

"Can you zoom in?"

The security guard manipulated the controls and the action in front of Sully's door was instantly twice the size. Despite the magnification, the video quality was poor—too poor for Sully to get as clear a look as he would have liked at the man's features. Still, even with the sunglasses, the passing familiarity to the man in the coffee shop—likely the same man driving the Peugeot—was strong. He looked at the time stamp. The break-in would have happened some thirty minutes after the accident. And Sully was long past the point of suspecting it had been no accident.

It was strange to watch these two men do their work, considering that at the time this event occurred Sully was in a hospital bed. The man at the door made quick work of the lock, which told Sully these were professionals. Even the security guard, now watching as avidly as was Sully, grunted in appreciation. When both men disappeared into the room, the guard once again sped up the playback but he had to slow it less than a minute later as the door opened and the men emerged, one holding Sully's computer. He looked at the time stamp. The toss of his room had taken less than four minutes.

Sully watched as the two men returned to the elevator, then disappeared inside it.

"Wait a minute," the security guard said. The seat under him creaked as he shifted. He tapped a few keys and the screen changed to show the interior of the elevator. The two men were standing with heads down, aimed away from the camera. When they exited onto the first floor the guard again tapped keys, changing to a view of the hotel lobby. The progression of cameras on this level allowed Sully to watch the men until the moment they exited onto the street. When they disappeared from view, Sully leaned back in the chair. He stayed that way for several seconds. Then he turned to the security guard.

"Thank you," he said. He rose and walked out of the room.

On his way to the elevator he was acutely conscious of the fact that the man who had spent the last hour helping him could be watching him travel through the lobby—could, in fact, follow his progress all the way to his room if he so chose. But he decided he was too tired to contemplate that irony. Instead, he turned his faculties to considering his course of action.

The first choice—and the most enticing—was to return to his room, pack the things that hadn't been stolen, and return home. After all, he and Jason had submitted their proposal to the Defense Department and their collective livelihood rested on the acceptance of that pitch. Yet, even as he considered it, the thought returned to him tainted with the blood of a woman who had eschewed personal safety for truth.

Whatever it was that Elena had uncovered, it had meant enough to her that she had risked her life to share that information with him. That, alone, was enough for Sully to work against the inclination toward abandonment that threatened to overwhelm him. The problem, though, was that ignoring his first impulse left him with little on which to draw. On the face of it, he had a mystery—a puzzle to solve. Yet, he also had few clues—virtually nothing to take and run with.

The elevator stopped at his floor and moments later he was in the hallway, the same one he'd observed from the security office. After a moment's hesitation, he crossed the burgundy carpet and keyed his entrance to his room. When the door closed behind him he took a few seconds to review the room. Then, as if awakening from a dream, he moved to the dresser and pulled out his clothes. In ten minutes, he'd packed everything he'd brought with him and was once again waiting for the elevator. Not long after that he was in the lobby, headed for the exit.

A line of taxis typically ran in front of the Duke but there were none when Sully exited. He had to wait nearly five minutes until one pulled up. Sully climbed into the back seat, pulling his suitcase behind him.

"Dove vuoi andare?" the driver asked.

It was a question for which Sully wasn't prepared. All he could think of was getting out of the hotel, the place of his violation. His destination after that was an unknown.

"City center," he said. The driver pulled away from the curb, turned the car around, and headed deeper into Rome. During transit, Sully did what he should have done before getting into the cab: he tried to affix a solid destination to the trip's end. And it didn't take him long to do so.

"Antica Vineria," he said.

The driver acknowledged the request with a slight nod. A few moments later he turned the cab onto Viale Bruno Buozzi and less than three minutes later they were heading south again on Lungotevere dell'Armi.

When the driver left him at Via della Croce, bag in hand, Sully took a moment to breathe deeply of the unique smell generated by the many cafes and restaurants that lined the narrow, cobbled streets, and the steady flow of people that passed through the shadows of the three-story buildings that rose on either side.

Several tables lined the walls, extending into the street. Most were occupied by people taking an early dinner and as Sully looked at them it came to him that everything that had happened to him since he'd walked from the hotel that morning had happened within the space of ten hours. It hardly seemed possible. What supported that realization, though, was the growing pain in the back of his head. The Dilaudid had been wearing off for a while—slowly at first, so that he'd hardly noticed, but all of a sudden, in a rush. Even in the few moments that had passed since he'd stepped from the cab he found it growing more difficult to concentrate, to focus on anything beyond the insistent pounding in his skull. He knew he needed to dull the pain somehow if he was going to think clearly enough to plan his next move.

The green door to Antica Vineria stood open and he entered, his eyes taking a few seconds to adjust to the lower light. It had been years since he'd frequented the place but he found the barstool as if he'd been there the day before. He ordered a Baladin and then sat nursing it for some time. The bar was busy but quiet—a perfect place for Sully to lose himself in his thoughts, his eyes moving over the many bottles shelved like books along the walls. And the Baladin did much to ease the pain that had forced him into the bar in the first place, although he avoided considering the wisdom of drinking a beer while some amount of painkiller still coursed through his blood. When he'd emptied the glass, the bartender brought him another. He was halfway through it when something like clarity came to him.

So far, he'd focused almost entirely on the math, despite the fact that the equations and figures accounted for a small percentage of what Elena had sent him. He didn't fault himself for it; he gravitated toward the math elements in any problem. But in doing so he had ignored the lion's share of the available data: the shipping manifests. The fact that Elena had forwarded pages of them baffled Sully but the sheer volume of them compared with the rest of it warranted greater attention than he'd thus far devoted.

The bartender replaced Sully's empty glass with a third. He took a long draught.

The problem, as Sully saw it, was how he could delve deeper into the mystery of the shipping manifests. His earlier review had shown the shipping addresses blacked out. Neither were there listed weights, and no item notes. Without further information, the scanned pages felt like a dead end.

He leaned back in the stool, feeling the stretch of sore muscles in his back and neck. The pain in his head had settled into a subtle throb but weariness was threatening to slip in and take its place. He beat it back, knowing he still had much to do. But even as he thought it, the reality of it hit him. The fact that he was even considering staying in Rome to play detective meant he'd bought in—that he'd made his choice between flight and fight. It was a sobering thought—

one he decided to chase away by draining the rest of the glass.

He stood and pulled €20 from his wallet. He set it on the counter and exited through the green doors and into a Rome evening. He needed to find somewhere to stay—a low profile place where he could pay cash and not leave a name. A place from which he could plan for what the next day would bring.

Chapter Seven

Sully paused just outside the tall iron gate, his hand on the latch. On the other side of the bars the aged stone and brick building rose three stories, the topmost of which narrowed to a structure just wide enough to house a door leading out to the roof of the story below it. It had been a long while since he'd passed through the gate and into the home that had been in the Rossi family for generations—the smallest of the four they owned in the city.

Elena had laid claim to the place in Rome's Testaccio neighborhood, long appreciating the clustered stately homes, the effusive green of trees and hedges, and the privacy walls that created quiet fiefdoms in one of the wealthiest parts of the city. She'd joked about the size of the place for one person—that she could avoid whole sections of it for weeks at a time—but Sully knew she loved the Old World feel of it.

There was a quiet creak of metal on metal as he lifted the latch. He closed the gate behind him and took the walkway up to the front door. Green, like that of Antica Vineria. The door would be locked. The police who would have canvassed her home, looking for clues related to her murder, would have seen to that. But they didn't know Elena as well as had Sully, who reached up and felt along one of the bricks that arched around the doorframe. It made him at once pleased and saddened when his fingers touched the key. The former because it allowed him entry to her home; the latter because he'd used it often in far better circumstances.

Before slipping the key in the lock he pulled a pair of vinyl gloves, procured that morning, from his pocket and put them on. Once he was inside, he closed and locked the door. That done, he turned to take in the place. The entryway opened to a staircase straight ahead, a sitting room to the left, and a dining room to the right. Sully knew that the hall leading behind the staircase opened to a living room and a large kitchen, which had been Elena's favorite room in the house.

But he didn't advance into the house right away. Instead, he stood on the stone floor and took in the place, letting what he saw run up against the images he pulled from the past—looking for something that might shed some light on why Elena had been killed. But aside from a few decorative changes he could see nothing amiss in the two rooms he could see.

He took the hall past the stairway. The living room looked like something out of a real estate magazine, not even a periodical out of place. Sully knew the police wouldn't have spent much time here. He moved to the kitchen, where he found abundant evidence of a woman who loved to cook: bottles of wine, olive oil, seasonings of all varieties, fresh basil drying above the sink. He spared a few moments to remember some of the meals she'd cooked him here—but he didn't linger on the memories. He didn't think it likely the police would make a return visit to the house but he knew that at some point members of Elena's family would come to go through her things.

Which was precisely the reason Sully *was* here.

He thumbed through a stack of papers on the counter, finding utility bills, a credit card solicitation, a few receipts. The fact that they were askew, not neatly stacked, told him the police had also gone through them. Glancing around the room, he found little else to raise his interest so he went back to the stairs and started up.

His guess was that the thing he was truly looking for—aside from any ancillary items that might shed more light on whatever Elena had been working on—would be in her room. He knew she kept a spare. She had two of everything important.

The stairs deposited him on the second floor, the hall splitting to run along both sides of the staircase. A total of five rooms lay behind him. Four more, including the master suite, lay ahead. When he entered it, he found the bed made. The dresser-top was neat, the bedside table devoid of clutter. She hadn't left in a hurry. Whatever it was that had made her call him hadn't been sudden or concerning enough to cause her to abandon her natural meticulousness.

He moved to the bedside table, hoping the police wouldn't have taken what he hoped was inside. They wouldn't have had a reason to—her father would have granted them full access to company property—but he could see a thorough forensic team scooping it up with other items of interest.

When he pulled open the drawer her spare company key card rested at the top of several other items, as if it had been waiting for him to come along and collect it. He lifted it from the drawer and brought it close enough to see her picture clearly. It pulled a half-smile from him, the photo of this vibrant woman he once knew so well. Yet, cognizant of the ticking clock, he let the moment pass and flipped the ID over, finding behind the plastic the other thing he needed.

Sully remembered that the security protocols for Rossi's companies forced a password change every thirty days for all employees with access to the systems. The frequency of the change caused any number of employees—Elena among them—to commit the cardinal IT sin: write the password down. In Elena's case, she kept it slipped into the ID card holder—a small, folded slip of yellow.

Now that he had what he'd come for, he took one last look around the room before walking out. There was no reason to linger. Elena was dead and whatever she had been was not to be found in a room, or a building. He took the stairs down, exited to the porch, locked the door, and slipped the key back onto its brick. He took the gloves off, slipping them into a pocket. Then he walked to the gate, passed through it, and let it shut behind him. He disappeared down the street. Not once did he look back.

*****

Rossi Global Shipping boasted offices the world over—small shipping hubs, logistical centers, server way stations, and regional management facilities that facilitated the work of the corporate behemoth in Rome. Sully could have had his pick of any of them. He could even have waited until he was back in New York, where he could find the Rossi Global presence on W 36th Street.

The reason he'd decided against that was because of his belief that time was a dwindling commodity. Regardless of the fact that Elena had been the daughter of the company president, security protocols would mandate a deactivation of her access codes. For all Sully knew that had already happened. He would swipe the badge at an access door and security would swoop down on him in seconds. He could only take it on faith that whoever was tasked with that responsibility within the company either lacked a sense of urgency or would hesitate to perform it against the daughter of the man who signed the paychecks. Regardless, he was stuck doing the deed in Rome, where his limited Italian could prove a serious hindrance.

He turned onto Via dell'Arte and slowed until he found a parking space along the wide road. Once out of the car, he stood and looked up toward the top of the building that housed Rossi Global's corporate headquarters. A little research had told Sully that the company had a dozen facilities in and around Rome. At the outset—when he'd first considered the folly in which he was now involved—he'd tossed around some of the other, smaller locations. His time with Elena had informed him that virtually any of the computers on the

Rossi network would meet his needs. It was the credentials that counted, not the location of the terminal. What had stopped him from choosing one of the smaller offices, though, was the principle of anonymity in larger numbers. If he were to wander into a shipping facility in the Trieste district, a location that employed a few dozen people, it was unlikely he'd make it through the lobby without someone asking who he was.

So he stood on a street in EUR, Rome's business district, about to enter the mouth of the beast. He allowed himself almost a minute to talk himself out of it. Hands in his pockets, he stood next to the rental car and looked at the nineteen stories that housed Niccolo Rossi's billion-dollar company and told himself that he could walk away—that nothing had happened yet that he couldn't forget once he got back to the States and dove into his work with Jason. Yet even as he thought it he knew it for a lie. Had it been just the theft of his laptop, the tossing of his room, the possible attempt on his life, he might have been able to walk away. But there was no accounting for the blood of a woman who'd reached out to him, a woman for whom he felt inextricably responsible. He released a deep sigh and started for the entrance.

As he approached, he resisted the urge to straighten his tie. The suit was the same one he'd worn to Elena's visitation. A laptop case—almost empty—completed the illusion. He walked with purpose, slowing as he approached a trio of men also heading into the building. When they passed through the doors and into the lobby he was on their heels.

The lobby was a large open space with a single desk tucked into the wall to Sully's left. A bank of elevators lined the far wall and Sully was relieved to see that there didn't seem to be a check-in point between entrance and elevator. He and his trio of unknowing compatriots headed for them, with Sully trying to look as if he belonged with the group. A quick glance showed two security guards in sight—one stationed behind the desk and another to the right, occupying a spot about half-way between entrance and elevator. It was this one whose eyes moved over the four men. Elena's badge hung from Sully's jacket pocket and he hoped the guard wasn't observant enough to spot the woman with the long, dark hair in the picture. He didn't breathe easily until the man was behind him.

They reached the elevators just as one of the doors opened and a half-dozen people spilled out. Sully and his newfound friends took their places and one of the men pushed the button for eleven. He looked at Sully, his hand hovering over the panel.

"Twelve, please," Sully said. He had no reason to pick that floor, save that he wanted to exit after the others had already gone.

Sully was silent as the car rose and the others ignored him. When the doors opened on eleven no one else got in and Sully went the rest of the way himself. When the door opened again Sully strode purposefully into the hall, displaying a confidence he didn't feel, but there was no one there to witness it. The floor seemed empty. A long hallway ran straight from the elevator, bisecting the building and ending at what looked like an open office door. Another hall ran along the front of the elevator, stretching left and right before turning in an L shape parallel to the center hall.

Sully went right, passing a restroom and a door with a sign he suspected said *maintenance*. When he reached the end of the hall he looked left and saw a line of doors—some closed, some open. The only thing to the right was an exit to the stairwell.

The first door he reached was ajar, the light off. Sully pushed the door open a few more inches and looked inside. It was a small office, complete with the computer Sully needed. He slipped inside, found the light switch, and shut the door. As he circled the desk he took note of the fact that the surface was essentially bare; there were no personal items on it. It gave him hope that this office wasn't in use, that he had as much time as he might need.

He sat and tapped the spacebar on the keyboard and the screen went from black to blue, the Rossi company logo in the center. A thing that looked like a credit card scanner was affixed to the monitor. Sully unhooked Elena's badge from his pocket and fished the folded yellow slip from the caddy. Then he ran the badge through the scanner. Immediately, a query box labeled *Password* replaced the Rossi logo. He typed in the password: Madeline43. Madeline was the name of Elena's cat at the time Sully worked in Rome. He could only guess the number meant she'd used Madeline as a password an additional

42 times.

The blue screen disappeared, replaced by a more faded blue laden with icons. Sully scanned them, his eyes flitting over various images with names and acronyms that meant nothing to him. So in the absence of direction, he clicked on one at random. When that didn't yield anything helpful he clicked on another, with the same result. He clicked on a half-dozen more until he noticed one that looked promising—a trio of files stacked on end. He clicked on it and after a few moments an application shell loaded and immediately filled with a text tree. Despite the Italian, Sully recognized it as a drill down menu.

And he recognized the number formations.

He picked the near empty briefcase off the floor and placed it on the desk beside the computer. From it he pulled printouts of the Rossi manifests he'd printed at an internet café that morning. The tracking app had a form field and he typed in one of the numbers. Nothing happened for a few seconds and Sully imagined the program was sifting through the database. After a few more seconds a query box appeared, overlaying the shipping program. In bold font was a single word: *Ristretta*. Below that, a command: *Inserire la password.*

Sully's eyebrow rose. The fact that he was logged in as Elena, a senior executive in her father's company, meant he should have had nearly unfettered access to company records. Unless his earlier fear was proving true and her access had been terminated. Except that he'd been able to log in, which meant her credentials were still in the system.

He typed her password into the query box and, after some processing, the screen produced what looked like a shipping manifest, only it was one with more detail than the pages in Sully's possession. He scanned the page, noting that the contents still weren't detailed on the manifest. What made that unusual was that the items had been insured—for a considerably large amount, Sully noted. And no insurance company in the world would insure a mystery item. He slipped that nugget away for later processing and scrolled down the page, to the shipping addresses—both origin and destination.

The destination was a city in Brazil: Forteleza. The address of origin was local: Piazza del S. Uffizio. Sully recognized it as a plaza adjacent to Vatican City, an area heavy with a papal administrative presence. As a quick look around the room didn't turn up a printer, he quickly slipped out his phone and snapped a shot of the screen. Then he found the next shipping number.

When this number, too, resulted in the appearance of the additional password screen, Sully frowned. But he entered Elena's password and was rewarded with a new shipping manifest. Just as before, nothing was itemized. So he scrolled to the addresses. This time the receiving address was somewhere in Toronto. But like the previous one, the point of origin was Piazza del S. Uffizio.

It was as he raised the phone to record the information that he heard a sound coming from beyond the closed door. The sound of footsteps; someone walking past the office.

Sully froze and listened but the sound lasted only a few beats and then was gone. Still, he waited in silence several more moments before releasing the breath he'd been holding.

"What in the hell am I doing?" he asked himself, as the absurdity of the situation hit him. "I'm in a foreign country committing corporate espionage against an ex-girlfriend's father."

The thought was sobering enough to remind him that every moment he remained in the building was to risk being found out. He entered the numbers more rapidly, each time prompted for the password. He captured each resulting page on his phone and, while he didn't spare the time it would have taken to review them all in any detail, he could see that the destinations of all fourteen shipments were foreign cities, most in the western hemisphere. Of equal interest was that all the shipments originated in Rome. More specifically, the shipping addresses were centered in and around the Vatican. The weights of the shipments also caught his eye, ranging between 50 and 800 kilograms. If his guesstimate was accurate, the Vatican had shipped out some four tons of unknown materials over the course of a few weeks.

He leaned back, the chair creaking under him. In a fashion, he'd accomplished what he'd set out to do; he'd learned more about the shipping manifests Elena had sent him. However, he'd learned nothing solid enough for him to be able to draw any conclusions, save that the Vatican had moved some very heavy things very quickly. He sighed, the sound overloud in the quiet office.

"There has to be a list of what was shipped," he said to himself. The problem was that he didn't know where to look, except to spend time poking around in the system. And with the digital security he'd already witnessed, he doubted the efficacy of that approach. Even so, he leaned forward, prepared to resume his work—which was when the office door opened.

The man standing in the threshold, hand on the door handle, wore the same uniform as the two guards in the lobby. Aside from the uniform, the first thing Sully noticed was the lack of surprise on the other man's face—as if he'd opened the door expecting to find someone.

"Can I help you?" Sully asked in his suspect Italian, forcing an edge of authority into his voice. He knew it wasn't his obvious foreignness that would do him in; Rossi Global was large enough to employ any number of foreigners. What would get him caught was acting as if he didn't belong.

The security guard did not answer immediately. The man's eyes moved over Sully, then over the near-bare office. Then he raised his other hand, bringing a phone to his lips.

"Confirming someone in 1242," the man said in Italian. "Stand by." He turned his attention back to Sully.

“I have a report of unauthorized network access coming from this room,” the guard said.

Sully evinced a frown.

“That’s strange,” he said. “I’ve been in this office for two weeks.”

He moved his hand to the badge that hung from his coat, pulling the guard’s eyes to it—a suggestion that this was nothing more than a security glitch. He saw the man’s eyes narrow. Sully’s hand covered most of the badge, Elena’s picture. He saw a hint of doubt cross the guard’s face but it vanished almost before Sully could register it.

“Can I have your name, sir?”

“John Anderson,” Sully said. “I’m with Rossi Global in New York. I’m here for a few weeks working on the Amsterdam Project with Vincenzo Bianchi.” He picked the names out of the air, forcing believability into every syllable. He was rewarded by a renewed flicker of doubt. Rossi Global was too big for the guard to know everyone who worked in the building.

Sully used those few seconds to stand. The papers he’d brought with him were still scattered on the desk.

“I’m sorry, Mr. Anderson,” the guard said in passable English. “I’m sure this is a mistake but I’ll need to run your ID through the system. May I see your badge, please?”

“Of course,” Sully said. He came out from behind the desk,

forcing an exasperated smile to his lips. His hand still hovered over the badge. His heart was beating faster; he could feel it in his neck.

The guard released the door handle. He still held the phone in his other hand. When Sully was a few steps away he pulled the badge from his jacket and extended it. The guard reached for it, his fingers closing over the plastic. His eyes moved off of Sully—which was when Sully balled up his fist and drove it into his stomach.

The guard doubled over, releasing his hold on the badge. Sully, in mild disbelief over what he'd done, stood there for a moment as the other man went to a knee. The urge to run washed over him. The stairs were near; he could be on the street in minutes. But his papers were still on the desk. And the guard still had his phone.

The guard was coming out of the initial shock of the attack. He looked up at the American who stood over him. He started to bring the phone up.

Sully hit him again—a solid blow that connected just behind the guard's ear. A wave a pain cascaded through Sully's hand as the guard crumpled to the carpet. Sully spared little time admiring his handiwork. Heart pounding now, he raced to the desk, grabbed the laptop case, and shoved the papers inside it. He was turning for the door while still zipping the case.

The guard was still down and Sully felt a flash of panic that he'd seriously injured him—or worse. Then he saw the Italian's hand move; he heard a groan. It was reassurance enough to send Sully stepping over him and into the hallway. He made a left; the stairs were straight ahead. He heard the ding of the elevator and the slide of the door before he reached that hallway and he passed through it quickly, his peripheral vision spotting the two uniformed men heading his direction. He reached the exit and hit the door release just as the security guards reached the spot from which they could see their compatriot sprawled in the doorway of office 1242. Sully heard a shout just as the stairwell door slammed shut behind him.

He started down the stairs as quickly as he could go. Someone slammed into the door above him but he didn't look back. Hand on the rail, he propelled himself around the landing corners. There were shouts from behind: orders to stop. On the sixth-floor landing, as he took hold of the rail to change direction, his foot found a wet spot and flew out from under him. He went down hard, his thigh bearing all of his weight into a stair edge. From his prone vantage point he could see legs on the landing above him. Despite the pain, he pulled himself up and started down again. He could hear more yelling behind him but he could pick out enough of the Italian to know it wasn't directed at him. His pursuer was giving updates to someone else. Then he heard a curse, followed by a thud as his pursuer hit the same wet spot that had downed Sully. He could only hope the man had been injured enough to slow or stop the chase.

By the time he reached the first floor he was almost spent. His head, the injury from the hit and run still fresh, pounded and every step sent rivulets of pain down his leg. He lowered his shoulder and hit the door hard, entering the lobby off balance and drawing shallow draughts of air. He took just a moment to get his bearings, to find the exit, then he propelled himself toward it.

Every eye in the sunlit atrium found him but all he could see was the exit. Then movement entered his periphery. He had no time to brace himself before something struck him; he hit the floor hard, the laptop case sliding across the tile. Then the man who had tackled him was punching him in the ribs. The blows forced the air from his lungs and he struggled to draw breath. But it was the pain in his skull that clouded his vision. He felt as if his head would burst. Then, for a few beats everything went black.

When his vision began to clear, it did so through bright spots that moved and shifted. His attacker still straddled him but the rabbit punches had stopped. The man had raised himself to one knee.

Sully feared he was going to black out again and if he did he knew he would wake up in a jail cell. So, struggling to focus, he shifted his weight onto his left shoulder. The movement caught the guard by surprise and Sully capitalized on it. Through the bright spots, he located the guard's belt; then he aimed his punch below it.

As the guard doubled over, Sully used the last of his strength to roll the man off of him. Then he found reserves enough to struggle to his feet. The blackness reached out for him again but he fought it to a draw. He saw the laptop case by the exit and limped toward it. There were still eyes on him but no one made a move to stop him as he bent and retrieved the case. Without a pause, he stumbled through the door. Less than two minutes later the rental car had disappeared into Via dell'Arte traffic.

Chapter Eight

The morning was quiet enough for Sully to hear the bells ringing in the Palazza di Giustizia, which he remembered seldom happened with the amount of traffic and noise that filled the space between the Palazza and Piazza di Monte Savello down which he walked—or limped. His path ran in tandem with the Tiber and he looked out over it as he neared Santa Maria della Pieta. As with the road, little moved on the river but he knew that would change as the day grew longer.

As he closed the distance to the church, he watched as a bus filled with tourists—the ones who did not mind an early start—rumbled past, black smoke bellowing from the tail pipe. There were a half dozen places that constituted a list of the tourists' likely destination and he knew that the small church that was his own destination was not on that manifest. The sheer size of Vatican City created the opportunity for the existence of a large number of seldom-visited spots, even in one of the most heavily traveled 109 acres on the globe.

When the sounds of the bus receded, leaving him, once again, with the feeling of having the entire city to himself, he sent his gaze out once again over the Tiber. As he followed its flow around the curve of the holy city he found himself breathing in the morning air more deeply, trying to pick up the scents that came off the water. It was one of the first few moments of peace he'd allowed himself since escaping from Rossi Global the day before.

He'd holed up in a dirty hotel in Campo di Fiori—a place where he could pay cash and field no questions. He'd remained in the hard, musty bed most of the night, nursing his injuries with ice packs, aspirin, and scotch purchased from a corner pharmacy and small grocery store respectively. However, even as exhausted as he was, he slept fitfully, and he was awake before the bars closed at 2:00 AM. He got up, downed four more aspirin with a finger of Glenmorangie, then shuffled to the window, where he could see the bar patrons spilling out into the street. He watched them for some time, as the crowd swelled then ebbed. When the street was quiet again he went back to bed, sleeping for another few hours. He awoke before 6:00 AM. By the time he'd showered and taken several more aspirin, which had done little to touch the near constant pain in his head, he had a plan of sorts—one that involved an old friend.

The road narrowed and Sully moved from it, choosing a narrower path that took him under the Beatific Arch and toward the Chapel of St. Paul. A set of stone steps left the path on his right, leading to the small church, and he watched from his elevated position as a young priest, stifling his yawn against the hour, followed a cobblestone path from a small reflecting garden to the open door of the church. Sully's path took him past St. Paul and farther from the river, the feeling of seclusion deepening, until the walkway spilled out into an alley that traveled along the backside of a two-story building of white stone. He followed the uneven pavement to the entrance, walking in beneath the inauspicious inscription that had announced the Holy See's contempt for the people who had occupied the adjoining land three hundred years ago, when Benedict commissioned its construction.

Santa Maria della Pieta had remained stylistically untouched for a hundred and fifty years, which made it feel older than other structures with a longer history but a more vigorous restoration schedule. Inside, the dim lighting took his vision for a few moments but when his eyes adjusted, he crossed through the church's single nave until he reached the raised altar.

He was alone in the church; he'd beaten the man he'd come to see. The fact that the Cardinal had asked Sully to meet him here, rather than in the man's office, was something Sully found interesting. It was a strange place for a morning meeting between old friends. And while Sully was just grateful Rinaldi had agreed to meet with him on such short notice, he couldn't shake the feeling that Rinaldi had known Sully was going to call.

He sat and turned his gaze to the fresco above him. The Blessed Virgin looked down on him, her sublime expression fixed, unchanging. Like that of the Luce behind the altar: the Madonna in her exalted form, hand reaching for the globe entrusted to her care.

He sat in the pew for what seemed a long while, as the sun's movement through the morning sky worked an incremental light trail along the altar. He didn't hear the Cardinal enter. One moment the man wasn't there; then he was. Sully stood and the older man pulled him into a too-tight embrace, patting Sully's back with a large, heavy hand. The good-natured blows sent fresh lines of pain shooting up to Sully's skull and he was the first to pull away.

"Hello Arturo," Sully said.

"My friend," the Italian said, "it's good to see you."

And, despite the circumstances that had brought him here, Sully had to agree. Rinaldi looked much the same as he had when Sully last saw him, maybe three years ago: a solid man finally giving ground to his sixty-five years; a full head of silver hair; sharp, dark eyes.

"How's life on the Curia treating you?" Sully asked, a hint of mischief in his own eyes.

Rinaldi blew a short draught of air out of his nose. "The same as always," he said. "Machinations upon machinations." Then he waved a dismissive hand before gesturing to the pew.

"Thanks for seeing me on such short notice," Sully said, after the two men sat. Then he raised an eyebrow. "Although I'm wondering why we couldn't have met in your office."

Rinaldi gave another dismissive wave.

“Every moment I get to spend out from behind my desk is time well spent,” he said. Then he made another gesture meant to take in the whole of the church. “And it’s been a while since I’ve been in this place—to see the Madonna keeping her watch.”

Sully nodded his own appreciation for the Luce but before he could say anything the Cardinal’s face took on a more serious look.

“I think the better question, though, is what could be so important that you had to see me right away.”

Sully waited a few moments before responding. During the walk to the church he’d considered what he would ask his friend—how much he would reveal—but now that he was here he understood that even the small questions would bring probing returns from the Italian. And Sully wasn’t sure he’d be able to answer those. Still, he knew he had no other choice. Not asking the questions would make this trip—indeed, everything that had happened over the last few days—mean nothing.

“Arturo, over the last few months your church has shipped more than two hundred boxes—some eight thousand pounds of freight—to several locations around the globe via Rossi Global. Do you know what’s in those boxes and why you’re moving them?”

The Cardinal’s first response was silence, of a kind that seemed to suck all other ambient noise from the church. It was the sort of reaction Sully expected from such a question. What interested him most, though, were his friend’s eyes, what secrets they might tell. But if the Cardinal held any mysteries, he kept them to himself.

"I don't understand," Rinaldi finally said. He leaned back in the pew. "What boxes?"

"Freight shipped to New York, Toronto, Mexico City, Brazil, and a number of other places. Shipments that originated from Piazza del S. Uffizio and handled by Rossi Global. All heavily insured."

His clarification produced more silence and when Rinaldi chose to break it, his words seemed measured, his accent more pronounced.

"While I can grasp the idea of what you are asking, I still do not understand why you, a friend whose vocation once had you instructing the brightest minds at Sapienza, are making inquiries about the Vatican's mail."

Phrased in that fashion, Sully had to admit it sounded absurd. He responded to the question with a wry smile.

"Let's just say that I'm looking into it for a friend," he said.

Rinaldi took and parsed that.

"So, we place that to the side then," he said. "Even so, what makes you think I have enough knowledge regarding the shipping history of this rather large institution to be able to provide you with any useful answers?"

Sully leaned forward, raising an eyebrow.

"You're the President of the Prefecture for Economic Affairs," he said. "Do you expect me to believe that anyone in your city can buy anything bigger than a candy bar without you knowing about it?"

That pulled a chuckle from Rinaldi, as Sully had expected it would. The Prefecture for Economic Affairs was not, in fact, charged with accounting for every dollar spent by the various departments and factions within the small nation; but Sully also knew that a shipping job the size of the one he was investigating would have brought a price tag that would not have escaped Rinaldi's notice.

Sully sighed, a weariness days in the making suddenly settling on him.

"I know it's been a long while since we've talked, Arturo," Sully said. "But it wasn't that long ago that you had a finger in every pie baking in this place. My guess is you still do. And I could really use a hand from someone in that position."

The silence birthed from those words was longer than the previous ones. It seemed that the cleric studied him for a long while but Sully could make out little of what was passing behind the other man's eyes. What he did feel, though, was that something had shifted. At first he wasn't even aware of it; it came to him gradually, like mountains separating themselves from the darkness with an approaching dawn. And so, when the old priest leaned forward and placed his heavy, aged hand on Sully's arm—when Sully noted the troubled look in his friend's eyes—he found himself prepared for it.

"I'm concerned for you, my friend," Rinaldi said.

Sully replied with a weary smile. He knew how he looked, how the events of the last few days had left their mark. He was surprised Rinaldi hadn't commented on the bruises and scrapes when they'd first embraced. Yet even as he thought it, there was something inside that told him the cleric was not referring to his physical appearance. It was that same part that had noted the subtle change in the atmosphere within the church.

"I feel better than I look," he said.

Rinaldi's hand tightened on Sully's arm. He opened his mouth to speak but then shut it. His eyes were, all of a sudden, infused with an earnestness Sully couldn't remember seeing from him. The man seemed to be fighting a battle with himself and, surprised by its onset, Sully could do nothing but remain silent and allow it to play out. He watched as the man's face reflected that inner conflict, then as it hardened into something that looked like resolve.

"I'm worried that you are chasing something much bigger than you realize," Rinaldi said. "Something that is best left alone."

Sully's arm was uncomfortably warm where Rinaldi's hand touched his skin but Sully didn't pull away.

"Now I'm the one who doesn't understand," Sully said but Rinaldi was shaking his head before he'd finished.

"Go back to the States," Rinaldi said. "Forget this quest you've begun. I have no more answers for you."

Sully could see that whatever it was that had stirred the

Cardinal to speak was receding and he couldn't let that happen. He had no idea what was happening—what he'd become involved in that had prompted a warning from a senior member of the Vatican hierarchy—but he couldn't lose the opportunity for clarity.

"I can't do that, Arturo. I've been run down and left for dead. I've had my hotel room ransacked, my laptop stolen." He stopped and made sure he had Rinaldi's eye. "And a friend is dead."

Rinaldi's sadness was evident yet he still answered with a headshake.

"Best you do not join her," he said, his voice quiet.

"I'm invested now. I can't leave. You know that." Sully paused, then added, "And I never said it was a woman."

Rinaldi removed his hand from Sully's arm and leaned back into the pew. The Italian studied his friend for several moments before releasing a deep sigh. But Sully still sensed the war waging within the man. As before, all he could do was remain still and allow it to reach its conclusion. Silence expanded to fill the whole of the church until the Cardinal broke it with a few quiet words delivered with the strength of a thunderclap.

"Go home, Solomon. Please."

It was Sully's turn to reach out—to place his hand on the arm of his friend.

"I can't."

Rinaldi responded with a grim smile.

"I know," he said. "So I give you what I can."

He turned his arm so that his hand clasped Sully's forearm.

"The Prophecies. 10-50." He pulled his hand away and stood. "I can do no more."

The Cardinal reached out and placed a hand on Sully's head and Sully saw the Italian's lips moving in some silent prayer. When he'd finished, he stepped out into the aisle and walked away, leaving Sully behind.

Sully remained in the pew for a long while after his friend had left, thinking over the meeting, over this thing that had gathered him up, over Rinaldi's final words. He might have stayed in his spot for much longer had he not heard tourist footsteps behind him or noticed a shadow disturb the shaft of sunlight that had fallen on the lilies that decorated the altar. He rose and, stepping out into the aisle, gave the Luce one last look before turning to head back the way he'd come.

Quatrain Century X – 50

The Meuse by day in the land of Luxembourg

It will find Saturn and three in the urn:

Mountain and plain, town, city and borough,

Flood in Lorraine, betrayed by the great urn.

- Michel Nostradamus[7]

[7] Nostradamus, M., & Garencières, T. (2001). *Nostradamus: his works and prophecies*. Urbana, IL: Standard Publications.

Chapter Nine

Sully leaned back in the chair and tapped his fingers along the laminate tabletop. A cup of coffee—heretofore untouched—sat to the right of his new laptop and, after a few more taps, he reached for it. He took a sip of the lukewarm brew and then let his eyes drift to the large, sidewalk-facing window of the coffee shop. The busyness of Piazza di Sant'Eustachio provided a suitable backdrop over which he could ponder the import of the quatrain.

Only a small portion of his attention was dedicated to keeping an eye out for members of the local law enforcement community—those who might be paying more notice to him than a law-abiding person warranted. As near as he'd been able to tell, his break-in at Rossi Global had not made the news. He was certain there would have been cameras in the lobby, if nowhere else. And so the fact that his face had remained off television and computer screens suggested powerful people within Rossi Global had chosen to avoid releasing any information about the event. The reasons for such reticence might have been of concern if Sully hadn't been otherwise occupied.

His eyes returned to the screen. It hadn't taken him long to link his friend's last cryptic words to Nostradamus. Under different circumstances, knowing the source of the reference would have caused him to dismiss the Cardinal's words as nonsense—merely a means of ending the conversation and taking Sully off the trail. But the previous Nostradamus writings supplied in the files sent to him by Elena gave Rinaldi's words greater weight; there was something here he'd meant for Sully to understand.

He read them again. Then a third time. He didn't know a great deal about Nostradamus—nothing beyond the standard jumble of mysticism, occultism, and obscure prophecies that served as fare for pop culture references. And the four lines on the screen in front of him seemed like nothing more than charlatanism—cryptic phrases thrown together to lift coins from the superstitious monarchs of the day. What he kept returning to, though, was that two very different people—people who Sully thought it unlikely knew each other—had seen fit to point him in this direction.

He released a deep sigh and then, despite his misgivings, picked up a pen and readied the yellow notepad on the table. By the time an hour had passed, the last of the coffee forgotten and cold, he'd filled a page of the tablet with notes and disparate thoughts garnered from hit or miss web searches. He put the pen down and scanned the notes. When he'd finished, he shook his head and leaned away from the table.

He didn't know what he'd hoped to find. All he knew was that he hadn't found it. He had the name of a European river that, according to the quatrain, was supposed to run through Luxembourg but didn't—even with the redrawn borders of the fifteenth and sixteenth centuries. Then there were the urn references, which undoubtedly meant the constellation of Aquarius. Lorraine had to refer to the region of the same name in France. And Saturn was, of course, Saturn.

He released a tired sigh. His head hurt—a dull throb just insistent enough to hinder his concentration. It made him wonder, yet again, about the wisdom of leaving the hospital without knowing the full extent of his injuries. What consoled him, though, was the fact that it was a few days later and he was still alive; even a slow bleed would have killed him by now.

He picked up the coffee and tried an experimental sip, grimacing as the cold, bitter liquid hit his lips. He set the cup down and returned his attention to his notes.

He could identify nearly everything in the four lines of the quatrain but, as with virtually all prophecies, there was no recognizable thread through the text—nothing to tie it together. It was what made it possible for anyone, anywhere to take the writings of someone like Nostradamus and make them mean anything they wanted them to mean.

He had *three* underlined on the page. Of all the disparate pieces of information in the verse, it was the one without a ready interpretation.

"It will find Saturn and three in the urn," he said to himself. On second thought, he supposed there were two things he couldn't qualify. In addition to the *three*, he didn't know what the *it* referred to. A quick read of the verse could have a reader believing the *it* was a reference to the Meuse but Sully doubted that; in his experience, rivers didn't tend to exhibit anthropomorphic tendencies, even in ancient prophecies.

"Something will find Saturn and three of something in Aquarius," he said. He considered the statement for a few more seconds before picking up his phone. He hesitated only briefly at the knowledge that it was midnight in Washington before making the call. Jason picked up on the sixth ring.

"I'm going to go out on a limb and assume you still haven't made it back to D.C.," Jason said. Sully could hear the sleep in his voice. "Otherwise you'd realize what time it is here."

"If it helps, I did hesitate for a whole second before dialing," Sully said.

"That doesn't help as much as you might think." There was a pause and Sully heard the sounds of his friend shifting in bed. There was a grunt, then Jason said, "Should I be worried that you're not back yet? Last time we talked, weren't you and my bottle of wine on your way to the airport?"

"I took a detour. And I drank the wine," Sully said. "But there's still a bottle in it for you if you're alert enough to help me with a puzzle."

Jason responded with a curse that sounded as if it had been muffled by a pillow. But Sully knew the lure of a puzzle would tempt his friend.

"What is it?" Jason asked.

Sully read his friend the quatrain, then went on to explain the trouble he was having identifying the various references. "Something will find Saturn and three of something in Aquarius," he said. "And I need to know what both of those somethings are."

When he'd finished, he was met with silence—one that stretched out for a long while. Sully was about to ask Jason if he'd fallen asleep when the other man spoke.

"This is what you called me after midnight to ask?"

"With the promise of a good bottle of wine in it."

"Which you'll probably end up drinking before I ever see it," Jason grumbled.

Sully smiled but didn't answer. Despite Jason's grousing, he knew his friend would be parsing the puzzle. It wasn't long before Jason responded.

"The *it* would have to be a telescope, wouldn't it?" He paused and Sully thought he heard the strained sounds of a yawn. "I mean, once you remove the possibility that the word has some mystical meaning—and the only reason I'm making that assumption is because not making it leaves us with far too many options to consider—then you're left compiling a list of things that can *find* something within a constellation. And the only thing that comes to mind at the moment is a telescope."

"I guess that makes sense," Sully said. "Although if I'm remembering correctly, the first telescopes weren't invented until after Nostradamus' death."

"You're kidding, right?" Jason asked. "We're having a discussion—one without a hint of irony, I might add—about a guy famous for making wild predictions about the future and you want to quibble over the fact that telescopes weren't around when he may or may not have written about them?"

"Point taken," Sully said. The absurdity of the situation was not lost on him. He was lingering in Rome, discussing ancient prophecies with a much put-upon friend, and considering the very real possibility there existed a conspiracy between the Roman church and at least one head of industry that had already resulted in at least one death. Not to mention the attempt on his own life, as well as the fact that, with yesterday's infiltration of the Rossi Industries headquarters, he'd crossed into the world of corporate espionage. A noise somewhere between a snort and a chuckle escaped him.

"I'm glad one of us finds my interrupted slumber funny," Jason grumbled.

Sully shook his head, a half-smile forming.

"If you knew what my last few days have been like, you'd appreciate my relative composure."

A few moments passed before Jason responded and when he did, concern shaded the question. "Are you going to tell me what's going on?"

Sully released another sigh. "You're certainly due an explanation." He stopped and his eyes moved to the window, to the busy street beyond it, to people wending from home, to work, to breakfast—to whatever constituted their personal normalcy. "And I promise you one while we share that bottle."

"Who said anything about sharing?" Jason asked but the humor attached to the response was a shadow, the concern, receding only a moment, returning. "We're waiting to hear back on what's probably the biggest grant request we've ever submitted and you're in Rome, calling me in the middle of the night with questions about ancient prophecies. Should I not be concerned?"

The honest answer, of course, was that there was ample reason for concern but Sully wasn't yet ready to have his friend carry that burden.

"Let's just say I'm involved in an academic exercise that's taking a bit more time than I anticipated and leave it at that, okay?"

A few seconds passed before Jason answered. "I guess I can buy that for now," he said.

"So, what are your thoughts about the *three*?"

"I haven't a clue," Jason said. "And, frankly, the fact that you'd expect me to come up with something even remotely plausible on an hour's sleep and an absence of good Italian wine is bad form, even for you."

Sully couldn't help but smile at the jab, even as he knew that as soon as the call ended, Jason would probably forgo the next few hours' sleep to research the question. The image of the two of them sitting in some high-end bar in New York, talking and laughing about all of this, came to him but it was like vapor, hazy and impermanent, fading after only a moment.

"You'll let me know when you have something?"

Jason's answer was preceded by a snort. "Presumption at its finest. And, of course I will."

Before Sully could say his thanks, something drew his eyes to the window. At first, he couldn't put a reason to it—couldn't identify the thing that had tugged his attention to the world beyond the glass. His eyes flit over the portion of that world he could see and finally settled on a single moving form. When his vision focused, a frown settled over his face. There was something familiar about the dark suited man crossing the street, his aim seeming to point him at the coffee shop. Identification came before the man had taken another two steps and, with it, the one thing Sully wasn't expecting: indecision.

He still held the phone to his ear as the man reached the coffee shop, Sully losing sight of him as he reached a hand for the door. It couldn't be a coincidence, of that Sully was certain, but that was the only thing that was clear. The coffee shop was a public place with more than a handful of witnesses; and Sully, in truth, did not know how the newcomer was connected to Rossi, or to the events of the last few days. It left him in a state at which mans' two most visceral responses—fight and flight—found an equilibrium that kept him rooted to the chair.

"If it were me, the thing I'd be focusing on is *betrayal*," Jason said.

Sully, who'd forgotten the phone, was slow to parse the statement, save for a small, involuntary shudder that the last word sent coursing down his spine. It seemed to fit the man who, now inside, found Sully's eyes with his own.

"I don't follow," Sully said.

"When you get right down to it, most of the quatrain is pretty mundane. Some geographical mentions. An obscure number *three*. The requisite hints of astrology. Really, all the standard stuff that makes for good prophecy."

Even with his attention divided, Sully thought he tracked with Jason.

"Including some suitably murky catastrophe," Sully supplied.

"Betrayed by the great urn," Jason said. "Really, everything else is build-up. You find out what the betrayal is, then you have yourself an interpreted quatrain."

That made sense to Sully and he chose to ignore the slight hint of mockery in his friend's voice.

"Then make that priority number one," Sully said. "Thanks, Jason."

He ended the call before Jason could object and then Mats Koning settled into the seat opposite him. Neither man spoke as Sully set the phone on the table. Then, Sully reached for the cup of room temperature coffee and took a swallow, careful to keep the grimace from his face. Only when he'd returned the cup to the table did he speak.

"Mats Koning, if memory serves."

A corner of the other man's mouth rose. He looked exactly as Sully remembered from their brief introduction at Elena's viewing: a trim man with Germanic features, perhaps early fifties, wearing another non-descript dark suit. And the same icy gaze.

"Good morning, Dr. Knight," Koning said. His eyes took Sully in, then swept across the table as if to catalog everything on it.

"To what do I owe the pleasure?" Sully asked, for the moment opting to act as if the meeting was nothing more than a strange coincidence.

Koning did not respond immediately. The corner of his mouth rose a fraction more, his face taking on a decidedly sardonic hue.

"You've been a busy man," he said.

Now it was Sully's turn to eschew a quick response. He leaned back in his chair and aimed his own half-smile at his unexpected tablemate.

"Can I assume, then, that your familiarity with my schedule means you've been keeping tabs on me?"

"Tell me, Dr. Knight, what were you expecting to find at Rossi Global?"

Sully's mouth drew into a thin line. He'd already deduced that the lack of media coverage about his excursion suggested those in charge at Rossi Global—if not Nicolo Rossi, himself—wished to keep the event out of the news. But caution still steered him away from self-incrimination.

"I'm not sure I know what you're talking about," he said.

"We have you on video."

At Elena's viewing, Sully had wondered how Koning was connected to Rossi. Now he found himself wondering if he was speaking with the head of security for Rossi Global. Almost immediately, though, that impression felt wrong. He remembered the way the men had talked, their body language, the tension; none of it fit that of a CEO of a multi-billion-dollar corporation speaking with a subordinate.

"Rome is one of the biggest cities in the world. I'm sure I've been captured on a thousand video cameras over the last few days."

"Perhaps," Koning said. "However, the footage of you coming

through the lobby *hot*, as they say, stands out."

Sully considered a continuation of the verbal repartee but, as if someone had placed a heavy pack over his shoulders, the weight of the last few days suddenly settled on him.

"Why are you here?" he asked. "What do you want?"

"I believe I've made that clear," Koning said. "I want to know what you were looking for at Rossi Global."

Sully sighed. "If you think someone who looks like me was at Rossi Global, and if you've captured that person on video, then I'm reasonably confident you know what they were looking for. I'm sure you have video of them rifling through a file cabinet or something."

If nothing else, Sully was rewarded when the look on Koning's face shifted to open irritation.

"I suppose a confession doesn't matter," Koning said. "We both know what you were doing. Only one of us, though, understands how dangerous your course of action is."

"If by course of action, you mean catching the next flight back to New York and beginning work on a big government contract, then I have to admit to not understanding the danger."

The irritation on Koning's face deepened and then manifested itself in a more direct approach.

"I'd like you to come with me, Dr. Knight." The way he said it—the words infused with absolute certainty—indicated a man seldom denied what he wanted.

"There's already been one attempt on my life," Sully said. "And the more we talk, the more I'm beginning to suspect you had something to do with that. So you'll forgive me for not jumping up and following you out the door."

Koning shifted in his seat, his coat falling away for a moment—just long enough for Sully to see a flash of gray metal against the white shirt. Even after the coat had again covered it over, Sully's eyes hovered over the spot.

"I see you're beginning to understand," Koning said.

Sully looked up, meeting the other man's eyes.

"What is it that I'm supposed to understand?"

"That this isn't about you, Dr. Knight. That there are stakes high enough to make the life of one person inconsequential."

It was the only kind of statement that could make Sully abandon the deflecting tactic he'd adopted. Despite himself, he leaned forward.

"What is it you don't want me to find?"

"Come with me and I'll tell you."

For one instant, Sully wanted to rise and follow the man wherever he would lead him. In only a short time, he'd become invested in whatever this was, convinced by what he'd found, as well as by the barriers raised to keep him from finding more, that it might be worth it. What kept him from rising, though, was his suspicion that no answers would be forthcoming, that Mats Koning would put a bullet into the back of his head at the earliest opportunity. The man's smile told him as much; it was the smile of a snake.

"It's tempting," he said. "But I believe I'm going to sit here and continue sipping some very cold coffee."

"Maybe I gave you more credit than you deserve," Koning said.

Sully raised an eyebrow.

Koning leaned forward, placing his elbows on the table, steepling his fingers. Sully's eyes were drawn to a glint on the man's ring finger, to a gray ring with a wide band. On the band was a spot of color, a dull red. Sully could see part of what looked like an X shape, the ends flared. "You think this stops with you," Koning explained. "That yours is the only life you're playing with."

Sully, his attention pulled from the ring, frowned, looking for the meaning in the veiled threat. Koning saved him the trouble.

"Cardinal Arturo Rinaldi," Koning said. "Dr. Jason Humphrey. Dr. Emily Hannah."

Sully listened to Koning intone the names of his friends and, as the implications of the list hit him, his eyes grew wide.

"*Now* you understand," Koning said. "Our actions have consequences, Dr. Knight. In this case, three people endangered by your probing into matters that do not concern you."

Koning was right: Sully understood perfectly. He understood that he'd placed his friends in danger—that his refusal to let the mystery stand had dragged them into whatever had killed Elena. He could feel the anger of that revelation coloring his face, could feel it threatening to overtake the mien of mild academic that was his normal skin, albeit a skin bruised and bloodied over the last few days.

"So once again, Dr. Knight," Koning said. "I need you to come with me."

Despite this second invitation, Sully didn't move. The anger that had taken him was growing, fueled by what he'd already understood as the absurdity of the situation. It was absurd that he was in Rome when he should have been in New York fighting for something that both he and Jason had spent months on; it was absurd that friends from his past were communicating with him in riddles; it was absurd that he was sitting in a coffee shop giving serious consideration to the words of a long dead mystic. The whole of it threatened to take the edge off of the anger, to send him into a fit of laughter. What kept that transition in check, though, was the gravity of all of it. One person was dead and Sully had no doubt that this man, or whomever it was he worked for, would kill anyone else who got in his way.

And it was this last that convinced Sully that he would not get up and leave with Koning. He knew his own life would be forfeit—but he was equally certain the others on Koning's list would meet the same fate, regardless of Sully's acquiescence.

He took a deep breath, clearing his vision, steadying himself against the flood of emotion—a flood that was, even now, receding. As it ebbed, it left something else in its place: a sense of calm he hadn't felt in days. He picked up his phone and slid it into a coat pocket. That done, he reached across the table and closed the laptop, then slid it off the table and onto the floor. Then he reached for the notepad and pen. He closed the book and set the pen atop it. He paused and looked up at Koning. The other man wore a small smile.

"Just one question," Sully said. He leaned forward again, his hands at the table edge, thumbs hooking beneath the metal strip that wrapped the laminate. "Were you the one who killed Elena?"

He saw the question hit Koning, saw the answer to it in the other man's eyes. Then Sully flipped the table.

He brought the table up with as much force as he could, propelling it into Koning. The table edge caught Koning in the nose and, rising from his seat, Sully put his own force behind it, a knee and both hands using the table to force Koning to the floor. Sully, his full weight in it, rode the table down, crushing Koning beneath him. He heard a clatter of something hard striking something equally hard and spotted the gun skittering out from under the table. He ignored it. Instead, he pushed himself upright and reached for the laptop. He considered the notepad, which had fallen behind Koning, but decided there wasn't enough on its pages to warrant the risk.

He stood there breathing heavily for a beat and his eyes traveled up, taking in the other patrons of the coffee shop, some already out of their seats, all with that muddled expression of surprise and defensiveness that comes from not having had time to process what has just happened. Rather than explain it to them, Sully headed for the exit. Seconds later he was out on the street, disappearing into the pedestrian crowd of Piazza di Sant'Eustachio.

Chapter Ten

Sully wound his way between the other pedestrians, instinct telling him to hurry but wisdom suggesting the best way to blend in with a crowd was to move at their speed. He'd turned right out of the coffee shop and crossed Piazza dei Caprettari, avoiding making that first right. Instead, he kept straight until he reached a narrower street, almost an alley carving a fissure between buildings. The street sign called it Via della Palombella and Sully took it, hurrying his steps once he'd separated from the crowd.

He knew Koning wouldn't have remained on the coffee shop floor for long and he mentally cursed himself for leaving the gun behind. Still, he suspected the inherent danger in walking around Rome with a gun that didn't belong to him outweighed the weapon's usefulness.

Tall, earth colored buildings rose on either side of him but the street wasn't long and when it ended, it emptied him into a wider road with more traffic. He stopped to get his bearings. He was in a district with a great many storefronts. A solid line of small cars and mopeds lined the opposite side of the street. A long, low wall bordered the side on which he'd stopped. A trio of girls sat near him on the wall. He could hear their talk and their laughter as he worked to put some order to the jumble of thoughts in his head.

For the first time since he'd fled the café, he could feel his heart begin to beat faster, his breathing coming harder. It was as if the false calm that had allowed his escape was giving way to the true emotions roiling beneath the surface. He did what he could to keep those emotions in check, knowing they wouldn't serve him here, but it was difficult to keep a finger hold on the false bravado.

He took a deep breath, held it for a few seconds, then released it. When he turned his head, he saw the trio of girls looking at him. When he made eye contact, they turned away, huddling together and giggling. While an innocent exchange, it told Sully he was more conspicuous than he wanted to be so he turned left and started down the street, passing a number of nondescript shops and eateries as he worked to build distance between himself and Koning.

The thought of the other man elicited a fresh welling of anger. In his mind, Sully could see him across the table, the snake smile firmly in place. He could hear him saying the names of his friends. That thought sent Sully fumbling for his phone. He pulled it from his pocket and raced through his contacts until he found Jason. His thumb was coming down on the button that would initiate the call when he hesitated.

From the moment he spotted Koning crossing the street, heading for the coffee shop, something about the man's presence had unnerved him. At the time, he'd hadn't the luxury to figure out what it was. Now, as he worked to put distance between them, the truth of it came at him in a rush. How did the man know where Sully was? Out of all of the coffee shops in Rome, Koning had found him in the one on Piazza di Sant'Eustachio. And as Sully replayed the scene in his mind, he saw in Koning's demeanor—the way he walked toward the door—a man who knew, rather than hoped, that his quarry was inside. It told Sully he was being tracked.

The revelation brought him to a halt, his thumb still over the send button. The scientist in him—the one used to calculating numbers and probabilities in seconds—raced through the possibilities. He dismissed his credit cards; he hadn't used them in days. Equally unlikely was some use of the extensive video surveillance system throughout the city. While Koning seemed the sort who would have sufficient connections to access it, Sully understood the basics of such systems enough to know that looking for one man not engaged in any activity that would raise a flag in the system's security algorithms was challenging. With those two possibilities dismissed, Sully could see only one other.

He slid his thumb away from the send button. The phone also explained how Koning could include both Jason and Emily in his list. Even more telling, the inclusion of Emily's name meant that Koning and his compatriots were not only tracking Sully's calls, they were listening to them. Sully hadn't called Emily since leaving for Rome; he and Jason had only spoken of her.

He felt a fresh welling of anger but checked it, knowing that the only thing that would serve him now was a clear head. He looked up and took in his surroundings. He hadn't gone far since leaving the trio of giggling girls behind and, if his suspicion about the phone was correct, then Koning, and perhaps others of his ilk, would not be far behind.

As he'd walked, the wider Via della Rotonda had expanded into an even wider street. A solid rock wall, pockmarked with the passage of two thousand years, had replaced the facades of more modern buildings to his right. He could see, up ahead, the first of the massive Corinthian columns that marked the entrance to the Pantheon. He could also see a great many more people traversing the piazza in front of the ancient building.

Sully started off again, heading toward the piazza, where the mass of tourists and locals would provide some measure of concealment while he planned his next move. He followed the massive, curved wall until its smoothness gave way to the marble edifice of the Pantheon entrance, the three rows of columns now in full view. A fountain stood in the center of the piazza and Sully headed that way, where several people mingled, or sat along its ring of steps. When he reached it, he crossed around to its opposite side and turned his attention to the street down which he'd come. The aged grandeur of the Pantheon provided a suitable backdrop for his thoughts, his rapid review and discarding of options.

From his position, he could see a black van parked next to the Pantheon entrance, the word *Carabinieri* in large white letters on the side. There were other signs of a police presence, as well, including the trio of uniformed officers behind and to his left. Sully gave brief consideration to walking up to them and telling them everything that had happened over the last few days but two things stopped him. The first was that his story was, on its face, unbelievable. It was doubtful he'd get through half of it before the officers took him into custody and sent him for a psychiatric evaluation. The second reason, however, was the more compelling. It was a simple desire to figure out a puzzle.

Over a short period of time, he'd become invested in the mystery. And the few pieces that had been revealed, as well as the forces that were marshaled to keep the others hidden, hinted at something extraordinary—something worth the danger involved in figuring it out.

It was also something big enough for a man to offer up his own daughter.

It was the first-time Sully had put that thought to the test. He had no doubt that Rossi was involved in the conspiracy (a first time for that appellation, as well). He also thought it increasingly likely that Koning had played some role in Elena's death. The fact, then, that Sully had witnessed the two men in conversation at Elena's wake suggested that Rossi—while aggrieved—was also complicit. Sully found that difficult to accept, yet equally difficult to discount.

He took a deep draw of the cool air, a hint of moisture in it, and pulled his thoughts away from Rossi, from the prospect of filicide. Self-preservation was, at the moment, a more compelling motivator.

He pulled out his phone and spent a few moments looking at it, thinking through the information it held, the phone numbers he might need. In the end, there was only one number that mattered, and he'd long ago relegated it to memory. He powered the phone down and then flipped it over, finding the seam along the bottom. He slid his thumbnail along it ineffectually before reaching in his pocket for his keys. He wedged one of them into the seam and worked it back and forth until the pieces came apart. That done, he found and removed the two sim cards, slipping them into his coat pocket. A few seconds later, and after a few tugs, he had the battery out, even though he thought it unlikely anyone could track the phone with it powered down and with the cards removed. Still, the events of the last few days demanded he exercise as much caution as he could.

After slipping the pieces of the phone into his pocket, he took one last look around and then turned away from the Pantheon, crossing the cobblestone past a line of closely spaced yellow brick buildings and slipping into a narrow alley bordered by more of the ubiquitous store fronts and outdoor cafes. He came out onto a wider street that he took for a short jog left before turning right into another of the smaller avenues. Without the phone acting as an electronic

Judas, Sully thought that his odds of staying ahead of any pursuers were tilted in his favor. However, with that freedom came the necessity of planning his next move, now that he'd ruled out the only sensible option: abandoning the whole business and heading back to New York. He chuckled to himself as he considered what Jason would have said about that decision.

As he walked, he saw a trio of arched doors to his left, rimmed with brown painted brick, a small restaurant visible through the glass. Just past the last door stood an ATM, snug in a hollow in the wall that seemed made for it. He stopped in front of it and pulled out his wallet. He hadn't discounted the possibility that Rossi, Koning, and their allies had the means to track his credit card activity. The problem was that the longer he stayed in Rome, the more pressing the need for money would become.

He withdrew the maximum of 400€, slipped it into his wallet, then hurried away from the ATM. As he turned into another side street the scent of pastries reached him, reminding him how long it had been since he'd eaten. He slipped into the café, bought enough cornetti to sate him, and slipped out again into the street. As he chewed, he considered his next move and it wasn't long before his choices were winnowed to one.

He knew of three people in Rome with some knowledge of this business and two of them were people he had little desire to see. That left a return visit to the Vatican to speak with a reluctant friend.

As Sully waved down a cab for the mile and half trip to Vatican City, he thought over what he would say to Rinaldi. In their last meeting, the man had made it clear that he was unwilling to discuss what he knew. Sully could only hope that his meeting with Koning—and the mention of Rinaldi's name as one of Sully's allies—would change that dynamic.

*****

It had taken almost an hour, grudging help from a doubtful staff, and a few phone calls to arrange the meeting. Without his own phone, and the link to Rinaldi's direct line it provided, Sully had been reliant on others to pass his missive to his friend.

When the cab came rolling to a stop near St. Peter's, Sully had exited, paid the driver, and headed toward the cathedral. A long line had snaked in front of the entrance and, at the time, he'd felt sorry for the people waiting in it. But it occurred to him, at some point after he'd approached one of the ever-visible Swiss guards and before he'd finally made contact with Rinaldi's personal assistant, that all of those people had likely made it into the cathedral by that point.

Even so, he'd finally succeeded in communicating, in as cryptic a fashion as he was able, that he had to speak with the Cardinal. Rinaldi had acquiesced but rather than meet at the Cardinal's office, Sully had been directed to Rinaldi's personal residence, the Domus

Sanctae Marthae—the Vatican guesthouse. An apartment building for a number of the permanent residents of the city, the building now had the added distinction of housing the current Pope, who had eschewed the more extravagant Papal apartment in the Apostolic Palace for a residence closer to his fellow citizens. Which explained the fact that Sully's walk across the Vatican grounds was in the company of a member of the Pontifical Guard.

Despite the circumstances that had brought him here, Sully couldn't help but feel a hint of disappointment that Rinaldi wouldn't receive him in his office in the Governorate Palace. On the few occasions in which he'd been invited to Rinaldi's office, in the coveted central chamber of the Palace, Sully had looked out on St. Peter's Basilica, which he could see past the fading brown edifice of Santo Stefano, the ticking of the Thristle—Williton clock in the corner of the office providing background noise.

He'd spent hours in that office, talking through a wide range of subjects—enough so that Sully thought he knew what motivated his friend. Everything the man did, he did with one goal in mind. Every move he made was executed with a master gamesman's view of his own position on the board. Even when a pope was healthy, when it looked as if his reign would last for decades, the vying for position went on, if at a less visible level than when the College of Cardinals gathered, waiting for their chance to choose a successor.

That's why, as much as he knew that Rinaldi, too, appreciated the view from his window, punctuated by the old architecture of the Church of Santo Stefano degli Abissini, the Cardinal couldn't help but see it as a metaphor for all of the obstacles in his path. Despite the church's rich history, it was a cumbersome, antiquated structure that obscured his view of the papal offices.

Sully suspected that Rinadli was on the short list to succeed the current pontiff—one of perhaps a dozen men who might fill the role. Sully had no doubt that was why his friend was tied to Rossi. He could only hope that, if the man's conscience, alone, failed to make him amenable to answering Sully's questions, then perhaps the recent reshuffling of the game board would serve the same purpose.

The non-descript white and tan building that was his destination emerged slowly from behind St. Peter's. The building, relatively new, seemed out of place when set in the same scene with the much larger, Renaissance-style structure. To Sully's eye, it looked like any six-story apartment building one might find in any large city in the States.

Rinaldi's assistant told Sully that the Cardinal's apartment was on the fifth floor and Sully suspected that his silent, colorfully garbed escort would remain with him the whole way. In all likelihood, the guardsman would stand in the hall outside Rinaldi's door for the duration of their conversation. Sully could only hope that, when the discussion concluded, he would be leaving on the same genial terms he currently shared with his guide.

When the whole of the building came into view, Sully's eyes moved to the fifth floor, and he wondered which of the windows marked Rinaldi's apartment. Then several of those windows turned into dust.

Sully's mind barely had time to register the blast—the immediate and thick plumes of black smoke—before the force of it, even from fifty yards away, hit him, the heat and deafening sound coming with it, reaching him from across the parking lot. Then he had to shut his eyes against the debris.

When he opened them again, it was to a scene ripped from a CNN news feed. A thick cloud of dust obscured his view of much of the building but he could see large gaps in the exterior wall, licking flames visible inside. As he watched, a section of the wall separated from the whole and plummeted to the pavement.

He stood frozen in place and it was only gradually that he noticed the shaking of his arm. Then someone moved into his line of sight, the guardsman, his hand on Sully's elbow, face close. The man's lips were moving and it seemed curious to Sully that nothing was coming out. He watched the guard's mouth move, transfixed by the strange sight, until a hint of clarity began to break through, to suggest that maybe it was Sully's hearing that was the issue.

As if waking from a dream, he looked past the guardsman, to the Domus Sanctae Marthae, to the people now running from it, running toward it. He could hear none of it. Rather, he became aware of sounds but they came to him as if from a distance, as if passing through a thick wall.

The guard was shaking his arm again and Sully looked at him. He still couldn't make out what the man was saying but he had a good idea.

"I'm fine," he said, his own voice distant.

The guard stopped talking and he looked intently at Sully, his eyes questioning. Sully suspected the guard's hearing was equally impaired. But Sully could feel the tension in the man's body; he knew he wanted to aid the rescuers already converging on the building.

"I'm fine," he said again. He gently pulled his elbow from the man's grasp. The guard still appeared uncertain but, after another close look at Sully, he turned and ran toward the smoke obscured apartment.

Sully remained there, watching the man sprint away, Sully taking in the devastation. The blast had shredded most of the fifth floor that Sully could see from his vantage point. But it hadn't stopped there. The explosion had also touched the floors above and below, shattering windows and leaving large gaps in the wall. In those few short moments, he knew his hearing was returning because he could hear sirens in the distance, the sounds of people yelling; and all at once, as if spurred by the noise, his feet began to move. He started toward the blast site, aiming for a group of people converging by the main doors. As he ran, his eyes moved once again to the place from which the explosion had originated and, with the same suddenness with which he'd started moving, he stopped.

The blast had taken out the fifth floor—the floor where Sully would have been only minutes later. It couldn't be coincidence. An ice-cold finger traced its way up Sully's spine and, for the first time, it came to him that Rinaldi was probably dead.

Sully watched people running into the building—guards, Vatican staffers, one man in clerical garb—all seemingly heedless of the danger. Floors above them, fresh tongues of flame licked out of the openings in the edifice. He knew he should be doing something but indecision froze him. Rinaldi was dead and, but for the span of two minutes, Sully might well have been with him.

Koning had known of Sully's earlier meeting with the Cardinal. The man might have suspected that Sully, his resources limited, would reach out again. So Koning had removed that resource. Now it occurred to Sully to wonder if Koning had left someone behind to make certain the job was done.

Sully looked over the parking lot but, amid all the chaos, the people trying to help, those who had arrived just to marvel, he knew there was no way for him to identify someone who didn't belong. All that mattered was that, if Koning had someone near, that person likely knew that Sully had not been in the building when it blew.

All of this came to him in seconds and the gravity of it settled on him with equal speed. Still, he stood rooted to the spot—the prospect of leaving when he might be able to help doing battle with his desire to escape unwanted attention. What tipped the scales were the number of people already assembled to assist, as well as the ever-nearing sounds of sirens. In moments, there would be too many people here—well-intentioned amateurs getting in the way.

By the time the first fire truck pulled into the parking lot, heading toward the damaged structure, Sully was heading in the other direction.

Chapter Eleven

Sully was shivering—tremors that ran up and down the length of his body. Tremors that had nothing to do with temperature. He knew he was experiencing some form of mild shock, a coming down from the adrenaline of the last few minutes. He didn't know how far he'd traveled, except that it was several blocks, most of them through similar looking cobblestone streets that all seemed to be bordered by the same buildings, the same walls. He hadn't even tried hailing a taxi near where he'd exited the Vatican. Instead, he'd just walked, heading away from the chaos behind him.

While part of him was in autopilot, there was another part that remained alert, that glanced at passing cars that cast the occasional glance over his shoulder. If he was being followed, he couldn't detect it.

He could still hear the sirens behind him and suspected he could walk for quite a while before those sounds left him entirely. He reached a quiet intersection but there were no signs telling him where he was. To his left, twin arches split the road, a picture of the Madonna and child separating the cars. To his right were nondescript buildings, café awnings hanging out over the sidewalk. He went right, hands in his pockets, passing a trio of identical silver buses parked at the curb.

Beyond them were tables and Sully aimed for one, almost falling into the first chair he could reach.

He sat there for a long while—he didn't know how long—before his thoughts worked their way into some kind of order. During that interval, a server came out and he ordered coffee—a rote response. Only when she'd returned with it did something like clarity return, at least enough so that he could provide a reasonable facsimile of a smile as she set the drink in front of him.

After she'd gone, he forced up a measure of dispassionate calm and tried to consider, in as analytical a fashion as he could, what had happened. Rinaldi was dead; of that he was certain. He was equally certain that the explosion had been no accident, no gas leak mishap that had happened to coincide with Sully and Rinaldi's meeting. The stark truth of it was chilling. In killing Rinaldi—one of the most influential clerics in one of the world's preeminent religious institutions—the nameless organization responsible for Elena's death, as well as the attempts on his own life, had given Sully a clear look at their capabilities. Koning worked for an entity with a vast reach—an entity that could carry out an assassination in short order, and within a relatively secure environment. It was a display of power—and one not necessarily for Sully's benefit. After all, he couldn't shake his belief that he was supposed to have been with Rinaldi when it happened.

Perhaps more important, they had also demonstrated how far

they were willing to go to accomplish their goals—whatever those goals were.

As those facts sorted themselves in his head, he felt his dispassion slipping. Somewhere, in the dark recesses of his mind, panic stood ready to replace it. This morning he'd been running on anger, on a willingness to see through to its completion something that had caught him up, however unwittingly. Now, though, he was being forced to face the possibility that he was unequipped for the task. What had begun as an investigation into the death of a friend, and that had morphed into a mystery involving strange shipments from the Vatican, had turned into something much bigger—something that promised an escalating body count. Worse, Sully knew that one of those deaths was a direct result of his involvement.

Guilt started to manifest but he stopped it before it could take on any real form. The truth of it was that he was, in a very real way, responsible for the death of Cardinal Rinaldi. Had he returned to New York after Elena's funeral, the man would still be alive. But he also knew that the only reason he'd been able to endanger his friend was because of the choices that Rinaldi had made. Whatever the cleric's motivations for working with the people who had killed Elena, he'd ultimately paid with his life. Sully couldn't hold himself responsible for that.

He took a sip of the coffee and glanced through the coffee shop window. Movement on a television screen caught his attention. The television hung in the corner behind the counter and it had escaped Sully's notice when he'd first arrived, absorbed in his thoughts. He had no difficulty identifying the scene that played out on the screen. It was an aerial shot, a few hundred feet above the building. Sully turned to look in the direction of the Vatican but the buildings on the other side of the street blocked his view. He turned back to the television, where an inset over the aerial shot showed a reporter talking over the video of fire fighters aiming water toward the upper floors. It struck Sully as strange that the event from which he'd just fled was now playing out as a breaking news item that would captivate all of Rome—the entire world. Maybe that, too, was the result of shock: the self-absorption, the slowness to recognize the full magnitude of what had just happened.

He stood and walked inside, leaving his coffee on the table. The three café workers were all watching the screen, as were the only two patrons inside. Sully stopped near the woman who had brought his coffee and watched the action play out on the screen. The reporter was talking fast and Sully could pick out less than half of it but the word *bomba* was clear.

"Who would do such a thing?" asked the server, her eyes riveted to the screen.

It was a question aimed at no one and so Sully did not respond, despite their proximity, and despite the fact that, of the people in the room, he was the most suited to answer it.

"Do you think Pope Francis was inside?"

That question pulled a different response from Sully, one bordering on incredulity. Until the woman next to him had put voice to the question, he hadn't even considered the possibility of the pontiff being in the building. His tunnel vision had kept him focused on himself, on Rinaldi, and on the people who had detonated the bomb. When he removed that filter, he realized how the thing would look to the rest of the world. It would be viewed as an assassination attempt on the Pope, with Cardinal Rinaldi as collateral damage.

"I hope not," he managed to mumble.

Inside, his mind was working furiously. If the Pope had been in the building when it happened, if someone of his stature had been considered an acceptable loss in the effort to halt the meeting between Sully and Rinaldi, that said more about the people who had done the deed than anything Sully had yet witnessed. It also reinforced his growing belief that this was not a fight he could win.

The problem, though, was that it was also the kind of act that told Sully bowing out was off the table. The moment the bomb exploded, Sully lost any chance of cutting his losses, tucking his tail between his legs, and heading home. The ones behind the bombing wouldn't allow it.

All of this came to him in the span of seconds, as he watched the event play out in front of him, the unsteady overhead camera shooting down through billowing smoke.

"How many dead?" Sully asked, the words barely audible. The server responded with a sound of wordless sympathy.

Sully shook his head and started to turn for the door. No next move guided his steps, only the sudden need to leave the café, to distance himself from the accusing television. He had almost lost the screen to his periphery when a sudden flicker pulled his attention back. It was a change in camera angle, this one a steady shot of the Domus Sanctae Marthae. The curious thing was that the building was whole. It took a few seconds for Sully to understand that he was looking at footage recorded before the explosion. From the angle, he suspected the camera had to have been somewhere in the vicinity of St. Peter's. It occurred to him, then, that what he was seeing was security footage. His eye caught movement near the bottom, right of the screen—two people entering the frame, walking across the parking lot. The realization that he was looking at himself hit him just as the bomb went off, sending the steady shot reeling.

Before he could react, the scene had reset—the steady shot again. He watched, riveted, until he saw himself, along with his escort, appear on the screen, until the explosion once again sent the camera bouncing. This time, though, the technical director running the footage slowed it down, trying to catch the precise moment the blast ripped through the structure. Sully, though, couldn't take his eyes off of the two forms in the corner of the screen. He was on camera, on an endless loop for the world to see.

The footage was grainy and the two figures crossing the parking lot were small enough in the larger shot that Sully didn't think anyone could identify him. He doubted even a high-tech computer forensics lab would be able to grant the forms sufficient detail to make them usable. Despite that, though, he found his presence in the frames disconcerting. Even without a papal death thrown in, Sully knew how thorough the coming investigation would be. A terrorist strike at the very heart of Christendom would draw agencies from across the globe. In addition to the church's own investigators, Sully knew the Italian government would be involved, as would Interpol. In all likelihood, the event would even pull in the FBI. And that pooling of resources would, sooner or later, provide names to the nameless figures. After that, it wouldn't take them long to link Sully to Rinaldi, then to want to ask him questions about the meeting.

The thought worried him, although the longer he stood there, watching the building come apart over and over in slow motion, it occurred to him that his concern was misplaced. The way this thing was heading, he suspected that the people responsible for the bomb would kill him long before any investigators uncovered his name.

That thought nearly elicited a dark chuckle but it was gone before it took form. In its place came a sudden weariness. When, not long after, he turned to leave, he didn't look back at the television.

Chapter Twelve

Sully removed his finger and let the red shade drop back into place. The street in front of the hotel was quiet, and had been so for the several minutes he'd spent watching. It was one of the reasons he'd picked the New Gemini, tucked into a secluded portion of Via Guido Mazzoni. The lack of either foot or vehicle traffic made it easier to watch for someone who appeared out of place. From the outside, the narrow, five-story building looked a dump, as if close to being boarded up and abandoned. Inside, though, it was clean, if not extravagant. And management let him pay in cash.

He'd had the television on for a while but it was off now, the same footage replaying over and again, studio talking heads from all over the world sharing time with on-scene reporters. There was nothing Sully could learn by watching any of it.

Turning from the window, he moved to the room's lone chair and sat, reaching for the bottle of wine he'd purchased on the way to the hotel. It was a Vietti Barolo Rocche, an expensive bottle that, considering what he'd gone through since touching down in Rome only days ago, he thought he deserved. It was also the sort of bottle he owed to Jason when he returned to New York. If he returned.

He pushed that thought from his head and uncorked the bottle, then poured some into a paper cup he'd taken from the bathroom. That first cup, small as it was, disappeared quickly and he poured another, which went with equal speed. He nursed the third cup longer, finally appreciating the dense flavor, the hint of spice. He sat that way for a long while, letting the morass of the day's events play themselves out in his mind, allowing them to find their own order.

He glanced at the bedside table on which sat the now half-empty bottle. There were two burner phones on it, purchased immediately after the wine. He thought about using one of them right now to check in with Jason but decided against it almost before the idea was fully formed. He doubted his friend would have anything helpful yet. Too, the moment he made the call he would have to pull the battery from the phone and toss it.

That decision left him draining the rest of the third glass of wine in one gulp. From every angle he'd considered, removing Jason from the mix left him with a distinct lack of options, all of which he'd previously considered and discarded. Consequently, he did the only thing he could think of that came close to resembling forward progress: he retrieved his laptop from next to the table and opened it.

When it booted up, his fingers moved by rote to call up his email account and he'd nearly completed the process before he stopped. It occurred to him to wonder if the same technology his would-be assassins could use to track his phone calls might also be used to keep tabs on his email, or perhaps perform some kind of signal backtrack that would lead them to the room in which he sat. He let that thought stop him for only a few seconds, though, before entering the last few characters. In the situation he was in, he knew he had to take a risk or two. The only other option was to hole up where he was and wait out whatever would happen. And there were two things working against that course of action: a lack of a clear timetable and a limited pool of cash from which to draw.

When his email finally popped up, after hanging during the load long enough for Sully to start to give more credence to the technical savvy of his pursuers, the screen revealed more than a dozen new messages. Sully, though, only saw the two at the very top, the most recent ones. One was from Jason, sent less than thirty minutes ago. There was no subject in the subject line. But as much as Sully wanted to touch base with his friend, it was the email directly below that one that drew the bulk of his attention, that made him lean forward in the chair. The email address bore Rinaldi's name. He absorbed the details in what seemed a microsecond: the fact that the message had come from Rinaldi's personal account rather than the account tied to his office; that, like Jason's message, this one also lacked anything in the subject line; and that the timestamp had the message arriving less than four hours ago. Sully felt his pulse quicken; it would have been minutes before the explosion.

He opened the email in a rush. It was short—a single paragraph.

"These are unusual times, Solomon. And I fear my own time is running short. Even so, the oaths I spoke as a much younger man keep me from freeing my tongue as much as I suspect you'll need. I can however, give you this: Castel Gandolfo, 1933. I can also tell you that they've known since the House of Stuart. It is not enough, yet it is all an old man can give and still maintain at least a pretense of fealty to those old vows" – R

Sully read it again, the dulling effect of the wine gone. The fact that it was likely Rinaldi's dying missive lent the words a sense of gravity. Indeed, the fact that Rinaldi seemed to realize he'd been targeted, yet still felt the need to withhold all but the smallest scraps of information, told Sully that, whatever Rinaldi had been involved is, he'd considered his life worth the secret.

In moments, he had another browser tab open. The House of Stuart reference was probably too vague a clue to provide any immediate insight. Castel Gandolfo, though, had tickled something in Sully's brain and a search confirmed its existence as a town fifteen miles southeast of Rome. An Apostolic Palace dominated the landscape but there were a number of points of interests for any tourist. Sully thought he might even have driven through it once during his teaching days in Rome. As he scanned the available information on the town he quickly realized that the place—albeit populated by less than 9,000 people—was large enough to make Rinaldi's clue nearly impossible to parse. However, when he added the date, it took only a few minutes before he found what he suspected

Rinaldi had meant for him to find—the move of the Vatican Observatory from Rome to Castel Gandolfo. He ran a follow-up query in an attempt to tie this information to the House of Stuart in some way but came up empty.

Sully leaned back and let his mind run over this new information. It wasn't much; he didn't see how it was actionable. But he refused to believe that Rinaldi would have given him something he couldn't ultimately use. He drummed his fingers on the table, trying to connect a relocated observatory with everything that had happened thus far. The initial threads were tenuous at best but, the more he thought about it, the clearer the connection became. Messages from Elena had drawn him into this and those messages had contained a reference to Nostradamus. Days later, Nostradamus had resurfaced during his conversation with Rinaldi. Even after a few days of study, Sully still didn't know a great deal about the sixteenth century seer but he did know that the man had dealt in the metaphysical. More germane in this case, the man had also dealt in the astrological. And the fact that Sully's investigation had uncovered multiple references to Nostradamus, and was then connected to the movement of an observatory from one place to another, had to be more than coincidence.

"But what do I do with it?" he asked himself.

He reached for the wine bottle and emptied the last of it into the paper cup. He nursed it for a few minutes, his thoughts a jumble.

Chief among them was the wish that Rinaldi's devout sensibilities had not held so firm in his last minutes. He released a heavy sigh and returned to his inbox, opening the one from Jason. As he'd expected, the message began by questioning Sully's whereabouts. Sully could almost hear the sounds of exasperation—perhaps even worry—coming through. He wondered how many messages Jason had left on his voicemail.

As he read the rest of the message, though, his already low spirits sagged further. At the time Jason had sent the email—nearly three hours ago—he'd discovered nothing about either the mysterious *three* or the reference to *betrayal* in the quatrain. His friend had closed the email with an apology and a promise to keep looking. Sully sighed for what seemed the thousandth time and glanced toward the empty wine bottle. The bottle's depleted state produced another sigh. He sat there for a while, the previous weighty thoughts that had occupied his mind prior to reading Jason's email now fighting against his inclination to go out for a second bottle of wine. It didn't take him long, though, to push that desire to the side and weigh his options. And with those options more limited than he would have liked, it took him even less time to choose his next steps.

"A drowning man clings to whatever he can find that floats," he mumbled to himself. With a shake of his head, he rose from the chair, turned off the light, and stretched out on the lumpy, musty-smelling bed. He was asleep in seconds.

*****

Thick tree cover lined both sides of the road as Sully worked the rental down SS140. Only twenty kilometers from Rome, the parcel of land over which he traveled felt a world away. He had the windows down, a cool breeze entering from the driver's side and swirling with its like coming in through the opposite window. Despite his frame of mind when he'd left the hotel, he couldn't help but let the scenery do its work on his mood. As he drove, expanses of untended foliage spread out from the road, interspersed with the occasional building that told him he was nearing his destination. Low walls, some almost entirely obscured by vines, ran alongside the car. A few hundred yards ahead, the road disappeared in a hairpin to the left and Sully slowed to guide the car around it. When he came out the other side, the road ran straight for another kilometer before reaching another equally sharp turn to the right. On the other side of this second turn was yet another straightaway and, despite the fact that Sully knew he was getting close, the sense of remoteness gave the illusion that the road could go on forever. Then a town opened up before him, appearing as if from nowhere.

Sully's first look at Castel Gandolfo took in three and four-story buildings of the earth color ubiquitous in the local architecture. Those buildings—sparse at first—grew in number before giving way to newer, smaller structures, a number of cafes and small shops among them. Before he'd driven much farther, though, the larger buildings returned and stayed with him until he rounded one last corner to see a picture from a postcard—a pristine mountain lake stretching out in front of him.

Sully slowed just long enough to appreciate the view—the clear blue water extending to a green, rocky shoreline; a near cloudless sky taking over once his vision cleared the mountains—but he turned his attention back to the road before the beauty of the scene could distract him from his goal. As he guided the car through light traffic, he reached for a piece of paper on the passenger seat, then glanced at the directions he'd written on it. Looking up from the paper, he scanned the street signs until he found the right one, then turned the car onto SS216. He traveled for another kilometer before he found a parking area just a few blocks from the Vatican Observatory.

Exiting and locking the car, he turned to review the large traffic circle that, more than anything he'd seen so far, reminded him of the much larger city only kilometers to the north. It looked like a place where Sully could spend a long afternoon, strolling the streets, wandering into any number of small shops, finding a good pub where he could nurse a local brew and enjoy a fine cigar. He released a heavy sigh before setting off down the cobblestone street toward Piazza Pia.

Before starting out that morning, Sully had crammed as much research as he could about the observatory into the time it took him to eat a cornetto and drink a single cup of coffee. One of the more interesting things he'd learned was that the observatory, itself, was absent from the town—the Vatican operating telescopes in other locations. Castel Gandolfo hosted the Vatican Observatory headquarters—a collection of offices, classrooms, and labs housed in a repurposed convent.

The problem, as he saw it, was finding whatever Rinaldi had meant for him to find in what amounted to a decent sized compound, complete with living quarters and a museum—not to mention not knowing how easy it would be to even gain access to the place. His truncated research had not supplied enough information for him to determine how much—if any of it—was open to the public.

He reached a cross street and, glancing at the name on the sheet of paper he'd brought with him, looked past the street to the building beyond it, separated from the rest of the world by a tall, gray wall. Beyond that wall, the building rose to four stories, the façade faded white brick and irregular gray stone. There was a sense of age to it that seemed incongruous next to the newer structures that surrounded it. However, as much as he could appreciate the building on a purely aesthetic level, his perusal quickly shifted to the more pragmatic.

From what he could see, without circumnavigating the property, there was only one way past the wall and that right in front of the building's main door. From his vantage, he could see no movement around the property, no one in the windows facing the street. He stood there for a little while longer until, with a shrug, starting across the street toward the entrance. He'd almost reached it when the door—a solid one of time worn wood—swung open. Sully, whose hand had started reaching for the door handle, paused as someone stepped out. For just a moment, the man seemed equally surprised to find someone standing there but after brief eye contact and a nod, the man stepped past Sully and headed toward the street. Sully caught the door handle just as the door began to close and he stepped inside.

The dim interior briefly robbed him of vision but as his eyes adjusted he saw that he was in a large entry hall. The walls were of a brick similar to that of the building's exterior; the floor was a dark stone tile. There was a small room to Sully's right—perhaps an office of some sort. At the moment, it was empty and so Sully started deeper into the place, toward the spot where the entryway opened up into a larger room straight ahead and where a hall ran off to the right and left. Just shy of stepping into the larger room, Sully paused as he discovered that he was not alone. The room—spotted with an assortment of chairs and a few small tables, most lining the walls—held perhaps a dozen people. A mixture of men and women of varying ages, they stood talking in small groups, some holding drinks or small plates of food. A few wore clerical garb but the majority seemed to be lay people. Before anyone turned attention to him, he stepped away from the archway and into the hallway to his left. His research had mentioned that the observatory headquarters contained classrooms and a lecture hall, as well as places where students and guests could mingle. The fact that there seemed to be some event—perhaps some class—occurring was a boon. It meant less suspicion if someone caught him wandering where he wasn't supposed to.

Leaving the small party behind, he started down the hall. He passed three closed doors before he reached the end of it. Behind any one of those doors could have been Rinaldi's clue but he knew he couldn't open doors indiscriminately. He had to be judicious in his risks. Even so, those closed doors again reminded him how difficult—perhaps impossible—this could turn out to be. At the end of the hall was an open door and when he looked in, he found a room with a half-dozen computers spread over two long tables. There was no one in the room and Sully stepped inside. He noted the exit on the other side of the room before moving to one of the computers. All but one were powered down. The exception presented a screensaver showing a modified version of the Vatican Observatory's website home page. Sully jiggled the mouse and the screensaver disappeared, revealing a generic blue background and a few lines of icons. He recognized only a few. Of the rest, he suspected they were base programs for student computers, likely to reveal nothing of importance. Still, he gave a moment's thought to seeing if this system would grant him any kind of deeper access, but as with the closed doors in the hallway, he suspected his time could be used to greater effect elsewhere.

He left the room behind, entering a narrower corridor that offered access to stairs going up to the next level. Beyond the stairs, the hallway turned to the right. He glanced down it, guessing it would have to run behind the room in which he'd seen the people talking and eating. He chose the stairs. If he remembered with any accuracy, the upstairs held rooms for the resident priests, a small chapel, and a few offices. None of it sounded particularly promising but he'd lived long enough to know that luck, however fickle, was a very real commodity.

The stairs creaked beneath him. When he reached the landing, he looked up the remaining steps and saw no signs of life. After ascending the steps, he reached a level more open that the one below, highlighted by a large central area with several chairs and small couches. He could see several rooms around the perimeter, including an open door that looked to lead into a kitchen. As he advanced into the room, beginning to wonder if he'd made a mistake in abandoning the search of the ground floor, he heard voices coming from somewhere in front of him, from behind a closed door. It struck him immediately that the only reason he could hear voices from a behind a door was because the owners of those voices were speaking loudly.

Stopping, he strained to hear what they were saying but the words were too muffled to pick out. The only thing he did ascertain was that one of the voices was markedly louder. After spending a few seconds considering his options, among which was the choice to turn around, walk down the stairs, and out the front door in abandonment of the entire enterprise, he quietly moved to one of the closed doors opposite the occupied room. He turned the door handle slowly and was grateful to find no light coming from inside. Opening the door wider, he slipped in and then closed the door all but a crack. Then he waited.

From his hiding place, he could hear the argument running its course although, the longer he listened, the more he became convinced that any argument he'd initially perceived was of the one-sided variety. On those occasions when he heard a voice different from the principal speaker's it was much quieter. He waited for almost ten minutes before the muffled voices stopped. Sully, who had closed his eyes and leaned back against the wall in the darkened room, straightened and cautiously positioned himself so that he could see through the cracked door. Seconds later the door on the other side of the sitting room opened and a man stepped out; Sully could see a second man behind the first but his eyes were riveted on the closer of the two.

Mats Koning turned back to the room he'd just exited, stopping the other man with a look. Sully heard him speak but Koning's voice was quieter now—too quiet to make out the words. What he said, though, had a marked effect on the second man, whose eyes widened. But he made no response as Koning turned and walked toward the stairway. Sully remained in his spot as Koning disappeared from view and he kept his eyes on the man Koning had left behind. From across the sitting room, Sully could take his measure: the man's face held worry—and relief. Sully didn't have long to garner anything more, though, before the man exited what Sully could see now was an office, closing the door behind him. Then he, too, disappeared from view, headed toward the stairs. Sully remained in his concealment until the creaking of the steps stopped, and then he waited for a full minute more before stepping into the sitting room.

He hastened across the hall and tried the door handle. It was unlocked. He pulled the door open and stepped inside, pulling it shut behind him. It was a medium sized office, perhaps fifteen feet by ten, and spartanly furnished. It held a single large, wooden desk, two chairs, and a small file cabinet. A laptop was open on the desk. Beyond that, all Sully could see was a small, organized stack of papers. The whole of the office spoke of an almost obsessive orderliness.

He walked around the desk and sat. The screensaver hadn't yet activated and he hurriedly brushed a finger across the touchpad. He studied the desktop, seeing a number of the same icons and folders that were on the computer on the first floor, as well as some he was reasonably sure he hadn't seen, all labeled in Italian. He opened a folder that said *mostra* and a quick perusal of the resident files showed lists of items exhibiting in the observatory museum. Another folder seemed to be financials but a quick read-through pointed to nothing out of the ordinary. Sully tried the remaining folders and loose documents on the desktop—an arrangement as orderly as the rest of the office—and found nothing. He knew he was rushing; he couldn't count on the man who occupied the office staying gone for long. But, to this point, the entire excursion had been an exercise in haste. If he was going to find anything, he would need a beneficence beyond his power to grant himself.

With that truth in mind, he abandoned the desktop in favor of the deeper file folders. A half hour passed as he waded through a sea of correspondence, financial figures, and line items—all, as far as Sully could tell, related to the legitimate operation of an observatory. With a sigh, he leaned away from the computer and shook his head. He could spend another hour, and likely longer, without finding anything. He drummed his fingers on the desk, absently wondering when the office door would open and the man who belonged here—or maybe Koning, himself—would be standing there.

He raised his eyes from the computer and moved them over the office, as much to rest them from the glare of the screen as to search for anything he might have missed. In doing so, his gaze fell on the neat stack of papers on the corner of the desk. Raising an eyebrow, he reached for them. There were loose pages on top that looked like lecture notes. Sully put those aside and reached for the next pages, which proved equally unhelpful. Beyond those pages, though, was a steno pad. Sully opened it and began to flip through the pages. There seemed to be little order to the contents, which was surprising considering the state of the rest of the office. Sully saw what seemed to be more lecture notes, some disparate thoughts that didn't seem to connect to anything else, a grocery list, a trio of Hail Marys scribed in the same hand, and an oddly shaped cross doodled in one margin, the edges of the cross flared. Sully started to close the pad, about to set it aside, when something in the bottom corner of a page caught his eye.

In a flash, he had the pad back open, where he could see Koning's name clearly. The hand that had written the word—the same hand that had supplied the rest of the content on the surrounding pages—appeared to have given the name a sense of weight. It was darker than most of the rest of the writing on the page, as if the author had pressed the pen down. Sully quickly scanned the rest of the page, his eyes flitting over dates and times, none of them with any context. Halfway down the page there were a series of numbers, again with no framework. Regardless, Sully had a feeling he'd found something important. Perhaps it wasn't what Rinaldi had meant for him to unearth but it was clearly related to the events that had surrounded him since he'd touched down in Rome. And the best part was that it was portable; he could take the notepad with him. With a grim smile, he reviewed the rest of the page, his eyes drawn to the only other thing written in the same heavy hand as Koning's name. It was made up of three digits: 73P. And as if to emphasize it even more, it was circled. Even so, Sully had no idea what the short bit of text signified. The beauty of portability, however, was that once he was out of the building and holed up somewhere comparatively safe, he could spend as much time as necessary parsing the information.

He rose from the chair, holding the notepad like a prize, even as stiff muscles protested. He was about to start for the door when a thought stopped him in his tracks. He glanced down at the book in his hands and then his gaze moved to the laptop. The fact that he'd almost left the office without realizing that the notepad wasn't the only potentially important item easily liberated from the building simultaneously amused and chagrinned him. He bent and pulled the computer's power cord from the wall. Then he removed the other end from the computer and shoved it into his coat pocket. That done, he reached to close the lid. The lid was past the halfway point when he stopped himself, eyes wide. He had no idea if the owner of the laptop had password protected it. If the screen saver made an appearance, he would probably never regain entry to the computer's contents. He ran a finger over the touchpad and then, setting the notepad back on the desk, he found the control panel and turned off the screen saver. Now he could only hope that the battery power would last until he found a place where he could plug in.

With a satisfied grunt, he tucked the steno pad under his arm and lifted the still open laptop from the desk. Moments later he was in the sitting room, heading for the stairs. He didn't draw an easy breath until the front doors deposited him on the walkway and he was hurrying back to the rental.

Chapter Thirteen

Sully had eschewed coffee at another café for a different kind of drink at a different sort of establishment. He raised his glass and sniffed the wine before taking a sip.

His initial impulse had been to get out of Castel Gandolfo as quickly as he could and return to Rome, where he could find yet another cheap hotel in which to hole up. What had stopped him, though, was the chance that he would need to make a phone call. And if his suspicions about his calls being monitored were valid, then the call he had to make would mean losing a burner, as well as having to run again. Better to run from a place he was already leaving. In the meantime, though, he could try to enjoy a superior wine in a place with unparalleled atmosphere.

Arte e Vino was a restaurant on many a tourist agenda but when he'd arrived, well before the evening rush, the crowd was light. He sat at an old, weathered wooden table in a small room with voluminous hanging wine racks attached to walls made of irregular stone. It had an old-world feel to it. In fact, the accoutrements, including the old suit of armor standing sentinel in one corner, made Sully feel as if he'd stepped into a scene from the seventeenth century.

He'd left the stolen laptop in the trunk of the rental, after changing the password so he would be able to access it again. His own computer was open on the table. The waiter had looked at him with barely concealed indignation when he'd opened it but had supplied the wireless code, taken Sully's order, and left without a word. He opened the pilfered steno pad and placed it on the table, open to the page with Koning's name. Then, under the aegis of *know thine enemy*, he typed the name Mats Koning into the search field. Koning's presence at the observatory made three times he and Sully had been in the same place, at the same time. He'd given the man little thought when they'd met at Elena's viewing. Then, when Koning had tracked him down in the café in Rome, and in the day following that meeting, Sully had had other considerations with which to occupy himself. Now, however, there was no escaping the fact that, if he was going to escape from this thing with his skin intact, he needed to know more about this man who seemed significantly more involved than Sully had first believed.

As Sully scanned through the results, though, he found little to put flesh on the skeleton. Mats Koning, 47, had held a number of high-level positions at several companies throughout Europe, with a short stop in Tokyo—his most recent stop a stint as vice president of operations for a manufacturing company based in Berlin. After his departure from that position, the Internet record was conspicuously silent. Sully spent a few more minutes going through any results that appeared promising but he could uncover nothing after the man left Berlin almost ten months ago. From the bits he could pick out prior to that time, Koning seemed to be a man with a decisive, perhaps even harsh, management style. The stories that accompanied his name were often filled with reports of employee layoffs, of leveraged buyouts, and of quick company turnarounds. What was missing, though, was anything that connected the man to the Vatican, or to Rossi, or to any insidious organization that utilized murder as a tool for accomplishing its ends.

Sully tapped his fingers on the table. From his dealings with Koning, as well as what little he could glean from the web search, he knew what sort of man he was dealing with. What he didn't know was whom he worked for now, or what motivated him. Or what weaknesses he had.

The waiter appeared at his side and slid a plate laden with the restaurant's famed rigatoni in front of him. Until that moment, Sully hadn't realized how hungry he was. He thanked the waiter and, the computer temporarily forgotten, dug in. Before he knew it the plate was empty and he was washing it down with the last of the wine. The waiter was there moments later, refilling his glass. When he left, Sully pulled the steno pad close again.

As he turned the pages, his eyes fell on the doodle he'd noted earlier—the cross with the flared edges. Sully could imagine someone absently creating it while pondering something else. For some reason, though, the image tugged at him, as if he'd seen it before but couldn't place it. To his eye, it looked similar to a Coptic cross, though not as ornate as the ones he'd seen. This design was much simpler, resembling what it was: a doodle. But he still couldn't shake the thought that there was something about it that demanded a closer look.

He leaned back in his chair and drank from the wineglass. Almost of its own volition, his free hand flipped a page, to where Koning's name had been written. His frown grew deeper. Then, as if someone had flipped a switch, a memory came rushing back. He was sitting in a coffee shop with Koning, just a few moments before he'd flipped a table on the man. He could see Koning place his elbows on the table, bringing his hands together. He could see the ring.

In moments, he was searching the computer, looking for a representation of the image on the steno pad—the same one on Koning's ring. It didn't take long before he found it and, when he did, he was confronted with the dual feelings of surprise and puzzlement. The red flared cross was one of the ancient symbols of the Knights Templar.

He scrolled through the images on the results page, the red cross showing in paintings, in family crests, on shields—a parade of images on items stretching through the centuries. His frown deepened. He was no historian. His knowledge of the Knights Templar didn't go beyond the most basic—that they were an order attached to the Catholic Church, and that they'd played some role in the Crusades. He had no idea how to process the presence of one of their symbols on a notepad he'd stolen from an astronomer's office, or on the finger of a man who wanted him dead.

The fact that he'd been presented with two instances of the symbol suggested that there was something there that warranted attention but, even as he considered that, he knew that there were only so many rabbit trails he could follow, especially if, in investigating the symbol, he'd be forced to consider the possibility that the Knights Templar still existed as an organization, and that Mats Koning might he one of its adherents. It was simply too much to handle at the moment.

He knew he had to refocus so he pushed the red cross from his mind and paged through the notepad until he reached the series of numbers, but his eyes ultimately settling on the bold and circled text: 73P. He entered the three characters into the search field. And when the results came back, the very first entry brought him forward in his chair. It was a Wikipedia entry titled *73P/Schwassmann–Wachmann.* He clicked through and read the introductory text, his curiosity more than piqued. When he'd finished, he absorbed the rest of the page, including the picture gallery at the bottom. It wasn't until he'd finished that he realized his heart was beating just a little faster. He clicked back and tried the next entry: a NASA article from 2006 that referenced the cyclical approach of comet 73P, with a back-story dealing with the fracturing of the comet a decade earlier. He read that article in its entirety and then a follow-up article that plotted the trajectory of the comet fragments during its 2006 passing.

When he'd finished, he leaned back in the chair. There were several more results for 73P but he suspected none of them would do much to add to the knowledge base he'd gained over the last several minutes. He absently reached for the wineglass and took a drink, hardly tasting the expensive vintage.

73P had to be the key to all of this. Contextually, it fit. Rinaldi sending Sully to an observatory; the coordinates and equations supplied by Elena; even the ramblings of a long-dead astrologer: all of it seemed to speak to a specific celestial body. And 73P fit the bill. The question, though, was why? From the information he'd read, he could find nothing about the comet that indicated there was anything remarkable about it; neither did the NASA articles express concern that there was even a remote chance of it striking Earth on any of its passes. He drummed his fingers on the table again and then reached into his pocket and retrieved a burner phone. He dialed the number from memory.

Jason answered on the third ring.

"Hello?"

"Jason, it's me," Sully said.

The line was silent for a single moment.

"Where the hell are you?" Jason shouted. "And why aren't you answering your phone?" He paused, then added, "And why are you calling from a different number?"

Sully, who'd pulled the phone away from his ear, returned it.

"It's a long story," he began, before Jason cut him off.

"Not this time," he said. "Every time I've talked with you since you left for Rome, it's been '*It's a long story, Jason*' or '*I'll tell you when I get back, Jaso*n' or '*I drank the wine I was going to bring you, Jason*'. Now, you're going to tell me what's going on or I'm going to tell General Randall we don't want his money. Then you can go back to teaching undergrads and I can find a partner who won't go incommunicado at a critical career juncture."

Sully, who had once again pulled the phone away, couldn't keep the smile from his lips as his friend ended the tirade.

"I'm sorry," he said. "You're right, I owe you an explanation." He glanced around the half-empty restaurant, doubtful that the place provided the best setting for an extended conversation; although he doubted there was any good place from which to tell someone that people associated with the Roman church were trying to kill you in an attempt to cover up some sinister plot that seemed to center around shipping packages to a handful of places around the globe. He was about to suggest such to Jason when something his friend had said finally registered. "Wait, what was that about Randall?"

"He approved the grant request," Jason said in a grudging tone, as if reluctant to allow Sully to redirect the conversation. "We should have the money by Monday."

Sully absorbed that in silence. With everything that had happened over the span of the last week, the grant request had been pushed into the back corner of his mind. He couldn't help but marvel at that. Until last week, convincing Randall to accept their project proposal had consumed most every waking thought. The realization that he hadn't thought about it in days amazed him. It also drove home the seriousness of this thing that had caught him up—this thing that had also caught up some of his friends and colleagues, even if they were unaware of it. It was that last thought that decided it for him, that convinced him to tell Jason everything, regardless of the surroundings. If Jason was going to be in danger because of Sully's actions, the other man at least deserved to know as much about that danger as he could.

"Get comfortable," Sully said. "Because this might take a while."

Over the next hour, Sully told Jason everything, starting from the moment he'd met Nicolo Rossi's two associates at the viewing, to his exit from the Vatican Observatory, stolen laptop and notebook in hand. Through it all, Jason—seldom a man to avoid a clever aside—remained silent, which was a testament to how crazy the story sounded. Even Sully, who'd lived through it, found himself doubting some of it. When he'd finished, Jason maintained his silence for a while longer. When he did speak, his words came as no surprise.

"What I'm not hearing," Jason said, "is a good explanation for why you're not sitting in an Italian police station right now telling *them* this story instead of telling it to me."

"Because we're talking about the Catholic church," Sully said. "And I'm not naïve enough to think they don't have someone on the inside."

Jason's immediate response to that was still more silence. Sully could picture the look on his friend's face, the way his lips pursed when he was considering something particularly distasteful.

"I'm not buying it," Jason said. "The second someone ran you down with a car—or at least the second you woke up in the hospital—you should have called the police. You know it and I know it. The reason you didn't—the reason you're still in Rome pissing people off enough that they want to kill you—is because you're pissed off too. And because you hate to lose."

Sully had no immediate counter to the accusation and the reason was because he knew there was an element of truth to it. He liked to tell himself he had no other options when the reality was that the people who had brought him into this—the people whose faces were crystallized in that of Mats Koning—had made him angry. Angry enough to forget his obligations back home; angry enough to break into an office building and steal intellectual property; angry enough to put his life on hold to ferret out a secret that could, ultimately, kill him. When he thought about it in those terms, he understood how foolish it sounded. But knowing it did little to dampen his desire to stay here and see things through.

He was about to respond when it hit him. Jason's statement

had been absent any doubt about Sully's account. He'd passed right over the disbelief Sully would have expected, and right into a disagreement regarding the way Sully had chosen to handle the situation. Sully felt a swell of gratitude for that level of trust.

"You're right," he said. "I should have gone to the local police right away. At the very least, I could have hopped a plane back to Washington before things got out of hand." He took a deep breath and then let it out, as if releasing something in addition to the air. As he did, he noticed the waiter hovering. On some level, Sully had been aware of the waiter's increasing appearances at the table for the last several minutes. Sully looked around and saw that the crowd was significantly larger. In fact, there wasn't a free table. He'd been so absorbed in conversation that he'd been oblivious to the increasing number of diners. When he looked back at the waiter it was with understanding; the man wanted to turn the table. Sully nodded and the waiter placed the check on the table and left. "The problem now, Jason, is that things *are* out of hand. People have died—one of them just because I spoke with him." He shook his head and offered a sardonic chuckle. "I'm invested now, Jason. And I'm not leaving until it's finished."

"You're an academic, Sully," Jason said but there was a note in his voice that told Sully he knew he was fighting a losing battle.

"Then I'm smart enough to stay one step ahead of these bastards," Sully said. "If I can count on a little help..."

It was Jason's turn to sigh. He'd always been the counterpoint to Sully's more serious mien. To hear him so grave was disconcerting. But Sully knew he'd be able to count on his friend.

"I can't believe I'm going to say this," Jason said. "In fact, if I was in my right mind I'd call the FBI office here in Washington and tell them what's going on. Let them send someone to scoop you up. But I won't. Instead, I'll be just as much of an idiot as you and ask what you need me to do."

"For starters, I need you to find out anything you can about 73P," Sully said. "From what I can see, it's just a cyclical comet—one that's breaking itself apart as of about a decade ago. I need to know why there's so much interest in it."

"If there *is* any interest in it," Jason interjected. "Just because you found it written on a notepad in an office in an observatory without a telescope doesn't necessarily make it the reason people are trying to kill you."

"Point taken," Sully said. "But at the moment, I don't have many other leads."

"Which should tell you something about your chances of figuring anything out before you get yourself killed."

"Are you going to help me or not?" Sully asked.

"Sorry," Jason said. "You were saying?"

"While you're at it, see if there's anything else you can dig up about Mats Koning. The stuff I'm finding online is innocuous enough but there's hardly anything out there for the last year. Maybe another set of eyes?"

"So, I'm supposed to play Internet detective while you play international spy," Jason said.

"Something like that," Sully said with a smile—a smile that fled as quickly as it came. "And Jason, if I'm right that they're monitoring my calls…" He let the unspoken warning hang there.

"I'll be careful," Jason said. "And don't feel too guilty. If I'm a target, I was probably one before you knew any of us were."

"That's not as comforting as you might think," Sully said.

The waiter returned and took the check, upon which Sully had placed his credit card. Anyone watching his accounts would get his location but Sully would be long gone before they arrived. Maybe he'd even pass them on the road as he drove the rental back to Rome.

"One last thing," Sully began. Despite Jason's admonition against guilt, it was a feeling Sully couldn't simply shake off. Had he gone to the police early on, or abandoned the enterprise entirely, Jason probably wouldn't be a target. At this point, though, there wasn't anything Sully could do to make his friend any safer. That wasn't true, though, for someone else. "It's probably best if we keep Emily out of this for the duration."

"Done and done," Jason said. "The lovely Dr. Hannah is now out of the loop."

"Thanks, Jason," Sully said. "I'll call you later to see if you've found anything. It'll be from a different number."

"Got it," Jason said. "I'll see what I can dig up. And Sully? Don't get killed."

"I'll do my best."

"Do better," Jason said. "The good general has bequeathed us a great deal of money. And if he takes it away because you're dead, I'm going to find some way to bring you back so I can kill you again."

"Understood," Sully said with a chuckle. "I'll talk to you tomorrow."

The waiter returned with his credit card as Sully ended the call and the man looked relieved when Sully added the tip and then closed the laptop and stood. A busboy was clearing the table before Sully had gone more than a few steps.

On his way out of the restaurant he dropped the phone in the trash can near the hostess station.

Chapter Fourteen

A flash of headlights cut across the window as a car turned at the intersection adjacent to the hotel. Sully gave the intrusion little notice, since the event had occurred perhaps a hundred times in the hour he'd been in the room. The hotel had been poorly positioned, with most of the first-floor rooms facing toward the intersection subject to the steady flow of traffic. He'd been surprised to find that the windows had not been darkened, or at least blocked by a heavy shade. Of course, it wasn't the nicest of the hotels in the area; and, as with the one Sully had stayed in the night before, it had allowed him to pay in cash.

Even had he shelled out for a nicer establishment, though, he suspected the headlights would have stopped bothering him long ago anyway. He'd spent most of the last hour engaged in research. After returning from Castel Gandolfo, and without any immediate goals, he'd decided that doubling up on the research requests he'd given to Jason would not be a misuse of time. And, truth be told, he found the research fascinating. Studying the composition and trajectory of a comet wasn't that far outside of his typical field of study. He knew most of the terminology; and while he wasn't as adept at the math as was Jason—or Emily—he knew enough to understand most of what he was looking at.

Much of what he'd learned had required no advanced degree, such as the initial discovery of the comet in 1930 by two German astronomers: Arnold Schwassmann and Arthur Wachmann. Before its breakup, it had been a good-sized comet—some 1100 meters in diameter. It wasn't a monster by any means but it was certainly large enough to cause major damage on a regional scale. A land impact of an object that size would produce a crater more than eight miles in diameter and an explosive yield of more than 46,000 megatons. It was large enough to destroy a small nation. And Sully didn't want to consider what an impact of that magnitude would do to the atmosphere, or how an ocean impact would generate huge tsunamis that could devastate coastal communities.

It was all academic, of course. From everything Sully had been able to ascertain, 73P wasn't an impact risk. Yet, if that was the case, why were Rossi, and the Vatican, and whoever else working so hard to keep him from uncovering information about it. Unless Jason was right and 73P had nothing to do with it.

He pulled his attention from the screen long enough to open the bottle of water that sat near his elbow on the table. He took a long drink, his mind divided between maintaining an objective distance that would allow 73P to be a rabbit hole, and engaged enough for need to cloud his judgment. He knew he had to let the former hold sway but, considering his circumstances, he found that difficult to do. He capped the water bottle, placed it back on the table, and returned his attention to the screen.

After some thought, he minimized the browser tab and double clicked an icon on his desktop. As an astrophysicist, he possessed a great many tools with which to ply his trade—some of which he used often, others on rare occasion. The one he'd just opened fell into the latter category, even if he always found it fun to use on those times in which the opportunity presented itself.

It was high-end consumer astronomy software that allowed him to position and track virtually every known object in the night sky. Someone could use it to monitor planetary movement, locate stars and galaxies, and track objects by name. The breadth of available features made it a robust tool and one that fit his needs at the moment.

"Let's get a good look at you," Sully said, selecting *Find* and typing 73P into the search field. The simulated sky swirled in front of him, shifting to a view that contained a point labeled in red: 73P/ Schwassmann-Wachmann. Sully oriented the comet to the position of Earth onscreen and nodded. "You don't look that scary."

He manipulated the controls to set the comet in motion. As he watched, 73P went through its paces, approaching then passing perihelion. Its path brought it around, heading in the direction of Earth. He monitored its progress with a critical eye but as it passed the planet, it was clear there was no chance of intersection. He glanced at the time and date indicator in the top left. It registered 2017. He frowned, beginning to wonder if Jason was right. He leaned back in the chair and drummed his fingers on the table. On the screen, 73P kept moving, heading into aphelion. He kept watching, fingers still drumming, as the comet made its return. Once again, it reached perihelion, then began its slow track toward Earth. As he watched, Sully found himself leaning forward in the chair, studying the angle of the approach. By the time the comet slid by the Earth, Sully was fully engaged. To his eye, there seemed to have been perhaps a hairline of space between the two bodies as they passed one another. He reached for the computer and manipulated the controls, pulling the comet backward, running it past the planet in a reverse of its course. Then he ran it forward again, slower this time. When it was done, he found himself shaking his head.

"That's pretty damn close," he muttered.

He knew distances were difficult to interpret on this scale but the observable difference in distance between the projected 2017 approach and the 2022 approach was significant. From his research, he'd learned that the 2006 approach, some 5.5 million miles away, had been close enough to cause astronomers to expect meteor showers. The 2022 approach looked closer by a margin Sully found uncomfortable to contemplate.

He watched it again, slowing the pass down, and felt a line of ice move up his spine. "Pretty damn close," he said again.

Standing to stretch his legs, he walked to the window and

pushed aside the flimsy curtain. The parking lot was half full and he saw no one moving, save the cars navigating the intersection. The motel room was a bit stuffy and he thought to crack the window a bit but found it nailed shut. He smirked and reached for the temperature control for the heating/cooling unit and when it activated, it shook like a wet dog for a few seconds before settling into a rattling hum. He turned away from the window and looked back at the open computer on the table. The urge to leave the room in search of a bottle of wine came over him but he fought it off and forced himself back to the chair.

He'd stopped the animation at the point where 73P made its closest pass to Earth and he marveled, again, at the sliver of space between the bodies. It might be enough to slide a playing card through. Looking at the image, he found himself growing convinced that this was at the center of everything. The approach of 73P in 2022 had set the Vatican on edge. How that concern had grown to include Rossi Global, how it had set Mats Koning on his tail, and how it had left the bodies of two of Sully's friends in its wake, he could only conjecture.

"How did they know?" he asked himself. "And how is Rossi involved?"

Even as he asked the question, his thoughts returned to Rinaldi's message. 'They've known since the House of Stuart,' he'd said.

That didn't make a great deal of sense to Sully. The House of

Stuart of the British monarchy had held power for the first half of the seventeenth century—a time when the first telescopes were invented. While significant discoveries were made during those fledgling decades, the technology would have been woefully inadequate to catalog comets and make predictions about their courses. Consequently, Rinaldi had to have had some other meaning.

Sully almost rose from the table again; sometimes pacing helped him think. But he remained seated as he ran the problem through.

"They've known about it since the House of Stuart," he said. The answer came in a flash and, when it did, he wanted to kick himself for not understanding right away.

"It will find Saturn and three in the urn," he quoted. He quickly minimized the astronomy software and found his notes on Nostradamus' quatrains. When the document opened, he scrolled to 10/50 and read.

"The Meuse by day in the land of Luxembourg,

It will find Saturn and three in the urn:

Mountain and plain, town, city and borough,

Flood in Lorraine, betrayed by the great urn."[8]

He read through it again, even though he could quote the

---

[8] Nostradamus, M., & Garencières, T. (2001). *Nostradamus: his works and prophecies*. Urbana, IL: Standard Publications.

passage by heart. When he and Jason had spoken of it, they'd puzzled over the reference to *three*. He felt a smile taking shape. One of the things he'd picked up in his research was that 73P had an alternate name: Schwassmann–Wachmann 3. The smile turned into a frown, though, as he considered what the quatrain meant. Bringing up the astronomy software again, he eyeballed Aquarius and then ran the comet's path in reverse. When 73P's path took it right through the constellation, Sully felt that familiar shiver navigate his spine once again. But it wasn't until he adjusted the view to establish sight lines for someone viewing from earth that he was sure. From his viewpoint, he could see Saturn sitting snugly within Aquarius.

He let out a breath he hadn't realized he was holding.

"I'll be damned."

Sully couldn't help but feel a sense of satisfaction at having figured out a puzzle but he could feel the scientist in him beginning to raise some red flags. In a matter of minutes, he'd gone from looking for a logical answer to the problem to entertaining the idea that a man dead for more than four centuries had predicted an impact from a heavenly body it would have been impossible for him to know existed. It was an absurd idea—one that rankled his intellectual integrity.

It made more sense for someone to have seized on some of Nostradamus' writings and created their own doomsday scenario. Perhaps that had even occurred sometime during the early seventeenth century, during the time of the House of Stuart. It was entirely possible for some high-placed cleric of the time to have become enthralled with what he saw as prophetic writing and to have searched through the quatrains, picking and choosing those that fit together to create a plausible threat. Only hundreds of years later, when sufficient technology granted them the ability to do so, were they able to pin the prophecies to some real threat, and that only coincidentally.

There were a number of other quatrains in the collection he'd copied down from the Internet and he ran his eyes over the ones visible on the page, wondering what other writings had fueled the idea—an idea that had grown to encompass a far-reaching, deadly conspiracy.

"Of course," he said suddenly, straightening.

The notepad he'd taken from the observatory was with the stolen laptop, both on the bed where he'd tossed them when he first entered the room. He got up long enough to grab the pad and then returned to the table. He opened it to the relevant page and found the numbers in the center, the ones he had not yet been able to figure out.

2-15, 6-6, 10-50, 8-2, 10-70, 10-60, 10-64, 1-69

The meaning of those numbers had eluded him. At first glance, they'd looked like dates but several of the numbers were too large to fit that criterion. And he had become so focused on Castel Gandolfo and 73P that he'd failed to give the rest more than passing study. It was clear, now, once he replaced the dashes with forward slashes, that the numbers marked others of Nostradamus' quatrains. In fact, the one referencing Saturn and the urn was there in plain sight.

He had a sudden urge to laugh. It was absurd. The entire thing was absurd. He'd spent the last week running around Rome, fearing for his life, trying to solve a puzzle that powerful people clearly didn't want solved, only to discover that at the crux of it lay the barely coherent ramblings of a man who thought God was speaking through him. The only thing that kept his mirth in check was that, despite its origin, real people with real guns and real agendas had taken the idea and run with it. Too, despite the amateur nature of Sully's own investigation, the 2022 pass of 73P had all the appearance of a credible threat. It created a strange mixture of thoughts in his head—an odd twisting of mirth and gravity. What caused the latter to win out, though, was the fact that people were hunting him. Ultimately, it didn't matter if 73P would miss the planet by a million miles or strike it dead center; he was a target.

The question was how understanding what the Vatican wanted to keep secret—what they were willing to kill to protect—affected his plans. For that, he had no immediate answer. He suspected a good night's sleep would go a long way toward providing some clarity but, as tired as he was, he felt a growing urge to take a look at the quatrains listed in the notepad to see how they could be interpreted to support his burgeoning theory. And since he couldn't call Jason again until tomorrow…

He retrieved his own notepad and began, going through each of the quatrains demarcated by the nameless man at the observatory. It took him a while to find the right balance between wild speculation and at least moderately supported conjecture but the longer he worked at it, the easier it became. As he dug into each four-line verse, as each yielded up its clues, and as he used both the astronomy software and deeper research materials to test the veracity of his ideas, he found his amazement growing. When he'd started, he'd done so donned in the figurative attire of the skeptic. The longer he worked at it, though, the more difficult it became to wholly discount the possibility that Nostradamus possessed some secret knowledge, some way of knowing what the future would bring. He knew it wasn't possible; he lacked either sufficient imaginative or spiritual facets to his makeup to allow for it. Still…

When he'd finished, he studied his notebook, pages of which were now covered with thoughts, numbers, equations, and even sketches. Separately, most of it could be dismissed. In fact, all of the quatrains had been interpreted in multiple ways over the intervening centuries. Together, though, they wove a tapestry richer than their disparate parts. That realization, however, did not diminish the slight feeling of uncleanness that lay over him for even half-seriously entertaining any of it.

A yawn grabbed him and held on and, yielding to it, he pushed away from the table. After using the small bathroom that still bore signs of the last user, he turned off the light and collapsed into the bed. As tired as he was, though, sleep did not come right away. As the minutes ticked by, his room was periodically illumined by the turning cars but their twin beams cut through the curtains with less frequency as the night grew longer.

It wasn't the uncomfortable mattress that rendered sleep elusive; it was what seemed like a hundred different thoughts fighting for space in his mind. He was in a state sufficiently relaxed to see those thoughts swirl around each other, forming connections he might not have made with the light on; yet the freeform nature of the process also made it next to impossible to come to any meaningful resolutions. He was thinking too much to sleep but he was too tired to think about anything clearly.

He shifted so that he could see the clock. He'd lain there for almost an hour and suspected it would be at least that long before he nodded off. He considered getting up and continuing his research but he knew himself well enough to understand that, while he was too alert to sleep, any serious work he tried to accomplish would be poorly done. He sighed and shifted position, resigned to waiting it out.

A few more minutes passed before a small sound pulled him out of a near-sleep state that he hadn't realized he was falling into. Alert now, he heard the sound again. It was coming from the door.

It took every ounce of self-control not to launch himself out of the bed. After everything that had happened over the last week, his fight or flight response had a hair trigger but he was aware enough to understand that the sounds of him scrambling from the bed could speed him toward a confrontation for which he was not prepared. As quietly as he could, he swung his legs from the bed and then stood, pressing the bed with both hands to minimize any creaking sounds. Even as he did it, he knew he was probably being overcautious. There were several rooms off the hallway that held his own room and the sounds of other occupants entering and exiting their rooms were to be expected. Still, his experiences of late reinforced the need to listen to his instincts.

He padded away from the bed and flattened himself against the wall that separated the main room from the bathroom. He'd only completed that act when the sound from the door came again. It was a scraping, a sound of metal on metal. The hotel was without keypad entry, opting for standard door locks.

From his spot, he could see that the bed looked unoccupied. He'd lain on it without pulling back the blankets. Anyone who came through the door would immediately see there was no one in it, provided his eyes didn't have to adjust to the low light. He looked around the room, searching for something to use as a weapon but knew there was nothing. The single item he might have hefted was a table lamp but it was bolted to the table. For the second time in as many days, he cursed himself for not grabbing Koning's gun when he had the chance. He didn't have long for self-recrimination, though, before he heard a louder, more decisive sounding click coming from the door lock. Then there was silence.

Slowly, he stuck his head out—just enough so that he could see the door. It was still closed and he heard no sounds. The quietness that filled the room was like a physical thing, through which he imagined he could hear the beating of his own heart. Still, the door did not move. Seconds ticked by, the silence becoming a white noise, spawning a sense of expectancy that caused Sully's breath to come faster. Consequently, when the door finally opened—just a crack—he came close to jumping out of his own skin.

He remained against the wall, watching as the door swung open, as the dim light from the hallway brightened the room. It occurred to him, in a detached, clinical portion of his brain, that whoever was entering had waited until his lights had gone out, then waited until they were certain he would be asleep. Most nights, that would have been the case.

When the door had opened a few feet, just enough to allow a man to slip by, Sully saw a shadow fall on the wall of the room. After the shadow came the assassin; of the man's purpose, Sully had no doubt. As he slipped into the room, backlit by the greater light from the hallway, Sully could make out little except that he seemed slight of build. But as the intruder advanced, stepping beyond the reach of the hallway light, one of the cars at the intersection turned the corner, its headlights sending arcs across the room, splashing across the assassin's face: a woman's face. Sully's breath caught in his throat.

She wore dark clothes and a baseball cap but Sully's eyes were accustomed enough to the light that he could make out distinctly feminine features. Her gender, however, did nothing to make Sully doubt her intent; she led with a gun. She crept in slowly and Sully couldn't hear a sound as she moved. She hadn't seen him; her eyes would take a while to pick out much in the comparative darkness of the room. He knew she'd be going to the bed, where she expected to find him sleeping.

It would only be moments before she passed where he was pressing against the wall but Sully found himself frozen. He'd been expecting someone who would come in and try to kill him; he'd just never expected it to be a woman. It shouldn't have mattered. She had a gun and was clearly intent on doing him harm. Yet, the prospect of initiating violence against a woman was unsettling. These thoughts all played out in an instant and, in the end, he knew her gender didn't matter. She had a gun.

He prepared himself to launch at her the instant she reached the spot where she would have stepped past Sully's wall had it continued across the room but, as if warned by some instinct Sully couldn't fathom, her head snapped toward him just as her foot hit that imaginary line. He saw her gun hand start to swing toward him and so he did the only thing he could: he threw his body across the few feet of space that separated them.

He heard the gun go off in tandem with the collision of bodies, his shoulder catching the woman under the chin. His momentum took them into the dresser and he registered a sound like glass breaking. Pain shot through his arm and he felt his breath leave him as something—her knee, perhaps—caught him beneath the ribs. Off balance, he held onto his assailant with one hand as they fell to the floor, his free hand frantically trying to grab for the woman's gun hand. He barely registered the shards of pain that raced through that arm with every movement. When the fall ended, he was on top and it took him a few seconds to realize that she wasn't moving. Before taking his weight off of her, he worked his injured arm down to her hand but didn't find the gun.

Breathing heavily, he tried to push himself up but renewed pain in his left arm nearly overwhelmed him. He tried again, putting his weight on his right arm. The woman beneath him still didn't move; her eyes were closed and, in the dim light, he could see blood on her temple. Once he leveraged himself to a half-seated position he took time to examine his arm. It was soaked in blood, oozing from a wound in his bicep. Gingerly, he felt around the edge of the hole, wincing at the pain. Then he ran his fingers along the back of his arm, jerking them away when an encounter with a similar hole sent more pain arcing through the appendage. He resisted the urge to turn and look for the spot where the bullet would have entered the wall behind him. Instead, he looked around for the gun. He found it beneath the dresser where one of them must have kicked it.

He noticed, too, pieces of what looked like glass littering the carpet around them. He picked one up and realized it wasn't glass; it was more of a hard plastic. From his spot on the floor he looked up and saw that the television atop the dresser was shattered. He must have driven her head into it when he'd tackled her. He suspected she was out before she hit the ground. What he didn't know was if she was dead.

Placing two fingers on her neck, he felt for a pulse. It took him a while before he found it but once he confirmed she was still alive, he leaned across her prone form and fished the gun out from beneath the dresser. When he had it, he studied it for a few seconds before turning and tossing it onto the bed. Then, bracing himself against the pain, he pushed himself to his feet.

Once there, he paused to consider his next steps. While the fight had seemed to happen in slow motion, he doubted more than forty-five seconds had passed since he tackled the woman. He knew he would hear sirens any second. Regardless of the quality of the hotel, gunshots universally meant police. The problem was that at that moment, he didn't know how he wanted to respond to that threat. His initial impulse was to grab his things and run. But there was a part of him that wondered if waiting for the police to arrive would be the worse of the two choices. They would take him into custody and he would tell them everything. He'd walk them through every step he'd taken since touching down in Rome. They wouldn't believe half of it but maybe they'd believe enough of it to set into motion something big enough to cause the people who were after him to refocus their attentions. It was what he should have done when he'd woken up in the hospital after the hit and run. Had he sought help then there was no way to tell where he would be now. Maybe back in Washington with Jason, planning how to spend Randall money.

It was a tempting idea—but one he could not, ultimately, enact. Relating his story to the police would place him at the Vatican at the time of the bombing. There was simply no way to chronicle the events of the last week without including Rinaldi. And with the various global police agencies still combing through the wreckage, still reviewing all of Rinaldi's records and correspondence, the act of attaching himself to that investigation would mean weeks—if not months—spent answering questions. It meant he was on his own.

With that choice made, he began to move. He hurried to the bathroom, flicked on the light, and pulled up his shirtsleeve to reveal the bullet hole. Blood issued from it. He grabbed for a towel, wet it in the sink, and used it to wipe the blood from around both entry and exit wounds. Then he took a dry towel and wrapped it around the arm. His shirt was ruined but he didn't have another. Blood had stained his pants, too, but the pants were dark; no one would notice if they didn't look too closely.

Leaving the bathroom, he went to the bed, pulled the blankets back, then did the same with the sheet. He caught the sheet between his teeth and pulled until the fabric ripped. He tore off a long run of the sheet, perhaps six inches wide. He repeated that procedure twice more. He wrapped one of the pieces around the towel on his arm, winding it several times and pulling it tight. That done, he moved the arm around to test it. It hurt but he'd be able to use it if he had to.

He took the two remaining sheet pieces and returned to his

would-be assassin. She was still out cold. Rolling her onto her stomach—a procedure made more difficult because of the limited use of one arm—he pulled both of her arms behind her and used one of the pieces to secure her hands. He pulled the knot tight, then ran the sheet once around her leg for good measure. With the second piece, he made a knot around one of her ankles. He pulled that one as tight as he could as well, ran the fabric in a loop around her wrists, then brought the rest of it down to tie up her other ankle. Finished, he stood to study his handiwork. He was satisfied that if she woke before the police arrived, she wouldn't be able to go anywhere. Almost as an afterthought he knelt to go through her pockets. They were empty, which was what he'd expected.

As he stood a second time, he heard the first sirens in the distance. He hurried to the table, grabbed his jacket from the chair and put it on, having some difficulty getting his bulky arm through the sleeve. Then he gathered his laptop and the two notebooks. With those secured, he retrieved the observatory computer from next to the bedside table. That left only one thing and, despite the fact that he'd twice berated himself for not taking Koning's gun, he still hesitated.

The sirens were growing louder, forcing his hand. His lips tightened as he scooped up the gun and slid it into his pocket. Something caught his attention from the corner of his eye and he turned to look. He saw the bullet hole in the wall. His lips tightened even more as he turned away from the wall and hurried out into the hall.

Chapter Fifteen

Sully took his exit from the hotel at something just under a run but as he moved away from the building, he slowed. With two laptop cases in hand, he would already draw attention. There was no need to draw even more.

His arm throbbed as he walked, the small weight of one of the computers pulling at the wound. He knew he needed stitches but he also knew he couldn't go stumbling into a hospital in his condition. He had no idea what the laws were here but if they were anything like those in the States, the treating physician would be obligated to call the police in to investigate a gunshot wound. He wasn't sure what options that left him but he didn't have time to think about them now. Of primary concern was finding somewhere else to sleep—somewhere far enough from here that he would avoid getting netted in the neighborhood canvassing that would take in at least the few blocks surrounding his vacated hotel.

His foot caught on a sudden rise in the sidewalk and he stumbled into the wall of a building to his left, the elbow of his injured arm striking brick. Fresh waves of pain engulfed the arm and he came close to dropping the computer. He leaned against the wall for a few seconds. He could hear the sirens getting closer. He thought they were coming from behind him. Pushing away from the wall, he continued on, turning off Via Giovanni Giolitti onto Via Cavour.

He'd picked the hotel near Termini for its reputation as one of the seedier areas in Rome, as far as such designations applied to a city in which every district was generally safer than any neighborhood in any American city of similar size. But the reputation offered some benefits to a man trying to keep a low profile: namely, hotels that took cash, inebriated young people who occupied the time and attention of local police, and people with a tendency to look the other way. He was counting on all of these attributes now.

The large shop windows to his left were shuttered, many of them covered with graffiti. The brick between the windows had also been marked by the same criminal element Sully was relying on to help retain his anonymity. As he neared the corner of Cavour and Giovanni Amendola he saw a trio of young men standing on the corner diagonal to his own. He felt more than saw them give him a once over but he crossed the street without concern. Despite its reputation, any real crime other than pick pocketing was rare in Rome.

As he reached the other side of the street, his foot caught the curb, causing him to stumble for the second time in a few minutes. He cursed as he steadied himself; he knew it couldn't be blood loss that was causing disorientation. While the bullet wound was something that needed tending, the amount of blood he'd witnessed as he'd cleaned and wrapped it told him it had missed any major arteries, passing through the flesh on the inside of the bicep.

His ears picked up the sounds of laughter from across the street. He looked and saw the young men watching him, one pointing. He thought he picked out the word *ubriaco* in their comments. They thought he was drunk. He gave them a wave and continued on. When he reached Via Farini, he turned left. He knew there were some hotels in the area even cheaper than the one he'd left but he wasn't as familiar with this portion of Rome as he was with others. He navigated Farini for two blocks before making another left that would take him back toward the train station.

The sirens had stopped, which meant the police and other responders would be in the hotel now. He wondered at their reaction to finding a woman trussed up on the floor of the room. Despite his situation, and the pain that was now settling into a dull but constant throbbing, he allowed a small smile to grace his lips.

A small yellow sign hanging over the sidewalk caught his eye. It said *Hotel Atlantic*. Sully looked to the left, down the small alleyway that emptied onto Via Gioberti. Down the alleyway, he could see the entrance to the hotel. It looked small and secluded. And cheap.

He turned into the alleyway and, after parting with just under thirty-five euros, dropped the computers onto a bed in a room only marginally larger than a closet. He turned the light on in the bathroom and looked around. There were clean towels. He returned to the bed and, after some consideration, he took the computers and slid them beneath it. That done, he exited the room and made his way back to the street. He made a right, aiming for the green cross that marked a pharmacy just on the other side of Via Farini.

When he entered, he doubled the occupancy of the place, the clerk behind the counter looking up long enough to note his presence. Sully grabbed a basket from a stack by the entrance and then worked his way up and down the aisles, filling it with a variety of medical supplies, even as he tried to remain cognizant of his dwindling funds. When he had everything he thought he would need, he turned to food. He grabbed a few snack items, two bottles of apple juice, and a frozen sandwich. After brief consideration, he added a package of undershirts to the basket. When he reached the register, he added a bottle of wine and a corkscrew to the tally. He didn't look at the label on the bottle.

Back in his hotel room, he set the bags on a small desk and reached for the wine bottle. After uncorking it, he took a long drink straight from the bottle. After a second-long swig, he removed his coat. Then he gathered the medical supplies and took them into the bathroom.

Standing in front of the mirror, he began to unwind the sheet wrapped around his arm. He noted a small amount of red on the exterior of the sheet—a spot that grew larger as the layers of the sheet revealed themselves. When he'd uncovered the towel, he found it soaked through. But after he unwound the towel, he saw that the bleeding had stopped. The wound was raw and still looked open but it seemed smaller than it had the first time he'd looked at it and, even as he watched, he saw no fresh blood welling.

The wound was too large to have been caused by a .22 but it would have to have been a small caliber round. He'd yet to give the gun a decent look but he was familiar enough with them to know his assailant had shot him with a SIG Sauer. Probably a .380.

He removed his shirt, carefully pulling it down his arm. He wet a washcloth and gently cleaned around the entry hole. When he finished, he raised the arm above his head and turned his side to the mirror so that he could see the exit wound. He cleaned around it, too, and by the time he was finished the pain had pulled sweat from most every pore. Dropping the washcloth in the sink, he dried his arm with a clean towel.

He studied his handiwork; the probing around the wounds had caused fresh wells of blood but not enough to spill over. Even so, he waited to be sure before taking up a bottle of hydrogen peroxide. He uncapped it and held his arm over the sink. Just before he poured it out over his bicep, he brought his teeth together. The pain was blinding but all that escaped him was a small grunt. After he stopped pouring, he held his arm still while the antiseptic did its work, the stuff fizzing inside the wounds. After a time, the pain lessened and, grabbing another towel, he blotted the arm dry.

He opened a box of butterfly sutures and applied two of them to the entry hole, pulling the edges of the wound together, which was uncomfortable enough to cause him to lament leaving the wine in the other room. Doing the same to the exit wound was more difficult and required an additional suture but it wasn't long before he was finished. He rolled his arm in gauze and then wound that with a few lines of tape and then studied his handiwork.

It wasn't elegant, and he knew the butterfly sutures weren't meant for something as serious as this, but he wasn't going to bleed to death. Leaving the bloody washcloth and towels in the sink, he returned to the main room and immediately reached for the wine bottle. He looked at the food but whatever appetite had traveled with him to the pharmacy had long since moved on. In its place had come a feeling of great weariness. He opened a bottle of ibuprofen and washed down a trio of pills with the wine.

Before lying down on the bed, he took the room's lone chair and wedged it under the door handle. He tested it, yanking on the door. The chair held. Palming the light switch as he passed, he lowered himself carefully onto the bed. Sleep took him seconds later.

*****

When Sully woke, sun was pouring through the window. He blinked to clear his vision and looked to the clock on the bedside table. It said 9:38. He groaned and closed his eyes. Without moving his arm, he tried to gauge its condition. He didn't feel much more than a dull ache. He remained still for several minutes, allowing the events of the past twenty-four hours to come to some kind of arrangement in his mind. Eventually, though, the need to use the bathroom overcame his reluctance to move a centimeter from his current position.

With another groan, he came to a sitting position, careful to roll to his right. The slight jostling made the pain more pronounced but it was bearable—a good deal more so than it had been last night.

After using the bathroom, he studied his still-wrapped arm in the mirror. A single spot of blood the size of a dime marked the gauze covering the exit wound. He rinsed his face in cold water and returned to the room.

Retrieving the chair from where it was wedged under the door handle, he dragged it to the desk and sat. He picked up the now room temperature sandwich and then set it aside. Instead, he opened and ate a granola bar, following it with one of the bottles of apple juice. He followed a second granola bar with another handful of ibuprofen. When he finished, he reached for the empty trash can and pulled the small trash bag from it. Returning to the bathroom, he fashioned a crude rain-sleeve for his arm, securing it with the tape he'd purchased for the gauze. Even with the rain-sleeve, showering was cumbersome but when he finished, he felt better than he had in days. He dried and then dressed, donning his only pair of pants and one of the t-shirts he'd purchased the previous night.

Back in the room, he knelt and pulled the pair of laptops from beneath the bed. Leaving the stolen one on the bed, he took the other to the desk, where he booted up and then spent time scanning the local and national news feeds. His perusal of the national feeds was driven by a desire to keep track of the investigation into the Vatican explosion. To this point, the footage of the Vatican security guard leading him across the parking lot seemed to have avoided any worrying scrutiny. On the local level, his interest was divided between Rinaldi's assassination and the overnight activities from a nearby hotel from which a person of interest had fled on foot. From what he could determine, the event was absent from the local news.

Sully sighed. It would have been nice to have access to a police report, if for no other reason than to know how the woman who'd been sent to kill him had spun things. A night's sleep granted him enough mental agility to suspect how it had played out. She would have told the police that she'd met an American in a bar and gone to his hotel room, where he'd roughed her up and left her. She might have even given them his name. How she would have explained away the bullet hole in the wall and the trail of blood leading to the bathroom was an open question but, with the absence of a firearm in the room, she would undoubtedly pin that on him too. It caused him to question his decision to gift-wrap her for the police.

He closed the computer and returned to the bathroom, where he removed the dressing. He wrapped the raw looking wounds in fresh gauze and then gathered the remaining medical supplies. He shoved them, as well as the rest of the food, into his coat pockets, causing them to bulge noticeably. Rather than try to carry the last bottle of apple juice, he drank it. Then he gathered the computers and notebooks and stepped out into the hall. He left the half-full bottle of wine behind.

When he stepped out of the alleyway and onto Via Gioberti the sun was high and the streets were filled. The storefronts that had been shuttered when he arrived were open and streams of people moved into and out of them. Now that he was on the move, he had to confront the truth that he was unsure of his next steps. The only thing he was sure of was that those steps involved a few more burner phones.

Returning to the pharmacy, where it appeared the clerk from the night before still presided, he bought a pair of the phones, making sure they were active before stepping back onto the street. Then he set off. He had no direction in mind but moving with the flow of people made him harder to spot. As he walked, he filtered through the data in his mind, sorting it by importance. At the top of the list, alongside deciding what to do next, was to wonder how the woman who had tried to kill him had found him. When he'd dropped the rental off and collected the substantial deposit he'd had to leave in order for them to allow him to take the car absent a credit card, he'd gone straight to the hotel. The only thing that sounded plausible was that the rental company had done a search on his license at some point and Koning's people had caught it. That meant the shooter would have been waiting for him when he returned the car. He was forced to admit that he'd been dumb; he should have rented a taxi for the trip, even if that had meant pulling funds from an ATM somewhere in the city.

The flow of bodies moved both ways along the sidewalk but the wider stream was heading north, toward Termini. He suspected the train station was as good a place as any to regroup—to find a place that afforded him time to draw out an endgame of sorts. After all, if a potential impact of 73P was the thing the Vatican was protecting, the fact that he'd uncovered it meant that he had at least a modicum of control over how things played out. Of course, if he was wrong, if he'd misread the clues, then he was as good as dead.

That element of doubt made speaking with Jason a priority. All of the research he'd done, the connections and interpretations he'd made—he needed to bounce all of it off of his friend to make sure he hadn't taken those last few steps across the border into insanity. The problem was finding a way to have that conversation without Rossi, or Koning, or other minions of the Vatican closing on his position within minutes of the call connecting.

He followed the crowd across Via Giovanni Giolitti and into the wide-open space that ran in front of the terminal building. Bags securely in hand, he crossed the lot and entered the station. Inside, the place was bright and bustling with activity. It had a modern look, due in large part to an expansive renovation project less than a decade earlier. As Sully stopped to get his bearings, his eyes traveled through the place, taking in the two levels of restaurants and shops, the threads of groups and individuals navigating the wide concourses, the young people who sat along the walls, bags at their feet. The station had the look and feel of an airport terminal and there was a quintessentially European atmosphere to it all that Sully couldn't help but enjoy, despite the circumstances that had brought him there. It also afforded a multitude of places where he could sit, drink coffee, and wait for it to hit a reasonable hour in Washington so that he could call Jason.

He took stairs to the next level and found a café with seating that allowed him to look out over the level below. Sipping a cup of strong, black coffee he used the station's free wireless to go over the notes he would share with Jason. When he'd sat down, it would have been around 4:30 AM in Washington. He thought he'd give Jason until 6:00 AM before placing that wake-up call.

As he thought about that conversation, though, a cloud of doubt began to form over him. While Termini Station was large and crowded, the second he placed the call, the clock would start. His enemies had already demonstrated that they had considerable resources at their disposal. He had little doubt they would track him to the table where he sat within fifteen minutes. He wondered, though, if that was necessarily a bad thing. After all, they wouldn't kill him in such a public setting. They'd likely watch him, waiting for him to leave. And during that interval, he would transfer everything he'd learned to Jason. Sully knew that in any unraveling conspiracy, there came a point at which enough people knew about it to make containing it an impossibility. Even so, he had no doubt that they would make him pay.

They would take him when he was alone, as he would inevitably have to be at some point. His only hope of escape once the conversation was concluded was to buy a ticket to another stop and hope there was no one waiting for him on the other end. He chuckled at that, knowing it was wishful thinking. The second he boarded the train they'd make a call and have someone positioned at every potential exit.

He took another sip of the coffee and pondered that but he dismissed it almost immediately. There was little use worrying over things one couldn't change. With that thought, he finished the coffee. As he contemplated getting a second cup, a voice peeled through the terminal announcing the arrival of the Ancona. Sully had never been to Ancona but he knew it was some three hours from Rome by car. A great many of the trains leaving Termini Station traveled a good distance and the tickets were reasonable enough to cause many people, even locals, to eschew driving.

Acquiescing to the desire for a second cup of coffee, he started to rise when an idea struck him. Setting the coffee cup back on the table, he moved closer to the rail and leaned over until he could see the arrival and departure board on the lower level. He scanned the names. Frascati, Salerno, Venezia, Milano… With a smile, he closed his laptop, gathered the other computer and notepads and headed for the ticketing counter. Fifteen minutes later and twenty euros lighter, Sully had a one-way ticket to Naples in hand. Thirty minutes later, the train was pulling out of the station and Naples was four hours in his future. The train was relatively full but Sully found an unoccupied row with a small table that would let him work.

The row across the aisle was occupied—a young couple, backpacks at their feet. Both wore earbuds. He opened his laptop on the table and pulled one of the burners from his pocket.

"It's 5:30 in the morning," Jason grumbled but there wasn't a hint of sleep in his voice. Sully suspected his friend had been up for hours.

"I was going to call you ninety minutes ago but thought I'd let you get some beauty sleep," Sully said. Absently, he wondered if the call was already being tracked and, if so, how long it would take them to figure out he'd boarded a train.

"How kind of you," Jason groused.

"You haven't slept at all have you?"

"An hour or two," Jason admitted. "And only because I had to sleep off the bourbon."

Sully chuckled but the mirth was short-lived. "Is it too early to ask if you've found anything?"

"Nope. But to be honest, I haven't found much. And you already know most of it" Sully heard a series of key taps and then Jason continued, sounding as if he was summarizing notes. "It's a mid-sized comet. As of 1995 it broke into four pieces; by 2006 it was in at least twelve pieces. Next pass is early 2017 but, while it's going to be the closest pass in a while, it's not raising any red flags."

Sully listened and couldn't help the feeling of disappointment that accompanied Jason's analysis.

"I'm assuming you reached out to JPL?"

"Yes. And 73P isn't even on their radar. Pun intended."

Sully absorbed that in silence—one that Jason broke.

"What about you?" Jason asked. "You said you'd done some research?"

After Jason's disappointing news, Sully found his desire to share his findings dampened considerably. Still, he'd bought himself a fare for a four-hour trip…

"The question that kept hitting me in the face was why the Vatican—or their astronomers—came to believe that Nostradamus' prophecies center on 73P," Sully said.

"And you think you've figured it out," Jason answered.

"I think I've made some interesting connections, at least," Sully said. "If you can keep up."

"Repeated and excessive intake of hard liquor may have dulled my wits but I think I can follow along."

"I went through a number of quatrains and found quite a few that could link to 73P. Do you have a reference list?"

"I can't believe we're doing this but yes."

"Look at 3/34," Sully said. Then he read from his notes.

"Condom and Auch and around Mirande,
I see fire from the sky which encompasses them,
Sun and Mars conjoined in Leo, then at Marmande,
Lightning, great hail, a wall falls into the Garonne."[9]

"Suitably vague," Jason said.

"Hear me out," Sully answered. "The first thing to note is that the Sun and Mars will be conjoined on October 7, 2021. On the same date, 73P will be in Leo."

"And I'm guessing you could pick a dozen other dates where the same thing will be true," Jason rebutted.

"Absolutely. But that date puts it relatively close to the next planetary pass."

There was silence while Jason considered that. "Okay, but all of those are French towns, right? I thought we were dealing with Italy in this game."

"True, but 73P is in at least twelve pieces now, right? Isn't it likely that if there's an impact event, those pieces will hit over a larger area?"

---

[9] Nostradamus, M., & Garencières, T. (2001). *Nostradamus: his works and prophecies.* Urbana, IL: Standard Publications.

"A logical assumption but a tenuous connection."

"Fair enough," Sully said. "So, let's move on. Quatrain 1/69:

"The great mountain, seven stadia round,

After peace, war, famine, flooding.

It will spread far, drowning great countries,

Even antiquities and their might foundations."[10]

Seven stadia is approximately 1300 meters, which is reasonably close to the diameter of 73P before it started to break up."

"I think I see how this works," Jason said. "So, we have a celestial event that happens *reasonably* close to the time 73P and Earth play chicken and we also have a size that comes *reasonably* close to the size 73P used to be. Is that *reasonably* accurate?"

"Let's move on, shall we?"

"Quatrain 2/15:

"Shortly before the monarch is assassinated,

Castor and Pollux in the ship, bearded star:

The public treasure emptied by land and sea,

Pisa, Asti, Ferrara, Turin land under interdict."[11]

---

[10] Nostradamus, M., & Garencières, T. (2001). *Nostradamus: his works and prophecies.* Urbana, IL: Standard Publications.

[11] Nostradamus, M., & Garencières, T. (2001). *Nostradamus: his works and prophecies.* Urbana, IL: Standard Publications.

"Who's going to be assassinated?" Jason asked.

"I have no idea," Sully answered. "But that's the least important piece of the quatrain. In the second line Nostradamus is referencing two stars in Gemini that will be pointing directly at 73P—the bearded star—in the constellation Argo Navis."

"Is that a constellation?" Jason interrupted.

"It was in Nostradamus' time," Sully said. "In 1752, it was broken into four different constellations but the quatrain still works. In January 2021 73P will cross Castor; in June 2021 is crosses Pollux; in July 2022, it enters the ship."

"Interesting…"

"And you wanted an Italian connection? You've got one."

Jason's response this time came a little slower. "And the *public treasure* reference?"

The question—or the way his friend asked it—produced conflicting feelings in Sully. On one hand, he was pleased that Jason was following the logic. It meant Sully wasn't wholly grasping at phantoms. On the other hand, Jason's hesitation served to grant the idea a legitimacy that Sully, himself had not bestowed upon it. He reminded himself that his purpose was to create a plausible explanation for the Vatican's interest, not to prove that Nostradamus was a prophet.

"That one took me a while," he said. "But I think that's what Elena uncovered. I'd bet all the shipping manifests she sent, and the ones I grabbed from the Rossi Global computers, are for shipments of church antiquities out of the Eastern hemisphere. I think they're trying to move as many of their relics and holy items as they can out of the impact zone."

The silence that followed was sobering. Sully looked up from his computer and out of the corner of his eye he saw that he had an audience. The young people across the aisle had removed their ear buds and Sully had no doubt they were listening to every word. A flash of worry coursed through him but it was gone in a moment. It didn't matter if his fellow passengers heard him. Most of it made Sully sound crazy. And if, by chance, they thought he was revealing some secret information—detailing the plans of some global conspiracy—they'd have a hell of a story to tell once they debarked.

He didn't wait for Jason to speak before moving on. "Quatrain 6/6:

> *"There will appear towards the North,*
>
> *Not far from Cancer the bearded star:*
>
> *Susa, Siena, Boeotia, Eretria,*
>
> *The great one of Rome will die, the night over."*[12]
>
> And 2/41:
>
> *"The great star will burn for seven days,*

---

[12] Nostradamus, M., & Garencières, T. (2001). *Nostradamus: his works and prophecies.* Urbana, IL: Standard Publications.

The cloud will cause two suns to appear:

The big mastiff will howl all night

When the great pontiff will change country."[13]

"Except now you have the pope dying in one verse but changing countries in the next verse," Jason said.

"That puzzled me, too," Sully answered. "Except that I don't think the *great one* in the first verse is the pope. I think it's the city itself. Or Rome as the seat of Christianity. The church is going to move the papal seat somewhere else—probably somewhere in the Western hemisphere."

"I guess that makes sense," Jason said grudgingly.

Over the next half hour, Sully went through a number of other quatrains, pulling out the bits that could make a compelling case for 73P as the destroyer of Rome. When he'd finished, Jason was forced to grant at least the possibility.

"But why keep it a secret?" he asked. "If they believe it's coming—if they've believed for hundreds of years—why not give enough warning for everyone in the kill zone to get out of there?"

"I don't know," Sully admitted. "But my guess is that a few hundred years ago, there wouldn't have been any effective way to empty a several country area and relocate everyone. And so the church

---

[13] Nostradamus, M., & Garencières, T. (2001). *Nostradamus: his works and prophecies.* Urbana, IL: Standard Publications.

put a plan in place that would, at the least, preserve Christianity."

By this point, his fellow passengers were riveted, making no effort to hide their interest. Sully knew that Jason, on the other end of the phone, was equally riveted. He also suspected his friend of having that same feeling of uncleanness that he felt.

"Let's say I admit that you've made a compelling case for why the church believes the prophecies apply to 73P," Jason said. "That doesn't change the fact that, according to everything we know about the comet, it's not going to hit us."

"I've been giving that some thought," Sully said. "You remember when Shoemaker-Levy 9 broke apart? That was because of the gravitational effect of Jupiter. We were able to measure it, quantify it. But while we know that 73P has broken up, we don't know why. There are a few theories but nothing definite. And that makes tracking the trajectories of the various pieces a challenge."

"The Diophantine equations," Jason said, excitement in his voice.

"I once had a smart person tell me all about gravitational degradation," Sully said. "Something about throwing a series of variable at an object in motion to see how those variables affect the course."

"I'll be damned," Jason said. He lapsed into silence for several seconds. Then he asked the question that Sully suspected was coming. "So, are we now working under the assumption that 73P is actually an impact threat?"

Sully took a deep breath and then blew it out. He ran his free hand through his hair.

"I don't know, Jason. It's already projected for a close pass—a near miss in astronomical terms. And if we can't track the movements of its pieces..."

The young couple now wore worried looks. Sully gave them an apologetic smile.

"And we can't track the pieces because we don't have any of the data to plug into the equations."

"Not unless any of our contacts at JPL can supply them," Sully said.

"But you don't think Nostradamus..."

"I can't," Sully cut in. "I have to work under the assumption that this is some huge coincidence. It's the only way I can preserve my remaining intellectual integrity."

"That's rich coming from a man who at one time scored women by pretending to be into astrology."

Sully couldn't help but chuckle at the other man's ability to lighten any mood.

"Her name was Moonstar. Can you blame me?"

The rejoinder he expected didn't come.

"Jason?"

"Sully, I'm looking at your face."

"What?"

"I'm watching CNN. And I'm looking at your face."

Chapter Sixteen

The train station in Naples was much like its cousin in Rome, sharing that airport concourse feel. Sully, though, kept his head down as he exited the train and moved through the crowd, dual computers in hand. The phone he'd used to call Jason was powered down and in his coat pocket.

According to Jason, the global news agencies had finally gotten around to blowing up the video of him walking to his meeting with Rinaldi. Next to that grainy image was a large, clear photo of him from his MIT days. At first, Sully had wondered if the by-the-books investigation into the bombing had organically uncovered his connection to Rinaldi, or if someone behind the scenes had implicated him. That question was answered when Jason told him the CNN anchor also made reference to an incident in a hotel near Termini.

As Sully worked his way down the concourse, he couldn't help but wonder what the conspirators hoped to gain from plastering his face and name on every news outlet around the world. If he were to be taken into the custody of Interpol, or the FBI, or any other major police agency, they had to know he would spill everything he knew. The only explanation he had was that, if he was picked up, they had people in place to make certain he didn't survive past the day.

Of equal interest to him was when the assumed cause of the explosion had turned from a gas leak to a bombing. Through all of the coverage Sully had heard, all of the talking heads had spoken in terms of the former. Even Sully, who knew the event to have been staged, thought the assassins might have done it with the tools on hand, tampering with an existing gas line to create the explosion. Now, though, investigators seemed to have dismissed that theory in favor of a bomb secreted into the building.

As Sully walked, he remained alert for anyone around who seemed to recognize him. He doubted that would happen within the train station. From what Jason had been able to tell, Sully's picture had only recently begun circulating. That meant he remained unknown to anyone not actively watching the news on a mobile device.

He cast his eyes about, looking for the ticketing counter. As he did, a large video monitor caught his attention: his face starting back at him. His eyes went wide but he quickly lowered his head. The picture they were using was almost five years old. In it, he was clean-shaven, his hair was neat, and he offered the camera a smile. Even if the passing years had not changed his features much, he knew the stress of the last few days had altered his appearance a great deal. He thought it unlikely a casual observer would match him to the man looking down on the whole of the terminal.

His other concern was for anyone who might have been waiting for him to debark the train in Naples. He suspected it would have taken some time for the conspirators to determine he was on a train, and then to figure out which one. Then they would have had to alert a contact in Naples to watch for him. And unless they had a means of reviewing the security monitors in Rome to see what he was wearing, they'd be forced to watch all of the exits in search of a man who'd changed his physical appearance and clothing since the last time they'd seen him. Even so, he'd taken the precaution of removing his coat before leaving the train, which left him walking around the terminal in a t-shirt, the jacket tied around his waist.

When he reached the ticketing counter, he parted with fifteen euros for a ticket to Pescara departing in thirty minutes. With a nod of thanks, he headed for the bathroom, where he and his belongings spent twenty of those minutes hiding in a stall. When it was time to board, he walked through the train until he reached the bathroom. Inside, he slipped the phone from his pocket, turned it on, and dropped it into the trash can. He exited the train a minute later.

Returning to the ticketing counter he bought a ticket to Rome, trying not to wince at the sieve his wallet had become. He had almost an hour before the train departed and so he returned to the bathroom, where he stayed until it was time to board. Once aboard, he found a seat that left him without neighbors for a few rows in either direction.

As the train started its roll, he could feel his mood changing, could identify the tendrils of despair that were slowly twining about him. It had begun the second he saw his face on the train station monitor. Until that moment, he had held on to the belief that he would be able to extricate himself from the trouble he'd become involved in. He'd thought that if he kept one step ahead of those who'd killed Elena—who'd killed Rinaldi—that he would be able to find a way to beat them. Knowing that he was now wanted by every police force and intelligence agency on the planet had shaken him, had forced him to consider that he might not survive this.

Holding sway at the moment was the part of him that thought it advisable to track down the nearest member of the polizia and turn himself in. At least he'd avoid getting shot on sight by someone who happened to recognize him on the streets of Rome; as well, he might stand a chance of coming out of all of it with his skin intact.

Even as he thought it, though, another part of him rebelled against the idea. It was the part of him that embraced a challenge, that hated to lose regardless of the cost. The part of him that wanted to track down Mats Koning, who had to serve as a stand-in for the nameless, faceless cabal behind Elena's death, and break his nose.

The problem was that he seemed to be out of options. As he saw it, there were two prongs to his situation. The first was determining if 73P was a legitimate threat. And if it was, proving to JPL—and by extension, the rest of the world—that a threat existed. NASA knew 73P would make a close approach; they simply didn't believe the break-up of the comet would drastically alter its course. As the date neared and as they turned more resources toward tracking and analyzing it, the data would become clearer. However, if 73P was a threat, and they waited too long to respond, they could find themselves without the necessary time to do anything meaningful.

In truth, Sully considered it the lesser of the two issues. The study of 73P was an intellectual abstract. And his work in forming links between the comet and the writings of Nostradamus was a necessary evil.

The second problem, and the graver one for Sully personally, was dealing with a secretive, murderous group whose principals remained largely anonymous. Despite all he'd been through, he had only two names. And he was becoming convinced that Nicolo Rossi was nothing more than a bit player in the game. He'd become involved because his company had the infrastructure and the resources to help the Vatican move two thousand years' worth of priceless artifacts out of the country. That left Mats Koning—the man who had dogged his steps almost since the moment he'd touched down in Rome. However, he couldn't bring himself to believe Koning was any more than a hired thug. He likely knew a great deal more than did Rossi but that did not grant him any kind of status within the organization. How could Sully expose something so carefully hidden?

And even were he to prove that, within the Catholic church, there existed some secret society that accepted the prophecies of

Nostradamus as truth, that was a long way from proving an active hand in, or complicity in, murder. What he needed, what he was missing, was a paper trail—a record to validate Rinaldi's assertion that what was coming to a head now had found its seed during the seventeenth century. But with Rinaldi dead, he didn't know where to start. When he got back to Rome, it would be as little more than an aimless vagabond—one with a very large target on his back.

After four hours on the train from Rome, Sully's back was starting to rebel now that an additional four hours were expected of it. He adjusted his position in the seat, briefly closing his eyes. When they opened a half-hour later, he straightened in a panic. He looked around, taking in his surroundings, but no one had come to fill the seats around him; no one was looking at his with a glimmer of recognition. He released a breath he hadn't realized he'd been holding and settled back in the seat. His eyes were still heavy but he couldn't allow them to close. He was too exposed.

He reached for his laptop but before his hand closed on it, he changed his mind and grabbed the stolen computer. With so many other considerations, he hadn't delved into the contents of the laptop since he'd taken it from the observatory. He opened it and typed in the new password. When the desktop appeared, he began a methodical walk through the files. The contents were, in large part, mind numbingly boring. There were multiple file folders with records of every kind, from observations gathered from telescopes from around the world, to files containing classroom records. In truth, it seemed like the quintessential computer utilized by the academic head of a university department. Sully certainly didn't see anything incriminating.

He felt a yawn coming and indulged it, following up with a stretch in deference to his back. When he resumed his perusal of the observatory computer, he was marginally more awake. He went through several more folders, all of which yielded nothing. He was starting to suspect that the steno pad he'd taken contained a great deal more useful information on its single relevant page than was contained in the entire computer when he clicked on a folder titled *Recipes*.

As he went through the contents, the slight smile he'd adopted at the thought of files of favorite dishes pulled from cooking websites disappeared. At first, he wasn't certain what he was seeing. The folder held a combination of text documents and spreadsheets, interspersed with a handful of image files. It was in viewing one of the image files that the truth of what he'd found hit him. It looked like a depiction of a debris field—twelve crudely drawn rocks that formed something close to a line.

He snapped upright, all thoughts of sleep gone. He opened one of the spreadsheets and was greeted by a series of numbers. After ten minutes of study, he thought he had a basic understanding of what he was looking at. In his profession, he was used to developing and analyzing complex mathematical models that explained the movements of stars and planets, the theoretical processes occurring around the event horizon of a black hole, or the energy signatures of stars millions of light years away. He knew his grasp of complex mathematics exceeded that of 99% of the population. He also knew that what he was looking at was more akin to abstract algebra. It wasn't his strong suit. That did little to dampen his excitement, though. He knew he'd found the base data for 73P. More, he thought the documents also contained, if not the complete equations worked out to their conclusions, at least the roots of those equations.

With renewed energy, he spent the rest of the ride trying to work through the equations but when the train finally rolled into Termini Station he was no closer to solving them. Still, it was with a smile on his face that he exited the train, although he remembered to keep his head down as he walked through the terminal and then out into the street.

Chapter Seventeen

Sully stood outside of a red brick building. There were few people about but he kept his head down, a newly purchased used baseball cap pulled low. He had the observatory laptop with him, his own back at the hotel. Through the window he saw two employees, no one else. The wall behind them held shipping supplies. Other supplies were spaced throughout the small storefront and there was a copy machine along the back wall.

As he entered, a bell above the door jingled. One of the employees greeted him and Sully approached the counter with a reasonable facsimile of a smile, his eyes hidden behind sunglasses.

"I'd like to ship this computer," he said, proffering the laptop to compensate for his weak Italian.

The employee—little more than a boy—nodded and turned to the wall, from which he took a box that looked just large enough to hold the computer. Setting that on the counter, he turned to procure a generous amount of bubble wrap. He reached for the computer and Sully handed it over. The clerk wrapped the computer in the bubble wrap, taped the wrap together, and then placed the computer in the box. Once he'd sealed it, Sully provided the address. Back at the hotel, he'd emailed the relevant files to Jason but he hadn't mentioned that he was sending the computer. If Jason's email was being monitored—and Sully had no doubt it was—then Sully's enemies would have set watches at every shipping location within fifty miles of Rome.

Sully paid in cash and left, heading back to the hotel. Now, if something happened to him, at least the computer, with the data Sully had already recovered and what other treasures it might hold, would be on its way to safer hands. Sully had considered holding on to it, digging deeper, but he had a feeling that, for better or worse, he was running out of time.

Consequently, there was little to do beyond waiting for a return email from Jason—a simple message that would either prove 73P would leave Earth unscathed, or whether the predictions of a man long dead would be validated.

During the short trip back to his hotel, he did his best to avoid crowds. Since returning to Rome, he's seen his face plastered on far too many television screens and newspapers for him to feel comfortable spending more time outside than he had to. The only thing that was working in his favor was that the search for him seemed to be focused beyond Rome, the prevailing theory being that if he had been involved in the assassination attempt on the pope, he would have left the city as soon as possible.

Interestingly, there was another camp that seemed convinced that an unassuming astrophysicist with no history of violent behavior, rather than being the perpetrator of the crime, might well be another victim of it. Sully found himself appreciating that line of thinking, especially as it offered some hope that if he were picked up, or turned himself in, he might be able to spin the narrative in that direction.

Reaching the hotel, he slipped past the front desk and took the stairs to the second floor. Once in his room, he removed the glasses and ball cap and tossed them on the table. He then pulled off the used but still good condition black half-trench coat he'd picked up at a thrift shop.

When his laptop booted up and he went to his email, he was surprised to already see a response from Jason.

"It's beyond me. If you want to do this right, we need to pull her in. Agreed?" - Jason

Sully cursed. He'd wanted to avoid involving Emily any more than he already had. He understood the hypocrisy of it—his willingness to expose Jason to danger while working to protect her. But Elena's death still hung heavy over him and he was self-aware enough to understand that Emily served as a proxy for a woman he had been unable to protect. However, working out the math was vital and if Jason couldn't do it, he didn't see what other options he had. He emailed back, acquiescing, even if he suspected Jason had already shared the data with Emily.

Settling onto the bed, he turned on the television but shut it off less than five minutes later. Half of the stations he passed over seemed focused on the Vatican bombing; the other half were filled with Italian programming that he couldn't expend the energy to follow.

Waiting had never been his strong suit and to do so now, to be forced to rely on others to do the work for him, chafed. That wasn't all of it, though. He wasn't egotistical enough to believe he could do everything by himself. No, he suspected the reason he was on edge was because, for the first time since he'd arrived in Rome, he had no clear next steps. And in the absence of a goal, his thoughts were free to roam. It was where those thoughts chose to go that drove his angst.

In the quiet and solitude of a bad hotel room in a foreign city, Sully was forced to consider all that he had lost in the span of a week. He'd lost his reputation; he'd strained friendships; most importantly, he'd lost someone he cared a great deal about. The losses were mounting, sapping away at his resolve.

In tandem with that line of thinking came questions about his future. He couldn't help but wonder where he would be next week, next month. Regardless of how this situation played out, the actions he'd taken would undoubtedly have lasting repercussions. It was possible he would end up in jail—and that was if he didn't end up dead. But even if, through some miracle, he avoided both a cell and a grave, he shuddered to think of what havoc the last week had wrought on his ability to work in his field. If 73P proved to be a non-event, he would still always be known as a once-prominent astrophysicist who had bought into the prophecies of Nostradamus. The fact that he didn't believe the prophecies—that he had tried to approach things rationally—would go missing in the retelling.

Even as he thought it, though, the focus on his own reputation seemed wrong—something done to avoid considering more difficult truths. The foremost of those was that a woman he had cared for—a woman he had once thought he'd loved enough to avoid taking the job at MIT, opting to remain in Rome—was dead. She was dead because she'd stumbled into something she didn't understand. Yet, the truth of it was that she might still be alive had she not known an astrophysicist—someone who could decipher what she'd uncovered. It was the theft of her father's materials, with the intent of sending them to him, that had sealed her fate. It was a hard thing for Sully to accept.

He rose and walked the short distance to the desk, a piece of furniture present in every hotel room he'd ever seen, regardless of the price of the room. A variety of food items were spread across the top of it. He selected a candy bar and, as he ate it, he paced the room. His thoughts kept returning to Rossi. The man's daughter was dead and yet, when he'd spoken with Rossi at the viewing, the primary emotion the man evinced had been fear. It had taken awhile for Sully to realize it—to understand that the complex array of emotions he'd witnessed on the man's face culminated in trepidation. The realization tore at him.

Rossi had acted as if the loss of a child were the most natural thing in the world. He'd stood in the receiving line and accepted condolences; he'd professed amazement that his daughter had fallen victim to the relatively low crime rate of Rome. Yet, if what Sully now believed to be true was, indeed, true, then Rossi would have had to have known that his daughter had been killed by the people he now protected.

Sully's pacing had him reach the door of the hotel room. He turned and started back toward the window. It didn't sit well. Despite the fact that he'd had nothing to do with Elena's death, he still felt guilt. How much more so for Rossi?

He lost count of the number of times he paced the space between the door and the desk. In the interim, his thoughts went to Elena, to the time they'd spent together, to how he'd felt when he'd learned she was dead. And through it all, he tried to put himself in Rossi's place—that of a man who had just lost his daughter, a man trying to make sense of the world in which he'd involved himself, a man trying to protect what remained of his family. At some point in the pacing, a thought came to Sully. He stopped pacing, took a seat at the desk, and began to research.

*****

Sully stood on the sidewalk, looking at the house, an elegant one in Rome's Parioloi neighborhood. On the streets below and above were several embassies, as well as families that had held both power and money for hundreds of years. Sully knew that the Rossi family could lay claim to both; their money was old, their influence great.

Even so, on the few occasions in which he'd met the man, Sully had become convinced that Rossi was possessed of a grander vision, one that took in more of the world than even his current circumstances afforded. Sully suspected the man was driven by the fact that, regardless of his wealth and power, the family could lay claim to a historical heritage that more than hinted at true power—the sort of power that set the course of industries, that had the ears of kings. Rossi's line had borne witness to the rise and fall of a great many popes and had maintained a constant presence in the city. But the world in its present form made that kind of influence, that level of access all but impossible to maintain.

Night had long since fallen by the time Sully reached the front door. It took two rings of the bell to bring someone and the man who opened the door bore all of the hallmarks of a manservant. He took Sully's name and then led him into a drawing room just beyond the entrance. After the servant left, Sully made his way around the room. A bookshelf made up the entirety of one wall, holding a number of volumes that looked aged. Sully glanced at the titles, recognizing some. On the opposite wall was a minibar and, without invitation, Sully poured himself a glass of bourbon, despite the absence of ice. Settling onto a chair that, along with a couch, served as the focal point of the room, Sully made significant progress through the glass before the door opened to reveal Nicolo Rossi.

Until that moment, Sully had been unsure how he would have placed his money. He'd thought it entirely possible that when the door opened, it would be to admit a great many armed men and women. Instead, it was just Rossi, who held a half-full glass of wine.

"Dr. Knight," Rossi said. His voice was tired.

"Mr. Rossi," Sully said. He started to stand but the elder man waved him down. Rossi crossed to the minbar. There, he topped off the wineglass. Then he moved to the couch opposite Sully's chair and sat.

"I suppose I owe you thanks for not calling the police," Sully said.

Rossi responded with a half-smile. He emptied half of the wineglass. When he lowered the glass, he gave Sully a once-over. His eyes were glassy.

"We're all guilty of something or other, aren't we?" the man asked.

Sully took Rossi's measure. The man was drunk, of that he was certain. But he was aware enough to be responsible for his words.

"Mr. Rossi," he said, "I know about 73P."

If he expected the pronouncement to have any effect on Rossi, he was disappointed.

"I know that you've been using your company to move

antiquities out of the Vatican," he pressed.

Rossi looked at him from across the short expanse separating the respective seats. The man's lip curled. There was a hint of mockery in it.

"Rossi Global moves a great many things, Dr. Knight,' Rossi said. "We move things for the Italian government. We move things for the Saudi Arabians. We move things for the Vatican."

That last hung there, as if waiting for Sully to challenge it. Sully pounced on it.

"You're moving everything the church has collected over the last two thousand years to cities in the western hemisphere," Sully said. "Every artifact, every holy relic, every significant piece of church history. You're shipping all of it with blank manifests so that no one finds out that a meteor called Schwassmann-Wachmann 3 is going to level Rome and the surrounding area five years from now."

For the second-time Sully's accusation produced an unsatisfactory response. Rossi's expression didn't change. The man took another drink before saying anything.

"Rossi Global ships packages, Dr. Knight. We do so without censure."

"Under threat of personal harm."

For the first time, Sully saw a break in Rossi's façade. His eyes betrayed a hint of anger, of sadness.

"You were hired by someone within the Vatican to ship an incredible number of packages oversees," Sully said. "My guess is that most of them have gone by sea, with Rossi Global dedicating entire ships to the effort. But you've also sent a great many of those packages through the air. To New York, Toronto, Buenos Aires, Mexico City—a dozen other cities."

Rossi didn't answer. He sat there, swirling the wineglass.

"What I find interesting," Sully said, "is that over the last few years, Rossi Global has purchased a great deal of land—every bit of which is in the western hemisphere. Your own annual report mentions land acquisitions in several western cities."

Still the silence from Rossi.

"The church thinks that the pieces from 73P are going to strike Italy, France, and Switzerland. And perhaps some adjoining countries. Regardless, Western Europe will be in shambles for decades. Any company that wants to survive will have to make sure their base of operations isn't located in Europe."

Sully watched Rossi's eyes. He saw the requisite defiance first, but that slowly gave way to something Sully couldn't quite decipher. What followed next, though, was something he did understand: defeat.

"Was that the trade off?" Sully asked. "You act as courier for the church and they tell you when and where?"

Rossi's mood had taken a darker turn. Sully suspected that had the man had a phone on him, he would have used it to call the police. Even so, Sully pressed on.

"But an initiative like that couldn't have happened in a vacuum, could it? Some of your top-level executives had to know. The problem was that Elena was one of those executives. But you couldn't bring yourself to tell her why you'd set aside a huge percentage of your resources to respond to requests from the Vatican. Because, had she known, she would have been appalled that you were keeping it secret. She would have argued that the world had a right to know."

Sully paused and downed the last of the bourbon. When the glass was empty, he rose and crossed to the minibar. He poured himself another and returned to the couch.

"So, she stole some of your files, along with some other information she'd gathered, and she sent it to me. And agents of the Vatican killed her for it."

The anger he'd witnessed in Rossi's eyes earlier returned, with a fierceness that overcame the effects of the wine. Sully pressed on.

"But even though they killed your daughter, for some reason you still feel compelled to work with them." He paused, taking a drink. Rossi's expression hadn't changed. "So they must have something on you. Something that compels you to keep shipping their packages even after they strangled Elena in a train station bathroom."

He saw a tightening of Rossi's hand around the stem of the wineglass. Still, the man didn't speak and Sully couldn't read the expression on his face. After what seemed a long while, Rossi raised the glass to his lips. When he lowered it he said, “We are an old family, Dr. Knight. You know this, yes?”

Sully nodded, expecting Rossi to go on but the man didn’t say anything else. Instead, he raised the wineglass and drained the rest of it. In that brief action, the anger Sully had coaxed from Rossi seemed to leave the man. In its place was the weariness that had been there before. Yet, still the man didn’t speak. Sully sat there, studying Rossi. The man watched him in turn and there was something there, something in his eyes, that gave Sully pause. Almost on their own, Sully’s eyes moved to Rossi’s hand, the one wrapped around the stem of the wineglass. He saw the glint of metal, the red of an oddly shaped cross on the ring finger. Eyes widening, he looked up, meeting Rossi’s gaze.

The knowledge that he couldn’t have been more wrong hit him in a flash. His strategy in confronting Rossi had been predicated on assaulting the man’s pride, on angering him with the accusation that the head of one of the oldest families in Italy had been relegated to the role of courier. That the daughter of a man whose family elevated rulers had been killed and he could only sit impotently in the face of her death.

The ring on Rossi’s finger told Sully he’d miscalculated. Badly.

Seeing that understanding come to Sully, Rossi finally spoke.

"In this part of Rome, Dr. Knight, there are few estates owned by someone unable to lay some claim to having contributed in some significant way to Italian history. Were you to ask, most families would be able to point to specific instances in which one of their patriarchs said or did something noteworthy, something momentous." He paused, then leaned forward on the couch, the empty wineglass still in his hand. "But we both know, Dr. Knight, that the decisions that truly shape the future of any country are those made in secret. Those absent from the public record."

Sully had no response. Rossi had taken control of the conversation and both of them knew it.

"There are interests that transcend national boundaries, Solomon. Interests that supersede allegiance to either God or country."

"Or family?" Sully asked.

He saw Rossi's face cloud but Rossi would not be baited.

"A man's lineage is one of the few things that are truly his own," Rossi said. "A thing passed from parent to child, a thing one hopes grows richer with each passing." Rossi glanced down at his empty wineglass, as if noticing it for the first time. He rose and walked to the wet bar, where he refilled the glass. "But lineage is always intertwined with responsibility."

The spell Rossi had cast over the room was fading and Sully found himself growing irritated at the other man's attempt to create a sense of gravity.

"I get it," Sully said. "Your family has belonged to the Knights Templar for generations—maybe even since its founding. You're simply fulfilling the family mandate." Hearing himself acknowledge that an organization he'd once thought relegated to medieval history still existed, and that he might well be talking with one of its members, had a surreal sound to it.

Rossi turned from the bar to study Sully, who could see little in the man's expression beyond the detached appraisal one might give a particularly troublesome fly.

"Most men spend their lives so focused on their own small affairs that they fail to give more than a passing thought to larger things—the things that impact millions," Rossi said.

"So, you and your friends concern yourselves with those bigger things so that smaller men don't have to."

"You'd be surprised how few people think about the future," Rossi said. "And when I talk about the future, I'm not referring to next month, or next year, or even the next decade. The future with which I'm concerned stretches to the hundreds of years, sometimes even longer."

"Which is a fancy way of saying that you play with people's lives because you have a grand scheme that makes those individual lives expendable."

Rossi smirked, then released a sigh. He crossed back to the

couch and sank into it.

"You're parroting an argument a thousand years old, Dr. Knight. One wrestled with by people smarter than either of us."

Sully knew he had to regroup. He'd come to Rossi hoping to use the man's grief to force him to divulge his secrets. Instead, he'd become involved in something resembling a philosophical argument, which would likely fail to produce the information he needed.

"You talk about thousand year plans," Sully said. "Of important decisions made by great men. Of a family mandate that goes back farther than I can fathom." He paused to make sure he had Rossi's eyes. "But I can't believe you would sanction the murder of your own daughter, regardless of the stakes."

Sully saw the pain settle on Rossi's face.

"Even our organization is not without its factions," Rossi answered and Sully heard cold anger in the voice.

Sully allowed the moment to linger. He drank the rest of the bourbon and then set the glass on the table next to the chair.

"I don't have kids, Mr. Rossi. So I don't know what it's like to have one. I certainly don't know what it's like to lose one. But I can't imagine a father—even one concerned with the future of the world—accepting the loss of his own child as payment for that future."

He thought to say more, thought to ask Rossi how Elena's death had been unavoidable in an organization split into factions.

Factions implied disagreement; factions implied a divergence of visions for that future he claimed to be working toward. But, as he looked at Rossi, he decided it wasn't necessary. The other man already knew all of it. Sully could see it on his face, could find it in the weariness he wore like a heavy coat.

Rossi sighed and ran a hand through his hair. Then he drained the wineglass.

"I'm old, Dr. Knight. Old and tired. The future is a young man's game. I think even Rinaldi was coming to believe that at the end." At Sully's look of surprise, Rossi gave him a tired smile.

"I would give it all up to have my daughter back, Solomon. I swear to you that I would give up the family birthright and live in a hovel in Stazione if I could have Elena here right now." He paused and fixed Sully with a hard look. "Elena was my oldest. I have two other daughters. Did you know that?"

Sully hadn't. But it didn't take long for him to understand. Rossi had lost one daughter. He had two more who needed to be protected.

"Mr. Rossi, Elena brought me into this. And now I'm well and truly in. My face is on the television; it's in the newspapers. And it's because your daughter trusted me. For Elena's sake, I'm asking for your help."

Rossi had lapsed into silence once again. He looked into the bottom of his glass. He stared into it for a long while—so long that

Sully began to wonder if the man had forgotten Sully was there. Finally, though, Rossi looked up.

"There's a world coming that will be much different from the one we know, Dr. Knight. All I want is for that world to be a safe place for my children."

"I knew one of your children well enough to know that she would have wanted the world to be a safe place for everyone," Sully said.

Rossi chuckled and, after a moment, rose. He walked to the bar and refilled the wineglass.

"Elena cared for you a great deal, Solomon. I'm starting to see why." He drained the refilled glass in one draught. When he turned to Sully, his eyes were rimmed with moisture, whether from the wine or unshed tears Sully couldn't know. "Hadrian's tomb, Solomon. You'll find your answers at Hadrian's tomb. The Treasury Room. The way unseen. Numbers three, seven, and four."

With that, Rossi turned and left the room. Sully didn't wait for the servant to come and show him the door.

Chapter Eighteen

The baseball cap was pulled low as Sully approached Castel Sant'Angelo. He wore the sunglasses, despite an overcast sky, and avoided looking behind him, toward the walled portion of the Vatican, still crowded with agents and investigators. Silently, he berated himself for taking a chance like this. The information from Rossi was vague; he had no idea what he was looking for. Still, with Jason incommunicado from Washington, the alternative was to kill time in the hotel room.

Hadrian's tomb had been constructed in the first half of the second century and had been repurposed and renamed more than once over the almost two thousand years since. Now it was a museum, which made it easy for Sully to gain access. However, there were large portions of it that were off limits to the public. Among these were the stairs leading from the treasury room. He'd done his research before coming and knew where he needed to go; what he didn't know was what he was supposed to do when he got there. He also hadn't known what tools to bring, so he'd come empty handed, save for a small, bright flashlight.

When he reached the main entrance—a large gateway—he

paid the admission fee and entered. He followed the Ambulatory of Boniface IX around the interior structure, skirting the usual tourist stops. Passing through the prison area, he exited into the Angel Courtyard. Here he stopped, despite his desire to find what Rossi had meant for him to find. The angel looking out over the courtyard from a tall pedestal drew his eye. He didn't know the age with any certainty but his limited knowledge placed its origin sometime between the second and third centuries. The sculpture bore the marks of a hard passage through time, surviving the fifth century sack of Rome, the structure's use as a military fortress, and construction projects spread through the centuries.

The courtyard was quiet; it had a secluded feel. He soaked it in but the press of time intruded even here and, after a time, he left the angel behind. He passed through the Hall of Apollo, careful to keep from studying his surroundings in too much detail, lest he find himself tempted to linger, then into the Hall of Clement VIII. He navigated through a number of other halls and courtyards before finally entering a room that overwhelmed his desire for speed. The walls of the library of Paul III were decorated with sixteenth century frescoes and reliefs by a master of the craft. Sully was compelled to stop and take in the work, fraught with imagery and symbolism. He'd always been something of an art lover and a place like this brought that out of him, made him forget, if just for a short while, the burdens he carried. With a sigh, he turned away from his perusal and stepped under an archway, entering a much smaller room: the Treasury Room.

It had taken Sully some time to piece together Rossi's cryptic clue and, even as he stood in what he thought was the correct place, he understood that his inexperience in the field of ancient architectural labyrinthology, as well as the rushed nature of his study, left much room for error. Even so, he couldn't help but feel at least a modicum of pride at having been able to divine an answer that at least fit within the bounds of plausibility.

As he surveyed the room, the first thought he had was how closely it matched the painting, as if Uccello had packed up his easel yesterday rather than almost six centuries ago. Four chests of varying sizes sat in the center of the room, the largest a stone colossus as tall as Sully. Behind the chests ran a wall that was composed of a series of cabinets fashioned from old, dark wood. To Sully's left was a narrow, arched doorway that led to winding stone steps. A red velvet rope, incongruous against the ancient background, ran in front of the doorway. Sully's attention, though, was solely reserved for the old wooden cabinets.

It had taken Sully only a short while to connect Rossi's parting words with fifteenth century painter Paolo Uccello. While spending most of his life and career in Florence, Uccello had traveled briefly to Rome in the company of his contemporary, Donatello. That brief visit had spawned a handful of works, including a painting titled *il percorso invisible*: the way unseen. The painting was of this room, of the four chests, the wooden cabinets. A sparse canvas of grays and browns, deep shadows and meager light.

While he'd found the painting quickly, it had taken significantly longer before Sully discovered what made it of use. He'd spent hours studying the painting on his computer screen, examining it in as much detail as he could. When that study failed to yield anything of value, he'd attempted to research the story around its commissioning and creation but it had not taken him long to discover a significant lack of information regarding any of the work Uccello had completed in Rome. His time in the city had been short, the records of the visit nebulous at best. So Sully had once again turned his attention to the painting, his eyes moving over the simple, subtly beautiful piece. He scanned the four chests, looking for some clue in the front-facing carvings. He'd tracked through the scrollwork evident on the cabinets. He'd even tried to divine the patterns visible on the stone floor. At some point, he began to suspect that the painting might not hold an answer more pronounced than the room itself. Perhaps Rossi's clue had been meant to get Sully only as far as the treasury room. Maybe the rest of it—the numbers Rossi had mentioned—would only be of use once Sully was standing in the room.

He'd almost given up in favor of a few hours of sleep prior to setting out for Castel Sant'Angelo when, in a last look at the painting, he'd caught a glimpse of something he'd missed. Even then, he'd almost passed it over as whatever it was that had tickled his consciousness eluded him when he tried to focus on it. But he'd persisted and, after allowing himself to relax his focus, he'd let it present itself. The scrollwork of the wooden cabinetry was elaborate;

a mixture of hard lines and seemingly free-form swirls. And in the bottom left corner, where two of those hard lines came together, the scrollwork yielded up an answer.

Uccello had been a master of perspective—a mathematician who'd used his knowledge to add layers of depth to his work. And in those layers, sandwiched between two lines heading toward a vanishing point, was the number seven. Sully wasn't surprised that he'd missed it; it had been craftily done, the number near hidden. But once he'd known what to look for, Sully had found the other two numbers: three and four. And even if the discovery of the numbers hadn't been enough, at the convergence of a fourth set of lines was a symbol that had come to dominate this thing that had caught Sully up: the symbol of the Knights Templar. It was clear as day to anyone who knew what to look for, a match for the sculpture in Rossi's sitting room, as well as the ring worn by Koning. It had been strange for Sully to consider that Uccello, a long dead Italian painter, had possibly been a member of the Order identified by the symbol. Or, if not a member himself, at least intimately acquainted with their workings.

Standing in the room, Sully tried to locate the symbol but, even knowing where it was supposed to be, it still took some time before he found it and he only did so after taking a step and a half to the right. When he did that, the lines so expertly captured in the painting moved to give him the same perspective as a viewer of the painting.

Keeping his eyes on the symbol, he started toward the cabinet wall. Twice, the symbol slipped from his vision but he regained it and, before long, he was on one knee, running a hand along the carving just above floor level. He traced a finger along the symbol and shook his head at how carefully it had been concealed, yet still left in plain sight. It was nearly indistinguishable from the scrollwork around it. He applied more pressure to the symbol, not knowing what he was feeling for but suspecting that the placement of the symbol indicated something about the section of wall it occupied. He felt nothing out of the ordinary and so he leaned back, studying the wall. The symbol was confined to a single cabinet door, one of perhaps sixty that covered the face of the wall. The doors were absent handles of any kind but when Sully took hold of the ridge at the bottom and tugged, the drawer pulled open. There was nothing inside. Sully leaned back again, pondering his next move, when he was startled by noise behind him. So focused had he been on solving Rossi's puzzle that he'd forgotten he was in a public place, a place where anyone could walk in on him. He quickly shut the cabinet door and moved away from the wall, making a pretense of studying the largest of the stone chests as a trio of elderly women ambled into the room.

The women paused when they saw him but Sully smiled at them and then returned his attention to the stone chest. He remained that way for what seemed a long while, making his way around the chest, feigning interest, as the women—English, Sully thought—worked their own ways around the room, chatting quietly to themselves. Finally, though, Sully was alone in the room again and, recognizing that he couldn't count on remaining so, he hurried back to his original vantage point at the front of the room and then found the spot from which he could clearly see the number seven.

At the wall, he found the number, again wholly within one cabinet face, and opened the drawer. As with the first cabinet, it was empty. He frowned and studied the empty drawer, then reached his hand in and ran it along the inside, feeling nothing. As he did so, though, he pulled the drawer out further, the drawer sliding along, wood against wood, until it stopped with a click. At the noise, Sully's hand, still inside, stopped. He raised an eyebrow and, after a moment, reached for the cabinet drawer above the one marked with a seven. He pulled it open and it, too, came to stop with a click. After a moment's consideration, he closed it again then, leaving the original drawer open, he moved back to the front of the room. After a few shifts he located the number four and moved quickly to the wall, where he opened the drawer marked by the number.

Hurrying now, aware that he could be interrupted at any moment, he repeated the process, finding the drawer marked with a three and the one marked by the symbol of the Knights Templar. After the latter clicked into place, Sully stood and took a step away from the wall, anticipation coursing through him. But when several long seconds passed with no big reveal, that anticipation became something heavier, something darker. He started to bend toward the drawer, to push it closed when a sound like a soft click came from somewhere along the wall of cabinets to his left. Straightening, he looked in that direction but didn't see anything. He started along the wall, scanning the face of it, not sure what he was looking for but buoyed by the fact that the sound had to have been more than coincidence. As he reached the center of the wall, the part positioned directly behind the largest stone chest, he saw a seam in the cabinet wall where one had not been earlier. Moving closer, he saw that the seam was a small gap—a separation as a portion of the wall had moved forward, providing a narrow view to something beyond.

Pulse quickening, Sully slid his fingers into the gap to see if he could force the opening wider, only to find that force wasn't necessary. The detached portion of the wall slid forward as if on an oiled track. When it came to a stop there was a gap of almost two feet. The light from the treasury room illuminated a portion of the narrow hall beyond the new door, enough so that Sully could see smooth walls and a stone stairway that descended downward, into a darkness the meager light couldn't penetrate.

Standing in front of the opening, the competing entities of urgency and caution warred within Sully. He didn't want to run headlong into the unknown but the longer he stood there, the more likely it was that another group of tourists—or someone attached to the facility—would walk in on him. He let urgency win and pulled the flashlight he'd brought with him from his coat pocket and turned it on, its light immediately offering him a clearer view of the steps downward, the walls covered with what looked like carvings, perhaps frescoes. Just as he stepped into the opening, he heard a gasp from behind him. Turning quickly, he saw the three elderly women standing at the edge of the large stone chest, three pairs of eyes wide. Sully froze, flashlight still illuminating the hidden passageway. After a few seconds, during which neither Sully nor the Englishwomen moved or spoke, Sully brought a conspiratorial smile to his lips. He raised a hand, placing his pointer finger over his lips.

"Shhh," Sully said. Then, after a wink, he turned and stepped into the opening. Once inside, he quickly ran the light over the interior of the doorframe, looking for the lever he hoped was there. He found it to the left and when he pulled on it, the doorway slid toward him, sealing him in. Seconds later he heard a softer noise and imagined the four drawers that he'd opened also closing themselves. He could only hope that the women he'd left behind would not be able to recall which drawers had been opened.

Knowing that time wasn't his ally, he began to descend the stairs. The light from the flashlight was strong and before he'd gone more than a few steps, the beam fell on a wall—one that looked to block any advancement past the twelve or so steps. He continued the rest of the way and when he reached the bottom, he put a hand on the cold stone. It seemed formed of one solid piece, as if cut from the surrounding rock. To Sully's eye it didn't look like something placed there to block that which had once been passable; rather, it looked as if the stairs had been purposely designed to end at the wall. Turning, he looked back the way he'd come, shining the light on the steps.

He wasn't certain what he'd expected to find but a dead-end was certainly not on the list of possibilities. Too, rationality told him that no one would go through the trouble of creating a puzzle lock that opened a hidden door if the act of opening that door did not reveal something worth the trouble of figuring out said puzzle lock. With that in mind, he returned to the top of the stairs and then began a second descent.

He took it slowly, unsure what he was looking for. He'd found Rossi's unseen way and he'd found the numbers. The next part of this was up to him. As he descended, he looked at the walls on both sides. They were decorated with evenly spaced carvings: cherubs, demons, pagan imagery. He ran his hand along them, feeling the rough stone. Above several of the images, words were carved into the stone, descriptions of the scenes in Latin. The words, like the scenes they described, were worn, as if brushed by many hands.

When he reached the bottom of the stairs, and the barring stone wall, he entertained the thought that Rossi's real aim had been to set Sully to spinning his wheels—to force him to waste time investigating something just to keep him busy, to run him into a wall that was both physical and metaphorical. But that didn't gel with Sully's recollections from the meeting. Rossi had seemed a man broken—a man willing to part with secrets.

He started back up the stairs, convinced he'd missed something. Again, his fingers found the carvings, his eyes the Latin words: Maledicto Eve, Tentatio Christo, Diaboli in Paradiso. He mouthed the phrases, translating as he went, picking up on a theme of sin and punishment. He was halfway up the stairs when he saw it: Semita Visum. The way unseen. Sully stopped, flush with both excitement and confusion. He'd thought he'd found the answer to Rossi's cryptic clue. Now here it was again, in a second language. What worried him was that parsing the first instance of the phrase had taken him hours with his computer, as well as a good measure of luck. This time, he had no resources, no way to know what he was supposed to do.

He ran his hands over the phrase, and over the scene beneath it—a gate separating barren land on one side, a lush garden on the other. Both carving and inscription spanned three evenly cut stones, as did all of the others Sully could see. He pressed the stones they covered but nothing happened. He hadn't expected them to slide out of the wall, as had the wooden drawers in the adjoining room, but he had no idea what to do next.

He ran through what he knew. Rossi had given him *the way unseen*. He'd also given him the numbers he'd used to open the door. He'd provided nothing else, no trick that would allow Sully to pass through solid stone. He stood there for a time, holding the light on the carving, running through his options. It wasn't long before he realized something was bothering him, something he couldn't put a finger on.

He took a deep breath and turned away from the carving,

letting the light play over the other wall, trying to clear his head, to let what was bothering him come to the foreground. In that manufactured calm, he started to think about the numbers. The numbers had marked the drawers. The numbers had shown him which ones to open in order to release the door lever. That thought bothered him but he was having a difficult time figuring out why. He turned, facing the top of the stairs, the beam of light moving over the door, the lever mechanism visible from this side. He kept the light there, on the lever, letting his thoughts drift. And when the answer finally came, it was like a physical thing, a slap in the face.

"Why numbers?" he asked himself. The drawers could have been marked with symbology of any kind. Why numbers. Unless the numbers had a second, equally important purpose. He turned back to the carving.

Three columns of stone ran down from the bottom of the carving and, as Sully followed the lines down, he noticed that each carving was positioned so that it occupied the span of one step. Starting from the left, Sully counted down three stones. When he reached it, he felt around the stone then pushed it but felt no give. There didn't seem to be anything that differentiated it from the other stones. He tried the column to the far right but got the same results. He stood back and looked at the wall. There were eight stones in each column and Rossi had given Sully three numbers: three, seven, and four. Sully realized that what Rossi hadn't told him was whether to begin at the top or the bottom.

Returning to the wall, Sully counted up three stones from the bottom. When he pushed the stone it moved, sliding back perhaps an inch until Sully felt it click into place. Excited, Sully moved to the next column and counted up seven stones. When he pushed that stone and felt it give, excitement turned to triumph. When the last stone, fourth from the bottom in the third column, found its niche, Sully heard a click that he hadn't noticed with the other two stones. Carefully, he pushed on the wall—and felt another rush of adrenaline as it started to swing open on silent hinges.

The new doorway revealed another set of steps leading down into darkness. There was no way to tell where the stairs led. He shined the light down the stairs. The stairs, old and uneven, went down perhaps twenty feet and the feel of the corridor was colder, danker than the one in which he stood. At the limit of his vision Sully saw another wall but before he could despair, he saw a hint of an opening to the right. Hurriedly, he started down the steps but, before he'd gone far, he walked back up to study the still open door. From the back, he could see the iron hinges that allowed the door to swing. He also noted the vertical slide bolt that was held in place by the recessed stones. When he'd pushed the stones in, he'd created a divot into which a guard could drop, causing the bolt to slide down. It was a cumbersome mechanism—one that the user had to reset manually. But he confirmed that he could close the door and reopen it from this side. He considered leaving it open but decided that, if the women who had watched him disappear behind the wall had somehow been able to convince someone official that they weren't crazy, and if they were able to figure out the sequence of drawers he'd opened to access the stairway, then sealing this second door behind him would at least delay his discovery. He pushed the door back in place and then reset the lock. That done, he turned and headed down the stairs.

He took the steps as quietly as he could, mindful of the uneven cuts and varying lengths. When he reached the bottom, he saw the opening to his left, a crudely cut doorway into a narrow tunnel. The tunnel ran straight for perhaps fifty feet before curving away to the right. He stepped into the tunnel, his heart beginning to beat faster. It wasn't wide, perhaps three feet, and the rough-cut stone ceiling was only inches above his head. For a moment, he had a feeling akin to walking to his own execution.

He knew his actions bordered on the irrational. He was in the proverbial lion's den, following a clue given him by a man who had been aiding the enemy, a man who might still be working for them, however much grief he felt. For all Sully knew, when he emerged from the tunnel he could be met by a roomful of men with guns.

With that thought in mind, he felt for the gun in his pocket. He'd been uncomfortable carrying the thing around Rome but if there had ever been a need for it, it was now.

His steps—light as they were—echoed on the stone. The air smelled damp. When he reached the part of the tunnel at which it began to turn, he slowed. He inched along the passage, stepping lightly, until he reached the place where the tunnel straightened out. It ran straight for another hundred feet and ended in a door. Sully started toward it. It was a windowless door made of aged dark wood. The iron hinges were on this side. They were touched by rust. It had a black iron handle.

When he reached the door, he placed a hand on it, felt the cold of the wood. He ran the light around the door's edge, seeing no gaps. Then, after a moment's consideration, he clicked off the light. Darkness rushed in; so absolute, it was nearly a physical thing. He stood there, heard his own breathing. He placed his hand on the door handle and turned it. It made a small sound, like the brushing of metal across polished wood. He pulled the door open and saw only a continuation of the darkness. He turned the flashlight on.

The door had opened into an antechamber. Perhaps twelve feet by twelve, the ceiling was much higher than that of the tunnel. Sully entered and shined the light up to the rock ten feet above. The chamber had two doors—one to Sully's left, the other straight ahead. Moving to the one to the left, Sully gently tried the handle. It didn't move. The door, itself, was damaged, the wood splintered across the bottom, as if bashed from the other side. Sully shined the light through the small cracks at the bottom but saw only dirt and rock. He wondered if a cave-in had made the way behind that door impassable.

He moved to the other door. It appeared undamaged. When he tried the handle, it moved. He turned off the light before opening the door. Again, darkness greeted him. But when he turned the light back on, the scene was much different.

The light revealed a large room. The walls, still made up of the bedrock that underlay the structure above, were smooth and straight, with four precise corners. What interested Sully most, though, was that the room was not empty. Long, large shelves ran the lengths of two of the walls. The shelves were filled with books, some that appeared to be centuries old. As Sully stepped into the room and felt the dampness that had accompanied him since he'd left the surface, he wondered at the presence of so many tomes in an atmosphere conducive to rot.

A trio of tables occupied the center of the room. Two were made of wood that looked as old as the bookshelves, as old as the doors. One table, though, was gray metal and the chair next to it was twentieth century. All three tables held a variety of books—some that looked very old, others much newer. Sully also saw several notebooks. The most incongruous thing he saw, though, was a blackboard. It stood on a wheeled platform at the end of the metal table. Someone had written on it in chalk. Sully moved closer.

The writing on the blackboard seemed to have been the product of a single hand. There were a number of Latin phrases on the board, with translations in German below them. Since he didn't speak German, Sully concentrated on the Latin. He was able to pick out enough of it to know that some of it had been pulled from

Nostradamus' quatrains. It was that recognition that caused his excitement to build. He'd been looking for proof that the church considered the prophecies of Nostradamus to be true. It seemed he'd found that proof.

Along with the text on the blackboard, someone had also drawn a crude diagram that Sully recognized as a representation of the solar system. However, it seemed the scribe had used the Copernican model. There were only six planets. Sully supposed that made sense. That model would have been the one in use during Nostradamus' life.

Standing in front of the blackboard, Sully fielded a wide range of emotions—chief among them was one that bordered on exultation. He was standing in a secret chamber beneath one of the oldest structures in Rome—a chamber that had obviously seen relatively recent use, albeit the thick layer of dust on everything, including the books spread over the tables, suggested that no one had entered the room in a long while. Indeed, as he looked around the room, he thought it entirely possible that he was the first person to stand here in decades. That suspicion allowed him to breathe more easily. From all appearances, this place had been abandoned, possibly in the sixties or seventies. That meant it was possible the people who were after him wouldn't know it existed. What tempered that thought was that Rossi clearly had known. Of course, the other man's knowledge could also mean that Rossi was more highly placed in the organization—either the Knights Templar or the entity that had taken its place over time—than Sully had first believed.

After some consideration, he reached into a pocket and withdrew the pieces of his phone. The phone hadn't been whole since he'd disassembled it after his first run-in with Koning. He'd debated bringing it but, without purchasing a camera, there was no other way to record what he was seeing. He fielded a slight smile as he thought of anyone who might be monitoring the phone, who would trace it to Hadrian's tomb. He wondered how long it would take them to realize he was far beneath the tomb proper.

When he'd finished assembling the phone, he powered it up and took pictures of the blackboard. After that, he took shots of the books on the table, then the bookshelves. It was as he turned to get a shot of the bookshelf along the opposite wall that he saw it. He stopped in mid-turn, the beam from the flashlight frozen on the wall to the left of the bookshelf, frozen on the large, perfectly formed carving of the cross of the Knights Templar. Had he had any doubt that the ancient religious order had been a player from the beginning, or that some organization either tightly or loosely associated with them still had a hand in it, the presence of that carving would have removed those doubts. What Sully was involved in had its roots in the ancient past, to a time of myth and legend. It was a thing that had survived the passage of time with enough vitality to swallow him up, to make him a part of something with tendrils that spread farther into the past than he could fathom. It was a sobering thought. It was also a thought he couldn't spend any time entertaining, not with the threat of discovery hanging overhead.

He hurriedly opened the books on the table. A number were ancient, the language Latin. Among these, though, were newer books in French and Old English. He scanned through these and was unsurprised to find that a good portion of them seemed to be devoted to translations and interpretations of the works of Nostradamus.

He opened one, a heavy book with no title on the cover. But when he saw the title page, in French, his eyes widened. The title translated as *A Study of the Works of the Seer, God's Anointed.* More than the title, though, what amazed Sully was the credited author: Armand Jean du Plessis. Cardinal Richelieu. More than anything he'd seen thus far, this one book validated the church's interest in Nostradamus. He took a picture of the title page.

The next several minutes passed in a blur as he went through the shelves, reading titles, pulling some books out and ignoring others. Of primary interest were any books of more recent production—anything that indicated the church had recognized that the quatrains spoke of an impact event. He found a few of these and dutifully photographed the evidence. But it wasn't until he'd reached the end of the second shelf that he found the prize. It wasn't a book. It had no cover, no binding. It was a series of pages, held together by a paperclip. Written in German, it looked more like an academic thesis than anything else. The name on what passed as the title page was what drew Sully's eye: Arthur Arno Wachmann. The date was April 17, 1937. The paper was addressed to His Holiness, Pope Pius XI.

Sully released an explosive breath and he thought a silent thanks to Nicolo Rossi. The room was a time capsule—proof that the Catholic Church had accepted Nostradamus as a seer, a man touched by God, and had spent centuries trying to identify the prophesied threat. Sully had no idea when the chamber had come into existence—whether Hadrian's tomb had been here first, or if the tomb had been constructed over it. He also suspected that, throughout the tumultuous history of the church, the knowledge of this place—of the work to which it had been dedicated—had been lost and rediscovered more than once. He also suspected the work was now carried out somewhere else, somewhere with modern equipment, by men and women with lab coats and degrees.

Quickly, Sully took a picture of the title page. Then he snapped shots of the first five pages of the report. When he'd finished, he opened a message to Jason and attached all of the pictures he'd taken. He added no message to the files. When he'd pressed send, he had a sudden flash of Elena, on the last night she'd been alive, doing the same for him. The thought cast a somber pallor over his mood.

When the email was gone, Sully powered down the phone and removed the battery. Then he grabbed the bundle of papers and returned to the metal table. There, he took one of the French-language books that looked promising, as well as the two modern notebooks. From the remaining tables, he took three more notebooks and two tomes, one that had to date from the mid-sixteenth century. Then, treasures in hand, he plunged into the corridor, leaving the room behind.

Chapter Nineteen

By the time Sully made it back to his hotel, his arms were leaden from the weight of the books. He'd endured a few tense moments in leaving Castel Sant'Angelo, the employee at the gate eyeing the books. Sully had avoided eye contact but hadn't hurried. He'd hoped he looked like an academic doing research. And since there were no books accessible to the public in the museum proper, the gatekeeper must have assumed the same.

He dropped the books on the table and rubbed his arms, trying to restore feeling to them. Throwing off the coat, he settled onto the edge of the bed. There was a part of him that wanted to dive into the books and notebooks he'd taken but he doubted that would be an efficient use of his time. He was no historian and certainly no linguist. It was enough that he had the material, that he could display it as evidence to support his theory that officials within the Vatican were planning for an imminent catastrophe. Absently, he wondered how much the pope knew. Despite the fact that he was the leader of the church, the truth was that the investigation into Nostradamus' writings, and the subsequent work to move the seat of the church to another country, ran through, by Sully's conservative estimate, twenty-four popes. That meant control by some group outside of pontifical oversight. Some group with enough power within the Vatican to sanction the murder of a Cardinal. It was a web beyond Sully's ability to untangle.

He reached for his laptop to check email. There was one from Jason.

Call me. E got the math to work. - Jason

In a flash, Sully was up and reaching for his coat. *E* was clearly Emily. Sully appreciated Jason's attempt at circumspectness.

He left the hotel and walked for several blocks, doing his best to stay around people, despite the dangers that presented. He knew people often avoided looking too closely at the things closest to them; he was counting on the general far-sightedness of crowds to preserve his anonymity. When he had gone perhaps ten blocks from the hotel, he pulled out the last of the burners.

"She did it," Jason said without preamble, once he'd confirmed the unfamiliar number belonged to Sully.

"So I gathered," Sully said. "And the verdict?"

"There's a better than average chance that at least some of the pieces will strike in or around Western Europe."

Sully absorbed that, noting what felt like a ball of ice forming in his stomach.

"You're certain?" He knew the answer to that. Jason was one of the smartest men he knew and Emily was smarter. If Jason told him the odds of an impact were good, he could take it as gospel.

"She verified your data, plotted it, and worked out the math. I reviewed as much of it as I could but there was a point where my head started to hurt. We're talking about a dozen large objects acting against each other, and all of them being acted on by whatever force was responsible for breaking the comet up in the first place. We don't know what that is but we know what it did; from that we can extrapolate what it's continuing to do."

The excitement in Jason's voice belied his claim that the problem was beyond him. He might not understand all of it but the dynamics of moving bodies was something he knew.

"I get it," Sully said. "Giant rocks tumbling around, the forces from all of them acting on all the others. All it takes is for one of them to hit any other one."

"And you've got space pinball," Jason finished.

Sully stopped at a street crossing with more than a dozen other people. Out of the corner of his eye, he saw someone looking at him. He thought he caught the beginnings of a frown. Casually, he turned and started down the sidewalk.

"So, what do you want to do?" Jason asked.

Sully had given the answer to that question some thought, even as Jason and Emily were working to solve it.

"We notify JPL," he said. "We share our data, let them work it out for themselves. Once they verify, they'll have about five years to plan a response." It seemed the most logical course of action. No agency in the world was better equipped to handle a threat like the one posed by 73P than was NASA. The eggheads at the Jet Propulsion Laboratory would come up with something.

"Did it ever occur to you that they already know?"

Sully's response was silence. Until Jason had asked the question, Sully hadn't even thought to—even if it should have been the most obvious one. No entity on the planet tracked objects in space better than JPL. Their records were extensive and grew almost daily. And they had teams of astronomers who did little beyond track the objects they'd found, as well as look for new ones.

"You think they know 73P's going to hit?"

"I have no idea," Jason said. "All I'm saying is that someone figured it out, or else we wouldn't have gotten our hands on the data. And if someone who isn't associated with NASA could do it, then it's a safe bet that someone at JPL did it first."

The logic in that made sense but if it was true, what did the silence from NASA mean?

"They haven't told anyone," Sully said.

"And start a global panic?"

"If they know, they're probably already working on something."

"If they know," Jason agreed.

As he'd walked, Sully had entered an area that was less traveled than the one he'd left. He reached another cross street and turned to the right. As he did so, he glanced back the way he'd come. No one was following.

"We have five years before 73P strikes," Sully said. "And it would take every bit of that time to relocate all of the people in the projected impact zone."

"If they're planning on doing that at all."

Sully went silent.

"There are more than a hundred million people in Italy and France alone," Jason said. "How do you relocate that many people?"

"Methodically," Sully said. "And you start now. Will there be panic? Absolutely. But then you get down to the business of moving as many people as you can, as fast as you can."

Sully's path took him past a café with outdoor seating. He took one of the seats, his eyes scanning the road, the sidewalk.

"Sully, we're talking about transferring the entire populations of several countries to other countries—probably on our side of ocean. Whole nations abandoned; infrastructure allowed to collapse; borders breaking down; people from third world countries streaming in to either be caught up in the resettlement or to take up residence at ground zero and ride it out." Jason released an exasperated sigh. Sully could picture him running a hand through his hair. "Then you've got politics. You'll have some people who won't believe it—people who think the whole thing is some fabrication to weaken their country. What happens if the leaders of one of the major political parties in Italy determines the threat isn't credible and they decide to resist relocation. Are we talking about civil war?

"And that's just the tip of it. There are a thousand considerations—and almost all of them have something to do with violence. A lot of people would die, well before 73P arrives."

Sully couldn't discount any of it. Every word Jason had said was true. 73P was an event that would change the world. Ultimately, though, there was really only one thing that mattered.

"All of those people deserve a chance," he said. "We can't simply do nothing and allow Rome or Paris to disappear in the blink of an eye."

A server showed up at the table and Sully rose, waving her off with an apologetic smile.

"Besides," he said, "at some point 73P is going to be close enough for every amateur astronomer on the planet to realize what's going to happen. That might happen six months before impact or it might happen a few weeks before. But when it does, you'll see a level of anarchy a hundred time worse than what we could expect with a soft reveal.

"Besides," he added. "We're not warning anyone about anything. We're submitting research to JPL and asking them to take a look. In the meantime, we submit what we've got for peer review—

get enough sets of eyes on it that it will be impossible to keep it a secret."

"You realize that submitting anything to anyone won't carry a lot of weight if it has your name attached to it," Jason said, a hint of mischief in his voice despite the implication in the statement.

"I'm well aware of that," Sully said. "Which is another reason we need to do this. Publishing the data about 73P is the only way I can start to clear my name."

"And I'm assuming the files you sent me earlier are part of that?"

"It's proof the Catholic church has been researching 73P as an impact threat for almost eighty years," Sully said. "And that they were on the lookout for something like it since as early as the sixteenth century."

Sully's path had carried him back to a more populated area, which he suspected was a good thing. He'd been on the phone longer than he'd anticipated—more than long enough for the Vatican's minions to find him. With his week-long growth of beard, the baseball cap, and new jacket, traveling with a crowd made it difficult to spot him. Even so, he knew he needed to end the call.

"If I can prove that I was meeting Rinaldi to talk about 73P, and that he was killed because he was going to talk, I might be able to walk away from this with my reputation only temporarily sullied."

"Unless you're forced to talk about a certain prognosticating dead guy," Jason said.

At that, all Sully could do was sigh but Jason wasn't going to let him off.

"Last time we talked, you said you didn't believe he'd predicted anything; that it was just coincidence. Do you still feel that way?"

"Yes," Sully said immediately. "And I have no idea."

He laughed, then. It was the first genuine laugh he'd had in a week.

"I'll admit that there are a lot of elements about the appearance, location, and timing of 73P that are point for point matches to sections of Nostradamus' quatrains," Sully said. "But I don't think it's possible for me to take that last step. I have to believe that it's one enormous and immensely improbable coincidence."

"Which is what I was hoping you'd say," Jason answered. "Because between you and me, the whole thing's starting to freak me out."

"You know, I hear bourbon settles the nerves," Sully said.

"Good to know."

Sully chuckled again. When they subsided he said, "I'm going to find a place to hole up here. Can you get everything together and submit it to all the usual places? And a few of the more reputable unusual ones too?"

"As quickly as I can," Jason answered. "Because I wasn't kidding before. If this keeps us from being able to spend Randall's money, I *will* kill you."

"Fair enough," Sully said. He was about to end the call when Jason muttered an oath.

"There's something else," Jason said, his voice suddenly grave. "In all the excitement about the math I forgot to mention it. When Emily called to share her research, she didn't seem like herself. When I pressed her about it she said she'd been feeling odd. She described it as 'that feeling you get when someone's looking over your shoulder.'" Sully's immediate response was silence and he felt something settle in his stomach, an uncomfortable weight.

"I'm going to assume you told her to go hole up somewhere safe," he said.

"Somewhere even God couldn't find her," Jason affirmed.

Sully took a deep breath and then let it out but the sick feeling in his stomach didn't go away. In his mind, he was thinking of Elena, thinking of her fate, knowing he couldn't accept the same happening to Emily.

"Will she have ditched her phone?"

"I don't know," Jason said. "I doubt it. Unlike us, I'm guessing she has a bustling social life. Not to mention enough professional responsibilities to make both of us green with envy." He paused, then added, "Why? Are you planning on calling her?"

Sully ran a hand through his hair, wincing as it brushed over the head injury—an injury that seemed to him to have happened so long ago but that was, in actuality, still fresh. He cast his eyes around the street, again mindful of how long he'd been on the phone.

"I don't know," he said. "I might. If only just to make her understand how much danger she might be in. And to tell her to be careful."

"Both things that I can do," Jason reminded.

"I know," Sully said. "But I think I owe her an explanation—one straight from the horse's mouth, as it were."

Jason chuckled. "Or the horse's ass?"

"That too," Sully agreed. "Can you give me her number?"

Less than a minute later Sully was making a second call. The phone rang twice before Emily picked up.

"Hello?"

"Emily, it's Sully."

The silence that followed the pronouncement lasted perhaps three seconds.

"What in the hell have you gotten yourself—and by extension, me—involved in?" she asked, her voice the perfect blend of playfulness and seriousness he'd come to expect from her.

"That's a question that would require a lot longer to answer than I have to spare at the moment," Sully said, allowing a slight smile to touch his lips.

"Maybe," Emily said. "But when I feel like I have eyes all over me I think I'm due that explanation."

"And you'll get it," Sully said. "For the time being, I just need to know that you're safe and that you're going to keep your head down for the next few days."

His words met another silence—one longer and more substantial than the last.

"Jason told me you were involved in something dangerous—something stupid, to use his word—but I wasn't sure if I should believe him. I thought it might have been a new tactic to get me to say yes to a date. That is, until I started to see your picture all over the news."

Despite the circumstances, Sully chuckled but before he could say anything, Emily continued.

"I'm going to work under the assumption that you didn't try to assassinate the pope," she said and Sully was grateful to hear only the barest hint of a question in the statement.

"I didn't try to assassinate the pope," he affirmed. "But that's part of the very long explanation that I promise I'll give you when I'm back in the States. Maybe over a bottle of wine?"

It was Emily's turn to chuckle.

"Would that be the bottle of wine you promised Jason?"

"He mentioned that?"

"He's quite concerned about it," Emily said.

Sully was enjoying the banter—enough that he would have liked to have continued it. But he was well aware that his continued use of the single burner phone had crossed into reckless territory.

"And I'm concerned about you," he said. "Jason mentioned that you think someone might be following you?"

"I'm not sure I'd go that far," Emily said. "But I'll admit that the feeling of eyes on me that I mentioned earlier is making me itch."

"Hence my earlier request that you keep your head down until you hear from me again."

"I'm in my hotel room now. I'm supposed to be at the Pentagon tomorrow and I suspect I'll be as safe as I can be once I'm there." She paused. "Can you at least tell me who I'm supposed to be hiding from?"

"Believe me, it's better if you don't know. That way you can claim plausible deniability if…"

He trailed off, not wanting to place that weight on her, but she picked it up anyway.

"In case something happens to you," she said.

"Which it won't," Sully said.

"I'm counting on that. Because if anything happened to you, I'd lose a valuable buffer between me and your partner."

The words were light but Sully could hear the concern behind them. More than that, he caught the hint of uncertainty—a perfectly understandable response considering the circumstances. She was talking to a man wanted for questioning in a bombing, a man who had jetted off to Rome and become involved in something of which she only knew the vague outline. It was a testament to her fortitude that her voice was at all level. He was about to say something along those lines when a loud, sharp noise came to him over the phone.

"Emily?" Sully asked, his voice nearly a yell, but the inquiry was cut off by a cry from Emily.

Sully heard another, louder sound—something like wood splintering.

"Emily!" Sully shouted, drawing the attention of people on the sidewalk around him.

Emily didn't answer. Instead, he heard a dull thump, as of the phone falling to the ground. Then voices, loud but muffled. Sully heard a flurry of noise, another crash, and then nothing.

"Emily!" Sully called again but there was no answer, no noise of any kind. And in that vacuum, he felt something hard press up against his back.

"Start walking, Dr. Knight," came Koning's voice from behind him.

Despite the fact that he knew the voice, despite the knowledge that the thing pressed to his back was a gun, it took what seemed a long while before Sully could pull his attention from the phone, from the forbidding silence that seemed to pour from it like some physical thing. Ultimately, though, the immediate prevailed and he slowly brought the phone down.

"And if I don't?" Sully challenged, with more bravado than he felt.

"Then I shoot you here and walk away."

"With all these witnesses?"

"Who will tell of a man of indiscriminate age and height, wearing a plain, dark suit. An everyman, as it were."

Sully didn't answer. He'd looked Koning in the eyes before; he knew the man was perfectly capable of pulling the trigger and then strolling away as if off to meet friends for lunch.

"Where are we going?" he asked.

"Just keep walking until I tell you to stop."

Sully did as instructed. They were on Via Venti Settembre heading toward Goito when a dark sedan pulled alongside.

"Get in, Dr. Knight," Koning said. He emphasized the command with a nudge from the gun.

Sully stepped over to the car, opened the door, and got in. Koning followed. There were two men seated in the front. Neither turned to look at the new arrivals. As soon as Koning shut the door, the car pulled away from the curb. Sully shifted so that he could see

Koning. The man looked just as he had during their conversation in the café. The same dark suit, the same knowing calm—as if the intervening days had been only a minor inconvenience.

"The first thing you're going to do is call Dr. Humphrey and tell him not to release the information you've collected to 'all of the usual places,'" Koning said.

"And why would I do that?" Sully challenged. "We both know that I'm dead no matter what I do."

Koning did Sully the courtesy of acknowledging that with a slight incline of his head.

"Instead of your own safety, Dr. Knight, you should be thinking of the safety of those you care about."

Sully flashed the man a malevolent look but he kept his voice calm.

"You can't just make someone like Emily Hannah disappear," he said, trying to keep his voice level.

The sounds of Emily's abduction minutes before still echoed in his ears. "Me? Sure. I'm wanted for assassinating a Cardinal. But if you get rid of her, you have two connected scientists going missing at the same time. That kind of thing leads to questions."

Sully's words had an effect on Koning, pulling a small frown from the man.

"You're more resourceful than I would have guessed, Dr.

Knight. You've caused us a great deal of trouble. But my suspicion is that our procurement of Dr. Hannah will do much to make you more agreeable."

Sully had no response and so remained silent.

"The first thing I need you to do is contact Dr. Humphrey and tell him to cease his work," Koning repeated.

"The fact that you need me to do that means you haven't been able to find him," Sully said with a grin. The smile faded, though, when he saw Koning adopt a more sinister version.

"I'm in no mood for games, Dr. Knight. Or witty repartee. You will call Humphrey now. Otherwise, the quite lovely Dr. Hastings will die."

It was all Sully could do to keep from throwing himself at Koning and hitting him until his fists were raw and bleeding. Regardless of the position the man held within the hierarchy of the Vatican's secret organization, he stood as surrogate for them, responsible for all that they'd done, all that they'd taken. What stopped him from doing that, though, was fear for Emily—as well as the gun Koning still pointed at him.

"Why should I believe she's even still alive? For all I know, your men left her dead in her hotel room." He tried to keep the panic from his voice as he made the accusation but, now that he'd put voice to it, it seemed a distinct possibility—much easier than secreting her from a busy hotel in Manhattan.

"Because it's childish to think otherwise," Koning answered. "And you don't strike me as a man who enjoys playing children's games."

"It's not a game," Sully said. "You're asking me to withhold information that a comet is going to kill millions of people. All I'm asking for is some assurance that the person I'll willing to make that sacrifice for would still benefit from it."

Koning considered Sully for a long while—so long that Sully began to wonder if the man was simply going to remain silent until they reached their destination. Then the man pulled a phone from his coat pocket. He placed a call and then spoke a few words, too low for Sully to hear. The gun never moved. He handed the phone to Sully. "Hello."

"Sully?"

It was definitely Emily's voice. He heard an element of fear in it but he thought he also heard anger.

"Emily," he said, unable to keep relief from his own voice. "Are you okay?"

"Define okay," she said, trying for normalcy.

Koning reached for the phone. Sully leaned away.

"Just sit tight, Em. I'm going to get you out of there."

Emily started to answer but not before Koning yanked the phone away. When Sully leaned forward, Koning raised the gun higher. Emily's words were lost in the transfer.

"Now you're going to call Dr. Humphrey."

Sully sighed and then nodded. Jason picked up on the first ring.

"You've already used this number," he said.

"Jason, I need you to stop work on our project."

The pronouncement was met with silence.

"What's going on?" Jason asked after several beats.

"Jason, they have Emily," Sully said. He glanced at Koning to see if the man would stop him but Koning only watched. "If we publish our findings, they'll kill her."

There was another long pause. "Okay, I guess I'll stop. This is the sound of me stopping."

Despite the circumstances, Sully had to smile.

"But they won't let her go, will they?" Jason asked, as serious as Sully had ever heard him.

"I don't know," he said. "For their sake, they better. If they keep her away from that microchip project for long, the general will be pissed."

"That will do, Dr. Knight," Koning said, reaching for the phone.

"I'll be in touch, Jason," Sully said before handing the phone over. Koning slipped the phone back in his pocket. They drove for several minutes in silence. Sully looked out the window. They were heading toward Tiburtina. "You're going to kill her anyway, aren't you?"

Koning shrugged. His eyes were focused ahead but the gun never wavered. Sully shifted position, grimacing as if in discomfort. As he did, he slipped a hand in his coat pocket. He felt for the gun.

"Why?" Sully asked. "There are five years before 73P hits. Why would you keep that from the people in the impact zone? Why not warn them?"

Koning gave another of his half-smiles. "Dr. Humphrey said it quite well, I think. Five years of panic. Of global chaos. Of civil war—one with the potential to flare into a truly global conflict. Are you certain the world would survive it, Dr. Knight? It's entirely plausible that 73P will claim fewer lives were it to strike as a thief in the night."

"Which it won't," Sully said. "The world will have notice. Weeks, maybe months."

"During which the world powers save as many as they can," Koning said. "A shortened timeline strips away all but survival instinct. No politics, no religion, no motive beyond living."

"And millions dead," Sully said.

"Tens of millions dead," Koning amended.

The way the man said it, as if it were no more than a tactical consideration, almost made Sully shiver.

"When it's all over, when your tens of millions have died, how does the church explain why they quietly moved their seat of power to Rio, or Mexico City, or Toronto?"

"Perhaps they don't explain," Koning said. "Or maybe, in 2018, the Holy Father says he had a vision—that God told him to build a holy city in South America. That the church should establish a presence in the part of the world with the fastest growing Catholic population. Then, when Rome is destroyed, the Holy Father can claim to have been warned by God. Circumspectly, of course."

The hardness of it made Sully sick to his stomach; as did the logic of it. As much as he wanted to, he found it hard to dispute anything that Koning had said. There would be chaos; it was impossible to tell how bad it would be, or what form it would take. And were 73P to remain undetected until the moment it breached the atmosphere, the two-hundred million who died might well be the lesser death toll. What made the logic too difficult for Sully to accept, though, was that it negated the beauty of freewill; it robbed man of his right to know what awaits in the dark, to choose to rage against it or to slink off into hiding.

"And you will make that choice for all of them?" he asked.

Koning shook his head. "Not I, Dr. Knight. Not a bit player such as myself."

Sully felt his hand tighten on the SIG.

"You're right," he said. "It won't be you."

He pulled the trigger.

The sound was deafening. It seemed to expand, to fill the whole of the car. From there, things happened in slow motion. He saw Koning's eyes widen in surprise just before a spot of red blossomed on his white shirt. In his peripheral, Sully saw the man in the front passenger seat turning. Sully struggled to pull the gun from his pocket, felt it snagging on fabric. Desperately he wrenched the gun free. He brought it up, fumbling. He shoved his hand over the seat and shot. The man flinched as if struck. He grabbed for Sully's wrist and Sully pulled the trigger again. The man stopped moving.

The driver hunched down. Sully felt the car slowing. He looked toward Koning, saw the man slumped in the seat. The gun had dropped to the floorboards. The blossom of red was growing, soaking the shirt.

The car stopped and Sully reached for the door handle. He saw the driver start to turn but Sully brought the gun up level with the man's nose. Slowly, the man raised his hands. He kept them there as Sully felt for the door latch, then as Sully backed out onto the road. He backed away from the car, gun held in a hand not quite as steady as the one Koning had used. When he was several feet away, he turned and started to run.

Chapter Twenty

He didn't know where he was, save that it was somewhere in Tiburtina. It was a narrow street; more rundown than any place he'd yet seen in Rome. Tiburtina was an industrial area, holding what few factories Rome could boast. Sully suspected Koning had brought him here to kill him. His body would have been dumped in an industrial waste bin, or hidden in a wall somewhere.

He caught a glimpse of a street sign: Via Vertumno. It was quiet. No one moved on the street. A security fence cut off his view to the right; to the left was a building with a smooth tan wall, the surface interspersed with rusted metal doorways and a single equally rusted garage door.

Sully kept moving. He ran past an ivy-covered wall, after which Vertumno opened up into something larger. Belatedly, he realized he was still carrying the gun in his hand. He shoved it in his pocket and moved on.

Cars lined both sides of the street but Sully still saw no one. Up ahead, a newer looking red stucco building loomed, all of its windows barred. Beyond it, Sully could see several taller buildings, a mix of factories and low-rent office buildings. He was breathing heavy and his arm, nearly forgotten, throbbed. He stopped, standing in the middle of the road, considering his options.

That was when he heard a car approaching from behind. He looked over his shoulder and glimpsed the dark sedan coming. His eyes widened and he took off at a run, aiming for the closest shelter of the red building. He didn't know if they'd seen him through the ivy that obscured his own view of the street.

The building seemed newer than those around it. A wide, rolling door was open, revealing industrial shelves inside. Sully darted in and stopped to get his bearings. The shelves ran four and five deep in three directions. A quick glance at the contents revealed sections of boxes, as well as shelves that appeared to hold a variety of chemicals. The latter seemed grouped by the color of their respective warning labels. He saw a large section with red stickers along the wall to his right. He also saw a door against the back wall.

He ran to it but when he reached for the handle, he found it locked. He looked along the wall but saw no other exits. Turning, he started back toward the front of the warehouse to get a view of the other walls but as he moved, he saw a shadow slide across a line of boxes near the exit, presaging the dark sedan that rolled to a stop in front of the wide door.

Sully froze but, after a moment, forced himself to move. He went to the right, skirting a line of pallet jacks, heading toward a line of shelves laden with tall, wide boxes. He heard a car door slam just as he ducked behind a large box. There, he waited in silence, save for the sound of his own breathing. He'd retrieved the gun and, with it in hand, peeked around the corner of the box. At first he saw nothing but, as he watched, a man he recognized as the driver of the sedan stepped into the warehouse. He held a gun and peered around the warehouse. His eyes ran over the place where Sully waited but moved on with no sign of having seen him. The man stepped deeper into the warehouse and Sully shifted position, bringing his gun hand up. His movement stopped, though, as a second man came into view.

Koning's shirt was soaked in blood and he moved slowly. But he, too, held a gun at the ready. Rather than the weapon, though, what drew Sully's eyes was the man's face. Instead of the look of calm superiority to which Sully had grown accustomed, the man wore an expression of barely restrained rage.

"That was foolish, Dr. Knight," Koning called out. "You're killing Dr. Hannah."

Sully didn't answer. Koning made a motion and the driver started deeper into the warehouse, heading toward the back wall.

"Dr. Knight," Koning tried again, "whether or not you agree with the humanity of our approach, you can't dispute the numbers. Many more will die if you publish your findings. It would be reckless."

Koning remained by the entrance. The driver disappeared from Sully's view but, moments later, he heard the man try the door.

Sully tried to figure out which way the man would move next. If he went to the left, he could look up the aisle and see Sully crouching behind the box. Sully knew his current position was untenable. He backed away from the box and looked at the whole of the aisle. To his right, two boxes butted up against each other. One was thinner, creating a recess. It might be wide enough. But he would have to pass an open space, a six-inch gap between his box and the next.

He watched Koning, saw the man look toward the aisle where Sully hid. Then his head swiveled the other way. Sully moved, slipping over to the next group of boxes and secreting himself in the gap. The trade-off was that he could no longer see Koning. But, when he looked out from his new hiding spot and saw the driver come into view at the end of the aisle, he breathed a sigh of relief. The driver looked down the aisle, seemingly straight at Sully, but then he moved off again. He would make a methodical search; eventually, he would traverse each aisle, trying to flush Sully out. The aisle in which Sully hid was the second to last on this side.

Koning didn't speak again. Sully imagined the man standing near the door, making certain that Sully didn't slip past. He would allow the driver to flush their quarry. Sully lost count of the seconds that ticked by—seconds that ticked into minutes. His legs were beginning to cramp but he dared not move. He kept his eyes on the adjoining aisle and was rewarded for his vigilance when he saw the driver come into view, a half-seen shape merging into and out of boxes.

Sully knew how precarious his position was, caught between the two of them. When the driver finished his pass down that aisle, he would round the corner and begin anew in Sully's—and that was if he did not catch a glimpse of Sully through the gaps in the boxes.

For the first time, Sully looked at the print on the cardboard. They all seemed to hold cleaning supplies and paper products. The driver had almost reached a point in the next aisle directly across from Sully's spot. In ten more feet, the man would reach the end and turn the corner. Without considering the wisdom of the plan, Sully pushed himself to his feet on legs that threatened to give out beneath him. Marshalling as much momentum as he could, he threw himself into the stacked boxes of paper towels that separated him from his pursuer. The boxes, with Sully in tow, crashed into the driver. They weren't heavy but their size, along with the added force Sully's body had given them, brought the man down. Sully landed on the driver's legs and reached out his hand to keep the man from swinging his gun around. The driver tried to push Sully off, heaving with his free hand, and he nearly succeeded. In a panic, Sully raised his gun hand and then brought it down with as much force as he could muster, the butt of the weapon meeting the man's skull. The driver stopped struggling immediately.

Breathing heavily, knowing Koning was still out there, Sully pushed himself up, but then bent to collect the gun that was still in the limp hand of the man he'd felled. Turning, he scrambled through the shelving unit, back to his original hiding spot. When he looked around the box, Koning looked back at him. The man fired and the box between them rocked. Sully dropped and, reaching the gun around the box, fired off a shot of his own. Koning, realizing how exposed he was, made a run for the shelves just inside the entrance—shelves laden with plastic containers of chemicals. Sully lost sight of the man behind a large drum, to which was affixed a red label.

"What now, Dr. Knight?" Koning called.

"Now, I call Dr. Humphrey and tell him to release our data," Sully said.

"And kill Dr. Hannah in the process."

Sully's lips compressed. "We both know you never planned on letting her go."

He heard a mirthless laugh coming from the other man.

"You've proven to be quite the thorn, Dr. Knight."

Sully didn't answer. He kept his eyes focused on the shelves behind which Koning had disappeared.

"You'd condemn the whole of the planet to five years of war?" Koning asked.

"I would give them a choice," Sully answered. "And the human race might surprise you, Koning. Maybe we've evolved enough to keep from slaughtering each other."

Koning laughed again.

"You don't believe that any more than I do."

Sully opened his mouth to answer but then he understood. Koning had no interest in discussing philosophy. He was stalling. He would have called for reinforcements. Any minute, the warehouse would likely be overrun with a dozen armed men. From his hiding spot, he studied the shelves separating him from Koning. They were full of containers of varying sizes, with a variety of labels. Many were adorned with red labels—including the drum behind which Koning had disappeared.

Carefully, he edged out from behind the box. He raised the SIG and sighted on the drum. At the same moment, he saw Koning lean out. The man fired off a shot before Sully could react and the box in front of him seemed to explode. Sully squeezed the trigger on the SIG—and the world was filled with light. Sully reeled back, his vision taken from him. Around him, he felt pieces of debris raining down. They felt hot on his skin. He blinked to clear his vision, just as another explosion ripped through the warehouse. Once he could see more than spots, he chanced a look toward the entrance, where a conflagration raged. The drum that had concealed Koning was a blackened shell, the entire top portion missing. Sully knew instantly that Koning was dead.

The fire raced across the shelving units, towards lines of chemical drums. A lick of flame had reached shelves holding paper products. As Sully watched, the fire caught and held on the boxes. He pushed himself to his feet. His arm sent off waves of pain. Glancing down, he saw the bullet wound had opened; blood stained the shirt.

The main entrance was blocked by debris and fire and smoke obscured it. In a minute, another batch of chemicals could go. Grimfaced, he ran toward the back wall, to the locked door. As he reached it, he heard another explosion behind him, felt another wave of heat. The warehouse would be a smoldering ruin in minutes.

He threw himself at the door, leading with his good shoulder, but the door didn't budge. He tried again, then again. The heat grew more intense; smoke was filling his lungs. Stepping away from the door, he raised the SIG and emptied the remaining three rounds at the lock. When the magazine was empty, he threw his shoulder at the door again and felt it give. Once more, he put his weight into it and the door burst open, leading Sully out into open air.

*****

Jason picked up before the first ring had finished.

"Emily?" Sully asked without preamble.

"Randall got her," Jason said. "They tracked her chip to a warehouse in Brooklyn and the general had a special forces unit there in fifteen minutes."

Sully let go the breath he'd been holding.

"But now he wants an explanation," Jason said. "And I'm told someone is on the way to pick me up so I can provide one in person."

Sully rounded the corner, reaching the front of the warehouse. Flames poured out of the entrance and were beginning to crawl up the exterior of the building. Koning's car, parked too near the building, was covered in debris. He heard sirens in the distance, drawing closer. Of Koning's reinforcements, there was no sign. He moved away from the building.

"I'm sorry," he said with sincerity. "I didn't mean for you to get hauled before an angry general."

"Well, for the amount of money he's giving us, I can oblige a meet and greet."

Sully laughed—at his friend, at the absurdity of it all. He was standing outside of a burning warehouse in Rome, inside which were two men either dead or dying. He had a bullet wound in his arm and pain in most every part of his body. A week ago he'd been at a black-tie party in Washington.

"I'm glad one of us finds this amusing," Jason said. Then he grew serious. "What now?"

"Now you send the information out to anyone who will listen," Sully said. "We have five years to get ready. We're going to need all of it."

"What about you?" Jason asked.

Sully ran a hand through his hair. He watched as the first of the fire trucks rolled down Vertumno, two police cars trailing. Sully didn't answer his friend right away. Instead, he knelt and placed the spent SIG on the ground. Next to it, he set the gun he'd taken from the driver. After he stood, he began to walk toward where the police cars were parking.

"Don't worry about me," he said. "I have a very long, very strange story to tell and I think I just found an audience."

He ended the call, slipped the phone in his pocket, and raised his hands as he approached the officers.

Chapter Twenty-One

Sully descended the metal steps to the tarmac, his bag over one arm and his free hand marking his progress along the rail. He looked up, his eyes squinting against the glare of the sun over Dulles. The Gulfstream had taxied to a stop well away from the terminal and a trio of vehicles—two with the olive green and utilitarian look of military transports, as well as a dark sedan that undoubtedly also belonged to the government—sat only yards from the plane. Between Sully and the cars, a half-dozen people were waiting for him but Sully immediately picked the two he wanted to see from among them. He spotted Jason's smile even before Sully's foot touched American soil. Emily wore a similar expression, if one not as unabashedly exuberant as Jason's.

As he crossed to his welcoming committee, a pair of escorts trailed him.

"Welcome home, Dr. Knight," General Randall said, extending a hand. The man's weathered face was absent anything like a smile but the handshake was firm and lasted long enough to indicate at least a measure of warmth.

"It's good to be back, general."

"We have quite a bit to talk about, doctor," Randall said. "And, from what I've come to understand, some work ahead of us, so if you don't mind..." He gestured to the waiting sedan.

"Of course," Sully answered but he looked past the general's shoulder, to where Jason and Emily stood.

The corner of Randall's mouth curved in something that might have been a smile.

"Drs. Humphrey and Hannah insisted on being here," the general said. "And I think the ride to the Pentagon should give the three of you time to catch up."

Sully smiled a thanks to the general and stepped past him, extending a hand to Jason, who ignored it, stepped forward, and grabbed Sully in a rough hug.

"You're an idiot," Jason said.

"I can't argue with that."

Sully looked over Jason's shoulder to catch Emily's eye. When he winked at her, she shook her head but the twinkle in her eye remained. After a few moments, Jason released him and took a step back. Before either man could say anything else, Emily moved forward, took Sully's arm in hers, and gestured toward the car.

"Shall we?"

As they headed toward the sedan, General Randall and the other uniformed men broke away toward the other cars, one of Sully's escorts from the plane following them. The other headed toward the passenger seat of the sedan. Before Sully reached the car, a man emerged from the driver's seat and opened the door for Sully and his friends. When Sully slid in, he saw a darkened partition separating them from the men in front. No one spoke until the car was rolling toward an access road.

Sully was the first to speak.

"This is a nice car," he said. He barely had the last word out before Emily, who'd slipped in between Sully and Jason, backhanded him in the chest.

"Jason's right, you *are* a jerk," she said but her chuckle belied the comment.

Sully laughed too but sobered quickly.

"I'm sorry," he said. At the words, her smile slipped but Sully saw no anger in her eyes. "I had no right to put you in danger."

She was shaking her head before he'd finished.

"You couldn't have known what you were getting into," she said. She shrugged. "Besides, it was probably the most excitement I've ever had doing math."

"What about me?" Jason asked. "Is anyone going to apologize to me?"

"Were you abducted by international bad guys?" Sully asked.

"No. But I was really worried. And you know how I am when

I worry."

A few beats passed while Sully eyeballed his friend.

"You're smoking again," he said.

Jason responded with a rueful expression, drawing another laugh from Sully. But that mirth, too, faded. He opened his mouth but Jason cut him off.

"I know," he said. "You're welcome."

Sully adopted a half-smile and shook his head. He leaned back against the leather seat, feeling something leach from him, leaving him feeling truly relaxed for the first time in what felt like months. But even as he thought it, he understood how far off his internal chronometer was. It had been less than two weeks since he'd boarded the flight to Rome.

"Well?" Jason prodded. "Are you going to fill us in or should I ask Dr. Hannah to hit you again?"

Sully glanced at Emily to find her watching him with equal expectancy. He thought there was a good chance she would, indeed, hit him again with minimal prompting.

"Well, you might be interested to know there's a black site in Poland," Sully said.

Jason raised an eyebrow but Sully waved off his concern with a half-smile.

"For the most part, our friends in the CIA treated me pretty well. Personally, I think they were just glad to have an American there."

"I swear I'll hit you," Emily warned, raising her hand.

"Okay, okay," Sully said, raising his hands in a gesture of surrender. Still, several seconds passed before he spoke again—time he spent organizing his thoughts, wondering what was important to convey in the space of a short car ride.

"It took a while before anyone believed me," he said. "A lot of the principals were dead. And Elena's father wasn't talking."

"Even after the information he gave you?" Emily asked.

"In a moment of weakness. A grieving father forgetting his duty." Sully shook his head. "Rossi's insulated from all of it. He was hired to ship packages and there's no one around to prove otherwise."

"What finally convinced them?" Emily asked.

Sully gave her a half-smile. "The math," he said. "Your math. Yours and Jason's."

"Not the secret chamber under the Vatican with all sorts of incriminating evidence?" Jason asked. At Sully's raised eyebrow, he added, "The good general kept us apprised."

"The Vatican denied any knowledge of such a room and they wouldn't let any investigators anywhere near there. I don't doubt the whole place is cleaned out by now." He paused and frowned. "By the way, are they still flashing my picture around? I've been a bit out of touch."

"The official report is that you were there to meet a friend. An innocent bystander caught up in the dragnet," Jason said.

"I'll take that," Sully said.

He knew he was keeping things light—probably inappropriately so, considering the circumstances. But in this place, with these people, he had no interest in dwelling on the hellish uncertainty of the last few days—days that included grueling interviews by more men in suits than he could count, nights spent locked in a small room with only his thoughts for company, hours spent wondering if anyone would believe him, if anyone would look past the trail of dead bodies to see a man caught up by something and dragged inexorably forward. Among those thoughts was the question of who in Sully's own government was a part of it—who was positioned highly enough to sign Sully's death warrant. In the end, someone had believed him. And, apparently, someone with enough authority had remained unblemished enough to see 73P for the real threat it was. He could have told his friends all of that, and he likely would someday. Just not today.

"What happens now?" he asked. His handlers hadn't been clear on that during the flight.

"You mean now that the cat's out of the bag that a huge rock almost a mile wide is going to crash into Europe?" Jason asked.

"Something like that, yes," Sully said.

"You remember how I told you I'd kill you if your little excursion cost us the general's grant money?"

"I have a vague recollection of something along those lines."

"Well, you'll be happy to know that I won't have to give your eulogy. Which, incidentally, would have been awkward if I was the one who killed you."

Sully frowned. "We're supposed to go back to work on the gravitational physics of charged particles like nothing happened?"

"Yes and no," Jason said, a hint of a smile touching his lips.

Sully's frown deepened but before he could say anything, Emily cut in.

"Your exasperating friend and I have been asked to be part of the taskforce they're putting together to deal with the threat," she said. She delivered the news with the insouciance she often wielded to great effect.

He considered the news, then nodded. "It makes sense. You're two of the smartest people I know. And without you figuring out the math, we wouldn't even know about 73P."

"And we're getting paid," Jason said.

"So you mentioned," Sully said with a chuckle. Then he frowned, remembering what Jason had said. "What does this have to do with the project Randall agreed to fund?"

"You're on the team too," Emily answered. She took his arm

again and moved a little closer. “Someone had this crazy idea. Something about focused charged particles burning large holes in solid objects. I may have heard someone toss around the word *weaponization*.” She shrugged, then aimed a sly smile at him. “I wasn’t paying close attention so I can’t be certain…”

It took a moment for Sully to process what she was saying and, when the impact of it settled on him, he found that his first reaction was a laugh—a full and rich emotion pulled from deep within him. It was cleansing. When it subsided, he gave Emily’s arm a squeeze and then turned to Jason.

“There’s just one more thing,” he said. He reached for his bag and pulled it onto his lap. Unzipping it, he reached inside and when he withdrew it he held a bottle, which he proffered to Jason. “It’s a Bartolo Mascarello Cannubi. 1961.”

Eyes wide, Jason reached for the bottle. When he had it in his hands, he held it with reverence.

“I think I may cry,” he said.

There didn’t seem to be a witty response appropriate to the moment and so Sully made none. Instead, he leaned back in the seat, kept his hand on the arm of the lovely Dr. Hannah, and let the government sedan take him to whatever his future held.

Quatrain Century I - 81

Nine will be set apart from the human flock,

separated from judgment and advise.

Their fate is to be divided as they depart.

K. Th. L. dead, banished and scattered.

- Michel Nostradamus[14]

---

[14] Nostradamus, M., & Garencières, T. (2001). *Nostradamus: his works and prophecies*. Urbana, IL: Standard Publications.

Epilogue

From one wall, a large flat screen monitor cycled through a series of images. Measurements. Projections. Arcing lines through digitally rendered space. A shadow of a monster on an inexorable approach.

On a handful of desks, smaller desktop and laptop screens added their own data to the whole—parsing the same problem from a hundred different angles.

At the large oak table that dominated the room, nearly a dozen people sat. Half-empty cartons of Chinese shared the table surface with laptops and notepads. The air was filled with the noises of conversation, the give and take of intellectual discourse, the impassioned pleas to reason, the angry defense of shaky ideas. It was the strange kinetic energy of creation: the fashioning of new maths, the forging of new avenues in the sciences. All of it aimed to one purpose.

In the cacophony, though, was something else—something perhaps unexpected. Amid the passionate dialogue, amid the tension, even amid the fear that was always there as a subtle undercurrent, there was a noise vastly different from all the others. It was a thing that came without warning, that emerged from the tension to pierce it, to sever it. It was laughter. And it signified one thing: hope.

Reference

de Lacaille, N. L., (1763). *Coelum australe stelliferum,* H L Guerin & L F Delatour

ESO.org., Split Comet Schwassmann-Wachmann 3, http://www.eso.org/public/images/eso9608a/

Nostradamus, M., & Garencières, T. (2001). *Nostradamus: his works and prophecies*. Urbana, IL: Standard Publications.

67222121R00194

Made in the USA
Lexington, KY
05 September 2017